THE OCEAN KING

RUSS WATTS

For Elle and Ophelia.
This is for after you find Nemo, long after.

'Behold, I give unto you power to tread on serpents and scorpions, and over all the power of the enemy: and nothing shall by any means hurt you.'
Luke 10:19

CHAPTER 1

OCTOBER TUESDAY 15TH 08:39

"O'Reilly, get over there, now. We're moving on this. You've got a green light," said Ravensbrook.

Don O'Reilly clambered up the side of the bank as the gritty sand stuck to his body. As he nestled low into the dirty shoreline, he tried to ignore the stench that pervaded the air. There was a strong fishy smell mingling with what he could only assume was human excrement. He looked through his goggles and checked that Pozden was on his left flank, Carter to his right. They signalled back that they had heard the directive. Although it was dawn, Don felt the warmth on his back. The strong East African sun could cause severe heat stroke in less than an hour. If all went well, they would be in and out in even less than that.

Do it, do it now.

With a quick flick of his hand, Don motioned for the others to follow him, and he crept up the sandbank, still hidden from view by the town just ahead. Tufts of coarse Psamma scratched at his legs and arms as he climbed, but he focused on the mission. Over the crest of the sandbank, the target was most likely holed up inside. They had received intelligence that there were four guards posted at each corner of the building, armed with AK47s and a blind faith in what they were doing. A sapphire blue sky and a warm beach suggested this might be a tropical paradise, but Don knew otherwise. He did not have time to relax now, he was lead on this. The men behind him were depending on him. Their lives depended on him and the hostage's lives depended on him. The objective was a mosque, most likely used by the targets because they thought they were untouchable there. The Americans would never dare to touch a mosque, would they?

They reached the top of the sandbank and Don looked back at the ocean they had come from. The CRRC lay in the reeds, obscured from view, and only visible to those who knew it was there. Don counted himself lucky that he was going in with men he trusted completely. He had worked with Pozden and Carter before. They had been in the same team for five years, and Wilson had joined them early in 1990, just after Panama. Robert had been alongside Don for as long as he could remember.

Don gave the signal and Robert and Wilson went over the top silently, creeping through the tall sand reeds. There was no need to speak, as everyone knew their role. Don watched the seconds tick by, and waited a full minute, giving Robert and Wilson enough time to get in position. Once the front two guards were incapacitated, Pozden and Carter would join Wilson inside the mosque and begin retrieval of the hostages. Whilst Don organised the Evac' Chopper, Robert would lay the explosives around the mosque, and in twelve minutes, they would be out of there. It was a plan they had gone over religiously, and Don knew it by heart. He knew down to the last second how things would pan out.

He motioned for Pozden and Carter to move, and then scrambled over the top of the bank. The stone walls of the mosque were dark against the blue sky, and the large squat building cast a shadow over the path between it and the shoreline. There was a peacefulness that surprised Don. Behind the mosque were small buildings, grungy houses covered with washing lines and empty streets. There were no street-lights and no moving traffic. The air was hot and foul, and Don felt himself begin to get irritated. He couldn't explain why, but it was almost too quiet. A light dust blew over the road as the sun heated it up, and a thin stray cat ran from between two parked cars, squinting at Don as it ran. Around thirty feet to his left was a trailer, full of the carcasses of sharks, their fins had been removed and their bodies left to rot. To his right, the path stretched onwards for miles, the grey town simmering in the morning sun running along it, until a boatyard blocked Don from seeing any further. The town of Hobyo was close by, and the Mudug region of Somalia had been a haven for thugs and terrorists for too long. Don never asked why he was sent anywhere, only when he could go. The hostages were so close now, he could almost hear them breathing.

God, please let them still be breathing.

Don shrugged off the irritation he felt, and saw the two slumped figures on the ground by the main doors. The first of the armed militants were down, which meant Robert was already laying down the explosives. The reeds rustled as Pozden went past, crouching low as he approached the main entrance to the target building. The doors were painted a deep green, and over the years, had faded to a cool mint colour. The paint had cracked as the door weathered and weeds grew around it. Why did that door look so familiar?

Do it, do it now.

As Don reached for his Heckler and Koch MP5K, time slowed. His sand-encrusted hand felt like it was encased in concrete, and Don tried to reach the gun, but he couldn't move. It was falling now, out of reach, and as it hit the sand, it sank beneath the surface. Don looked up in surprise at the shouting voices. He recognised them as Somali, but was unable to understand what was being said. Confused, he turned his head towards the mosque. The bulbous dome atop it temporarily blinded him, as the first shards of morning sunlight bounced off it. There was more shouting, panicked voices, urgent screams in an unintelligible language, and then silence. Don blinked away the tears in his eyes as he saw the three men run toward him brandishing AKM's, firing their weapons randomly, their faces contorted by rage. Everything was happening in slow motion, and he reached for his gun again, only to find it wasn't there. A burst of gunfire erupted from the reeds six feet in front of him, and Wilson sprayed the advancing men with a hail of bullets. In turn, the men fell, one by one, their chests exploding in a mist of blood and smoke.

Don was frozen to the spot, as the doors to the mosque burst outwards and the hostages began pouring out. Terrified men and women charged out, running in all directions, some toward the beach, but others down the shadowy roads, not knowing where to find safety. Don looked up again at the mosque's dome and saw a lone figure standing on the roof in front of it. The man wore sunglasses and a yellow polo shirt. A red bandana covered his mouth, and he held an RPG-7 over his shoulder. It was pointed down at the beach, directly at Wilson who was still shooting, as more terrorists came from the two sides of the building.

He tried to shout, tried to warn Wilson, but Don's mouth refused to obey his brain, and his throat was constricted, as if tied in a noose. Don's eyes widened when he saw Robert standing in the doorway of the mosque, ushering the hostages out. As the last one left, a single shot rang out loud and clear, and Robert's left knee came apart. Blood spurted from his leg and he crumpled to the ground. Don tried to shout again, but his lips were tightly shut.

Robert, get out of there!

Wilson raised his weapon and shot the man on the roof, just as the RPG was fired. Like a freeze-frame shot, Don could see the rocket headed toward them, hanging in mid-air, a wisp of smoke trailing behind it. Wilson's face was pure adrenalin as he continued returning fire. The hostages had run wild and many had been caught in the crossfire. Bodies littered the street. Carter was running toward him, and Robert was being dragged inside the mosque by two of the terrorists. The rocket inched closer and Don's heart hammered in his chest.

All around him was gunfire and shouting. He could see the deadly bullets in the air, their paths unclear. The man on the roof was falling, and his lifeless body appeared suspended above the closing doorway. All Don could see of Robert was his boots, as he was dragged into the darkness. He couldn't see Carter anywhere. It was chaos. The rocket was closer now and Don felt himself falling. He was sinking into the sand, just as his gun had done. His body refused to listen to his brain, and Don felt powerless to stop himself from sinking, sinking down into the sand. The scene of carnage and death burned itself into his retina, as he sank further past his waist, past his arms, past his neck. The sand reached his chin, and Don tried to scream, but no sound came out. Finally, his mouth opened, but before he could cry for help, the warm African sand flooded in, choking him, stifling his cries, and filling his lungs. The sand burned in his throat, scratched his oesophagus, and Don couldn't breathe anymore. He couldn't see, or feel anything;

couldn't find the sun, the sky, his team. His arms tried to grab the last of the harsh sand reeds as he sunk, but they slipped from his grasp, cutting and slicing through his palms. Choking on the burning sand, Don closed his eyes and the world went a hellish, fiery black.

Coughing and gasping for air, Don jerked awake and released the pillowcase from his fists. He turned over and drew in a long breath, letting the fresh air fill his lungs. The dream had been all too real, and his throat was sore, as if it was still filled with sand. He knew he sometimes called out in his sleep, and wondered if he had been doing it again. Sometimes, the sound of his own cries woke him in the night. This time, the dream had kept going, and he tried to erase it from his mind. The memory was real enough; he didn't need to dream about it too. Unfortunately, the nightmare was one that resurfaced often, and no amount of therapy was going to rid him of it.

Reaching for the glass of water on the bedside table, he noticed the time. It was just before nine. Don swung his bare legs out of the warm bed, and planted his feet on the soft, but thin carpet. He gulped down the water and yawned. His naked body was cooling off quickly as the sweat dried. The sheets felt damp too, and he knew it wasn't just the nightmare that had made him sweat. As he walked over to the en suite shower, he kicked over an empty bottle of Bud, and it rolled under the bed, clinking as it joined the others.

One day, I'll get around to cleaning up, he thought as he got inside the shower. The instant hot water woke him up further, and he washed all over, before standing under the cascading water, letting it wash away last night. Too many times lately, he had been having that same dream. It felt good to be in the shower. It was only small, but it cleared his mind as well as his body. He could feel the sand draining away, the images of the rocket coming toward him fading, and he began to relax. So often now, when he woke up, he was more tired than went he went to bed. The Doctor had told him that alcohol was a stimulant, and that he should cut down. Don had agreed, made all the right noises, and then made his way to the nearest bar. How else was he supposed to fall asleep without a drink?

Don rubbed his chin and felt the rough stubble there with his fingers. He had just had three days off, and he was going to have to shave before heading into work today. Still, he could afford a few more minutes in the shower. He let his fingers run past his chin, up over his head, and through his short, clipped, greying hair. He knew he shouldn't, but he couldn't stop himself. His index finger found the groove that ran from his left temple, over his ear, and to the back of his head. It was shallow and smooth, and proof that not everything was a dream.

Reluctantly, he left the shower, towelled off, and padded back into his room. The bed was a mess and he could see more beer bottles lining the desk, deposited between photographs and books. His laptop was buried beneath a pile of paperwork, and he thought momentarily about checking his emails. As usual, he thought better about it, and decided if anyone needed him, they knew how to reach him. It was his boss, Zola Bertoni, who had made him get one so he could take his work home with him during the busy summer season. He never used it to work at home. If he needed to do anything, he preferred to stay late at work. Keep the office for working, and home for drinking.

He pulled open a drawer on the bedside table and pushed aside the half-empty whisky bottle, until he found his underwear. Then he opened the closet and grabbed what he needed: jeans, a black polo, and a pair of dark Merrell sneakers. He was on his feet much of the day at the park, and comfortable footwear was essential. The days when he could spend twenty fours on guard in bare feet, or crouched in a wet trench, unable to leave even to take a piss, were long gone. As he pulled the polo shirt over his head, he remembered he hadn't shaved. He crossed the room and looked in the mirror, as he pulled on his jeans. Did it really matter? Wasn't stubble fashionable these days? Besides, he didn't look that bad considering he was pushing fifty. He still went for a run occasionally, when he wasn't hung over, and he was in reasonably good shape. His arms still kept the muscle he had gained in his twenties, and he could easily pass for forty. No, the stubble stayed. He would shave tomorrow.

He straightened out the shirt collar and looked at his face. The scar on his face was almost invisible now. He had been far more self-conscious about it ten years ago, but things had been very different then. Now, it was just a part of him, a reminder of his old life. It was not something he wanted reminding of, but he was never going to escape it. Don avoided looking directly into his eyes for fear of what he might see, and looked around for his keys. They weren't anywhere he could see, but nothing was ever too far away in his apartment. He only had two rooms, the en suite bedroom and lounge where he was now, doubled as a kitchen and dining-room. The TV was still on mute, and he flicked it off, not interested in what the presenters had to say about the latest celebrity marriage, or how the economy was going down the shitter, again. The coffee table was a mess, testament to last night's excesses, and he spotted his car keys in the ashtray, an island surrounded by empty bottles. He picked the keys up and then poured himself another glass of water. He looked out of the window, between the wooden slats that shielded him from the prying eyes of Mrs Barkley next door. She was sat on the balcony reading the newspaper, a cup of coffee and a small plate covered with crumbs on the opaque folding table before her.

Coffee, that's what I need, good strong coffee.

Mrs Barkley was the self-appointed keeper of the apartment complex he lived in, and somehow seemed to know everything going on. She made it her business to know everyone, and Don had unfortunately picked the studio opposite hers to live in. If only he had known five years ago what he knew now, he would've picked a place on the other side of the complex, if not the city. Now that he was here, he really couldn't be bothered to move.

Don looked at his watch. Only nine thirty. He still had time to grab breakfast and do a drive-by before heading in. He thrust the glass into the sink and let it rest on the dirty plates from the weekend. They were submerged in the sink. Flotsam swirled around and Don decided he would wash up later, or else he was going to run out of dishes. The wallpaper above the drawers was peeling, the carpet was thin, worn down by years of abuse, and the light in the fridge was broken, but it was home.

He left the apartment quietly, hoping Mrs Barkley wouldn't hear him, and he could get down to his car. Avoiding the morning interrogation was almost becoming part of his routine now. As

Don turned the key in the lock and stood outside in the open hall, relishing the fresh air and scent of palm trees, he heard what sounded like a newspaper being folded. An elderly voice followed it.

"Mr O'Reilly, you were up a little late last night. At your age, you should show a bit more restraint."

"Pious, interfering, piece of..." Don whispered as he locked the door, before turning and offering his neighbour a great, big smile. "Good morning, Mrs Barkley, how are you today?"

"I'm fine. It's nice to see you up so early." Mrs Barkley looked at him over her reading glasses, her beady eyes trained on his. "I saw Jose this morning, you know, from thirty-four? He said Mr Gatterman from number eight had a fall last week. Well, poor old Harry hasn't had a visit from his daughter since the tenth. The tenth! Can you believe it, that poor man?"

Don nodded and slowly began to edge away. "Yes, yes, terrible, I know. I'm just on my way to work now."

"I've got some fresh apple pie if you'd like a piece, baked fresh last night. Let me get you some." Mrs Barkley got up, put her reading glasses on the table, and took hold of her walker.

"No, really, Mrs Barkley, I have to get going. Maybe later." Don edged further away and was at the top of the stairwell now.

"Nonsense, you need a good feed, look at the size of you! Don O'Reilly, you need a good woman in your life, someone to look after you. You can't live on TV meals your whole life. It wouldn't hurt to put a bit of meat on your bones."

"Okay, Mrs Barkley, see you later." Don disappeared down the stairwell leaving Mrs Barkley talking to herself. He could hear her still chatting away, her voice fading as he descended the steps to his car.

He was out of the lot in five minutes, pulling away from the Peterson Apartment Complex and onto Montezuma road. It was a reasonable neighbourhood, close to the State University, which meant lots of students living close by. Lots of students meant lots of coffee shops. He pulled into Mama Kitty's Coffee Shack, grabbed a large takeaway latte and a sesame seed muffin, before continuing onto Collwood Boulevard. The traffic was light, but steady, and the nightmare from last night was forgotten. Collwood

Boulevard soon became Collwood Lane, and he pulled up under a palm tree, right outside number seven. The shades by the front window were open and he turned the car's engine off. He sat in silence for a moment, staring at the house. It was small and tidy, just as he remembered it. The lawn was a little long, but nothing out of hand. The driveway led past a red letterbox, and he could see the silver Ford Escort that was parked.

So you're still at home, then, Don thought. He saw a figure walk past the bay window at the front and he slid down in his seat. The figure showed no sign that they had seen Don, and walked out of sight. Don took a sip of coffee and then a bite of muffin. He stayed in his car for ten minutes eating and drinking, watching the house for more movement. The same figure he had seen earlier, appeared once at a smaller window that led through to the guest room. It was a brief appearance, but it was enough for him to know.

Still mobile, that's good. And still breathing. Even better.

Don checked the time, and then put on his sunglasses. When he had parked, the car was in the shade, but already, the coolness of the shade was passing and this particular autumn day was shaping up to be a bright one. As he drove into work, away from number seven Collwood Lane, away from more memories and murky figures from his past, he checked off in his head what he had to do in the office today. It was routine now, as he had been doing it for close on ten years. His staff knew the procedures too, and it should be easy-going. He clocked off at seven today. Don began to plan on whether to hit the Fisherman's Arms, or the Old Station afterwards. He found it easier to get through the day when he didn't think about the bigger picture. Just figure out what's for dinner and remember to show up for work. Tomorrow would dawn, whether he planned it or not.

Tomorrow. It's just another day. It's a Wednesday, no big deal. There will be twenty-four hours, half of which you'll spend sleeping.

Except it wasn't just another day. Tomorrow was a day he definitely did not want to think about today. October sixteenth. It was burned into his brain, seared like the branding on cattle destined for the slaughterhouse. No matter how much he tried to avoid it, there it was waiting for him. And when it was gone, when October sixteenth was over, it would be there the next year, the year after that, and the year after that.

Don pulled up to the staff entrance to the Wild Seas Park. He rolled his window down and flashed his ID card at the waiting security guard.

"Morning, James, all good?" asked Don.

"All good, boss, all good."

The barrier lifted and Don pulled into his space behind the main office.

"Good morning, Don," said a female voice as he got out of the car. "I swung by the office earlier and Terrick said you were in today. I wasn't certain."

"Mrs Bertoni." Don shook her hand and had to admire the woman. The current betting was that she was fifty-five, maybe fifty-six, but she hid her age well. A red blouse blossomed out from beneath her black suit jacket. Her hair and make-up was immaculate, as always, and she wore a smart business suit, open-necked, showing off just the right amount of cleavage. Rumour had it that Mr Bertoni had paid for implants, and Don sure appreciated it. That being said, he tolerated her because he had to. She paid him to do a job, and he was good at it, looking after security at the park year-round. He had been on the end of one of her verbal assaults a few times down the years, and had managed to evade them for a while now. He hoped she wasn't about to chew his ear off for being late.

The current director of Wild Seas Park, Zola Bertoni, was proud of her Italian heritage, and it was no surprise that she had inherited her mother's temper. She made her presence known and liked to spend as much time on-site as possible. She looked at Don as a hungry leopard would gaze at an injured Springbok. He had grown used to it and chose to ignore it.

"Don, don't be an ass, call me Zola. Honestly, Fiona, Don and I go way back. He's been on the team for eight years now."

"Nine," said Don correcting her, "coming up on ten soon."

Zola's eyes fleetingly flared before she broke out into a smile and let out a childish giggle. "Oh my, it feels like yesterday. But sorry, I haven't even introduced you to Fiona, have I? She's joining our executive team today. Don, Fiona, Fiona, Don."

Don shook the cold hand of a younger woman dressed in grey.

"Pleased to meet you." The woman spoke in a soft voice and was in awe of Zola, watching her every move and hardly noticing Don at all.

I'll give you six months, tops, before Zola eats you alive.

"Don, do you think you could join me for lunch today? I have a few things I need to run past you. We want to make a few changes to the Christmas celebrations. I know, I know, they've been organised for months, don't tell me, but John has come up with some fantastic new concepts. I really think we can get away with making just some minor adjustments and be onto a winner." Zola winked at Don and led Fiona away. "Lunch. My office. Two p.m."

"Want me to bring anything?" asked Don, hoping she would tell him to forget it.

"Just your sweet little self," Zola answered, walking away.

Don shook his head and jogged up the steps to the security room. He punched the pin number into the keypad and the metal door opened quickly, letting him inside the air-conditioned offices of the largest marine park in the world.

Just have to make it to seven, he thought. *Just get through lunch with Vampirella, get the car home, and get to the Old Station. Then you can get blasted and put off remembering that tomorrow is the sixteenth. I'll deal with it later, much later.*

OCTOBER TUESDAY 15TH 19:25

Amanda dangled the last Herring just above the waterline and watched Poppy race up to grab it. Just as the dolphin was about to surface, Amanda threw the dead fish up in the air, and watched as Poppy somersaulted above the cool water of her enclosure, catching the prize in her mouth before disappearing beneath the water and splashing Amanda.

"You all set?" asked Don. As head of park security, he had to be the last one out for the day, before handing over to the night shift. When he wasn't going back to his apartment alone, he often took Amanda out for supper, or a quick drink. He often had to wait for Amanda, almost drag her out of the park, and today was no exception. He watched her wipe her hands on a rag and then scoop up a now empty bucket.

"Yeah, I guess," said Amanda, as she walked on over to Don. "Poppy just had the last one. I'm done now." The pool area was wet and she walked barefoot, preferring to trust her natural grip than any rubber replacement footwear. She smiled as she approached Don. "Sorry, you must get fed up of waiting for me. You know, I'd be perfectly safe, and you can trust me to lock up. Honestly, I don't mind."

Don crossed his thick arms before answering. "You know that's *never* going to happen. I could wait all day for you, don't you worry." It was almost seven thirty and he was getting itchy. He was thinking about that first beer, the best one, the beer everyone savoured the most after a day's work. It was always the freshest, tastiest one of an evening. By the tenth, they all started to taste the same.

Don had spent the last five years of his life flirting with Amanda, and it had never gone further than the odd drink. Both of them knew it was a harmless game. At twenty years his junior, Amanda could have her choice of most men. She was truly beautiful, and kept her body in good shape. Running around the park did that for her. At work, she kept her shoulder-length hair tied up, but the moment she left the park, she let it loose. Don loved her like a daughter. He had noticed in the last few months that she had seemed happier, and it was no coincidence, she was seeing someone new. The new guy, Hamish, actually seemed like the genuine article. She hadn't let them meet yet, but Don could tell he was special. He planned to probe Amanda tonight for more details. If Hamish truly was going to be the man who swept her off her feet, Don needed to make sure she wasn't in for a fall. He had picked up the pieces before, and hated it when men used her. She was too trusting, too willing to let herself fall in love, when she should be keeping her guard up.

Yeah, but then she'd end up old and alone like me. Better to let her get on with living, mistakes and all.

They left the dolphin enclosure and went into the female changing rooms. Don sat down on the wooden bench sandwiched between two rows of lockers, whilst Amanda showered. When she emerged, she got changed behind the lockers.

Don kept his distance and talked while he waited. "So Zola told me Shakti's not well. Something about a check-up last week throwing up some potential problems? I tried to get more information, but she wouldn't spill it. Sounded serious. You know anything?"

"She wouldn't tell me either." Amanda's voice carried over the lockers and Don could hear her dressing. Occasionally, it would sound muffled, presumably when she was pulling something over her head. "I talked to Jay yesterday, and he said they think it might be cancer. I don't know for sure, but that would be my guess. To be fair, our resident whale is getting old now. If it wasn't that, it would be something else."

"So what's Zola going to do? The star of the show can't go on forever, but it's a big stadium to fill. As much as I love Poppy and Pete, I don't think they'd put enough bums on seats."

"Tell me about it. Zola wants to get another dolphin, mix it up a bit. I told her, you can't just go out, buy a trained dolphin, and expect it not to upset ours, but she doesn't see things the way we do. It's all about the money. I'll bet she hasn't even thought about what effect Shakti's death will have on the staff. Jay can be a pain in the ass, but I could tell even he was cut up about it. If Zola had her way, she would pop down to K-mart and get a new whale. Like the Orcas are right next to the frozen yoghurt, aisle ten, right? That woman gets under my skin.

"She probably thinks Shakti can be replaced, but it's not that easy. There's more interest in the animals' welfare these days. We don't get as many people now as we did ten years ago. I don't have to tell you that. I don't know the numbers, but you can tell walking around the place that it's not as busy as it used to be. Even the school groups have dropped off. Did I tell you I lost my regular Friday class? Saint Augustine cancelled last week. They said it was no longer 'economically viable' to bring a group of thirty students along every week. Some of those kids live right by the most beautiful ocean on the world, and yet, half of them have never been to the beach. I'm trying to educate them, show them how amazing life is out there, and...I don't know, sometimes, it just pisses me off the way it works."

Don started to answer, but was cut off by the echoing blast of a hairdryer. He loved how passionate Amanda was about the animals and the school-kids. He had watched her work with them both, and she knew just how to deal with them. The animals, the dolphins most of all, responded to her more than any of the other trainers at the park. The kids, too, were enraptured when she spoke. It was as if they were the centre of the world, and she was showing them things they had never imagined.

The hairdryer was turned off, and Amanda came around the corner slinging a bag over her shoulder. "Well?"

Don watched as Amanda posed, smirking and giggling as she pretended she was doing a fashion shoot. Her long hair flew around her neck, and she wore a cherry-blossom shirt over skinny jeans and sandals. Don stood up smiling. "All right, all right, show's over. Carrie Underwood called, she wants her career back. Let's get out of here. You up for the Old Station tonight?"

"Hell yeah, I love that place. Best Caesar salad on the west coast." Amanda skipped out of the changing room and headed for the exit. "I am starving. I think I might actually pass out if I don't eat in the next two seconds."

"Well, there's this place I know. It's *real* close and we can be there in, oh, twenty seconds. It's a little chilly admittedly, and the ambience is a bit, well, dead. You do like Herring, don't you? Honestly, they pile it high and you can eat it straight from the bucket. No need for cutlery, you just get stuck in. Poppy and Pete recommend it."

Amanda raised one eyebrow and pointed at Don. "Ha ha, very funny, Doctor Jones. I think I'll pass. Let's get to a real bar."

"Excellent choice. I hear they do some fine cold beers too," said Don grinning. "And once you've stuffed your face, you can tell me all about Hamish."

Don locked the changing rooms and they left the building, chattering absently, laughing as they made their way to the security office, and eventually, Don's car. By the time they had reached the Old Station, Don had clean forgotten that tomorrow was the sixteenth.

CHAPTER 2

OCTOBER TUESDAY 15TH 18:03

Curtis discarded his woollen hat, and cast his jacket aside as he sat down. The small cabin was warm, the coffee warmer, and Curtis poured himself a fresh cup. Although the boat was gently rocking from side to side, he managed to pour and drink the whole cup without spilling a drop. That was what thirty years of being at sea taught you.

"Seems like the wind's dropped," said Hamish. "You leaving Roy up there on his own?"

Curtis poured himself another cup of coffee and sat down next to his son. "Roy can handle it from here. Been through worse than this." He took a sip of the hot liquid that warmed his bones, and stretched out his thick arms, rolling his shoulders to erase the stiffness. "You weren't with us for the winter of '98. Now *that* was a storm."

Hamish smiled inwardly. Every time they skirted a storm, or had some strong winds, his father would bring up the winter of '98. It was like a myth now, a daring tale of adventure and heroism, where his father and Roy would survive by the skin of their teeth, and still bring home the catch. Not just any catch either, but the biggest catch of the day. None of Curtis' competition brought anything home after the infamous storm of winter '98. "Yeah, I heard about that one already, Dad," said Hamish fake yawning.

"You did, huh? Then I guess you heard about the time I spanked your hide for backchat," said Curtis winking back at his son. "On more than one occasion, if I recall correctly."

Just then, the small fishing trawler they had called home for the last two days pitched sharply to the port side. Various drawers flew open and the cutlery tipped out, showering the floor with a variety of knives and spoons. A tin mug whistled past Hamish's head and he ducked, catching the portable radio as it jumped from its position on the shelf above. He shoved the radio back up on the shelf as the trawler levelled out, and noticed his father was sat perfectly still, holding his cup tightly, ensuring none of the coffee was spilt.

"I'm fine, don't worry, Dad, I got it covered." Hamish slid out from beneath the table and scooped up the cutlery that had made a futile bid for freedom.

Curtis grunted. "Don't be such a baby." He watched as his son stowed away the dishes and mugs, and cast an eye out the porthole window. The weather was calmer now, much calmer than the last ten hours. He gave his son a hard time, but only because he knew Hamish had to toughen up if he was going to take over the business. "I've been out on this ocean for thirty years," said Curtis.

"And she ain't got me yet," muttered Hamish beneath his breath quietly.

"And she ain't got me yet," said Curtis, not hearing his son. "You know, she's a tough bitch, but once you get used to her, you'll see how amazing it is out here. She can throw a tantrum now and then like all good women, but if it was plain sailing, life would be boring. Don't you reckon?"

"Yes, Dad," agreed Hamish, knowing if he didn't, he would get an even longer lecture than the one he knew he was about to receive.

"I've been fishing these waters for longer than I care to remember. When I started out on old Jack Morrow's boat, I was wet behind the ears, a little like you, you know. You can't expect to go straight into it. I know you want to get on with it, son, but you can't adapt to a life on the ocean just like that. You can't rush it." Curtis snapped his fingers and then took a swig of coffee. He'd been up for fifteen hours solid, and now they were approaching the fishing area, he needed to stay alert a while longer, at least until the nets were out.

"I know, I know." Hamish sat down. "Dad, let me take the wheel for a bit. You and Roy could do with a break. I know what I'm doing."

Hamish remembered the first day he had come out on the Mary-Jane. He was seven years old, and he had been amazed at the size of the winch on deck. He was even more amazed when he had gone inside the wheelhouse. His father had shown him the galley, the pantry, and then let him sit in the skipper's chair and pointed out what all the machines were for: sonar systems, radios, navigation controls, and the command console. There was an ELT, a GPS monitor, a Wesmar Sonar TE-33, and even an old Fathometer. He had forgotten what it all did the minute his father started talking about the next thing, but he still remembered that day clearly. Hamish had felt as if he was on board a space ship, and felt a kinship to the boat from then on. Of course, once he had hit his teens, he lost interest, and it was only more recently that he had gotten back into it again. His father had put a lot of trust in him these last few years, letting him get more and more involved in the running of the company and showing him how to handle the trawler.

Hamish got up to go and relieve Roy. "What's the First Mate been up to anyway? Roy's hardly spoken to me since we left the dock. He's in a foul mood." Roy was as old as his father was, and had probably spent more time on the Mary-Jane than dry land. He was also a grumpy old man, and rarely had a kind word to say to Hamish. It was evident he didn't like him, and Hamish was kind of pleased he had been so quiet.

"Roy's just got something on his mind. It's difficult for him to...look, just sit down, Hamish. I need to speak to you."

Hamish sat as instructed. A cloud had come over his father's eyes and he wondered if Roy was sick. Roy was a hard-ass, often outright nasty, but Hamish also knew how much the man meant to his father. They had been fishing these waters, sailing the western Pacific together, for as long as he could remember. "What is it?" Hamish asked nervously.

Curtis cleared his throat. "Show you can be responsible and then if you want the business, it's yours. I told Roy yesterday. It's only fair he knew."

"Really? Dad, are you... *Really*?" Hamish was staggered. He had not expected this, not now. "What about Roy?"

"Roy knows the business inside out, and he's a damn good fisherman. I've been friends with him since we were on the same football team back in high school. But he's an asshole. I know that, I've seen how he treats people. If I let him run the business, he'd piss off our partners, crap on our customers, and the business that I've spent the past twenty-five years building up would be gone in a year. You can't build up a good reputation overnight like I have, but you sure can destroy one.

"It's up to you now. I've still got a few years in me yet, but your mother...well, she worries you know. I can't carry on forever. We'll talk about it when we get back home, but it's up to you now."

"Thanks, Dad, I...I'm...Wow. Thanks." Hamish had hoped this would happen one day, but he never imagined it would be this soon. His father would be sixty next year, and he wondered if that had something to do with it. It was true, his mother did worry a lot, but then, she had never been one for the ocean.

"While we're at it, there's something else, son." Curtis leant back, and felt the surge of the ocean lift the trawler over a swell and then put her back down again. "Make an honest woman of her. Amanda is the best thing that could've happened to you. Don't let her get away. This time next year, you'll have your hands full. Trust me. Do the right thing."

Hamish blushed. "I know. I love her. I've been thinking about, you know, asking her." He hadn't talked this openly and honestly with his father in years. They were not the hugging types, and he was annoyed that he still hadn't been able to rid himself of blushing.

"Want my advice?" asked Curtis.

Hamish knew it was coming anyway, so he nodded affirmatively.

"Stop thinking, and start doing. Ask her. She'll say yes."

Hamish thought of Amanda, of her beautiful laugh and eyes. He couldn't say he had fallen in love at first sight, but it hadn't taken long. He had been invited out for a drink by an old friend from University. His friend had known someone else there at Flannigan's, and before long, they had randomly joined the birthday table. Amanda had been there as part of the group. Hamish had chatted to her, flirted, and managed to get her number. The rest was history. They had clicked instantly, and even though it was less than a year, Hamish knew she was the one. He wasn't quite so sure if Amanda felt the same way though, and didn't want to rush her. Christmas was a couple of months away, and he had started planning a romantic getaway. Now, he was desperate to get back and tell her the latest news.

"Right, enough daydreaming. You go relieve Roy. Send him down to the main deck. I want to look at the crane with him. I'll be there waiting." Curtis snapped Hamish out of his thoughts.

"Aye, Skipper." Hamish walked past the pantry and climbed the small steps up onto the deck, and then up into the wheelhouse. The storm was dying out, and the swells had definitely weakened. Hamish's mood was in contrast to Roy's, and as he approached him, he decided to play it safe and not bring up the topic of his father's business. He found Roy hunched over the wheel.

"Hey, Roy, Skipper said to meet him on deck. He wants to check the winching gear out. I'll take the wheel."

Roy said nothing and brushed past Hamish on his way out. He didn't even make eye contact, but zipped up his jacket and tugged a knitted, woollen hat down to cover his ears. Hamish watched Roy leave and join his father's side down below. The wind whistled across the deck of the Mary-Jane, as a salty spray splattered against its hull. It had been at sea for two days and Curtis had decided they should venture out into the richer, deeper fishing grounds. They had caught a respectable amount, but had a way to go before they would reach their allowed quota. Mary-Jane was not full yet.

Hamish checked the instruments, and they were on course, headed Northeast. He scanned the horizon and noticed something out of place. To the starboard, a flash of red appeared on the crest of a wave, and then disappeared. As the trawler came out of a trough, he saw it again. It was smooth and circular, like a red rubber ring, only larger. It dipped in and out of view again, and Hamish turned the boat around to head towards it. It could be a piece of debris, something that had fallen off a cargo ship, but the most common debris they came across, was driftwood or old shipping containers. This looked more like a raft, and Hamish had a bad feeling.

"Skipper, hey, Skipper!" Hamish leant out of the wheelhouse and hoped his voice would carry far enough over the wind to be heard. He could see his father standing beside Roy on the deck. There was no movement or acknowledgement from either of the men that they had heard him, so he tried again.

"Hey, Dad. Dad!" He turned back and saw the red raft bobbing up and down. He kept the trawler on a direct heading with it, knowing this was more than just random debris. It was a cocoon, a life raft; someone needed help.

There were other items in the water. As they drew nearer, he saw the evening sun light them up, its rays skipping off fragmented pieces of metal. Did a ship go down nearby? They had not received any distress calls or seen any flares.

"What's up, Hamster?" Roy looked at Hamish suspiciously, as he entered the wheelhouse.

Hamish bristled. Hamster had been his nickname throughout high school and it had annoyingly dragged on into college too. Roy took great fondness in reminding him of it at any opportunity. Hamish had left college and childish nicknames behind him when he left his twenties. Yet, Roy had made no secret of his scorn for Curtis' son. Hamster wasn't the worst thing he had been called.

"If you can't handle it, I can take over from here," said Roy reaching for the wheel. A mischievous smirk spread across his face as he removed his hat.

Hamish took a step back. "I can handle it just fine, Roy." He kept one hand on the wheel and pointed out the window ahead. "At least you're talking to me again. Look, Roy, there's something odd going on."

"You need me to fetch Daddy?"

Hamish knew the implications, but chose not to answer. He had plenty of experience of dealing with Roy, and found the best way of responding to his comments, was to ignore them. Any attempt at engaging him in a meaningful, adult conversation usually ended badly. It hadn't always been this way. Roy had been in and out of Hamish's life for as long as he could remember: the occasional Sunday BBQ, birthday parties, and random get-togethers when they were celebrating a big haul. The animosity had only surfaced once Hamish had joined the trawler. Two's company and all that.

"Look, Roy, there's a life raft over there. I'm telling you, we have to go check it out. There are other things in the water too. See?"

Roy wandered in front of Hamish and peered out of the window. "You see a flare go up?" he asked in a low voice.

"No, nothing."

"Anything on the ELT?"

"Nothing."

"You check the GPS? We've not strayed into a shipping lane, have we?"

"Jesus, Roy, no. I don't know what it is. We'll be on it in two minutes though, so I'm slowing her down. Go tell Dad, please?"

Roy looked at Hamish sternly. "You'd better not have fucked up, Hamster." He pulled his hat back on and stormed out of the wheelhouse.

As Roy left, Hamish knew the first thing he'd do when the Mary-Jane was his, would be to fire Roy's ass. Before then though, he would have to put up with him. He suspected that Roy knew his days were numbered. There was no way he would continue working alongside Hamish with Curtis gone.

Hamish scanned the ocean, looking at the various pieces of scrap floating in the water. The red life raft was close now, and he slowed the trawler down, pulling up as close as he could to it. The seas were calm and the wind had dropped to under twenty knots, so he killed the engines and dropped the sea anchor. He rigged the GPS unit to the engine controls so they would not go drifting off, and headed outside to join Roy and his father, grabbing a jacket on the way.

"What is it?" he asked as he joined his father at the rails on the main deck. The three men stood side by side, holding onto the clammy railing, watching the life raft edge closer on the current.

"Well, it's definitely a raft of some sort. Could be from one of the trawlers in Old Jack Morrow's gang, but we'd have heard about it. You sure there was no distress call, Hamish?"

"I'm sure."

Roy grunted and Hamish glared at him.

The red life raft was drifting closer to the boat now, and they could see it clearer. It was a six-man raft, orangey-red on top with two thick black bands of rubber around the base. The zipper was half-open, and the rubbery curtain that protected the raft's opening flapped in the wind.

"Looks like a Revere or a Challenger SOLAS," said Roy. "Jack Morrow wouldn't have one of those. Maybe it's a private yacht. Some rich banker got blown off course in the storm, tipped over, used the raft to escape. Maybe it was too quick for them to signal for help. Wouldn't be the first time some idiot with more money than sense got lost out here."

"Could be, could be." Curtis did not sound convinced, but had no other plausible explanation to suggest. The reflective tape on the canopy exterior was covered in a dark substance. Something dark had dried over it, something that looked worryingly like blood. "Look, let's bring it in. There might be someone in there that needs our help. Rich or not," he said looking at Roy.

Hamish saw the boarding ladder drift by, separated from the raft. "Hey, anyone need help over there?"

Curtis and Roy grabbed hooked boat poles and leant over the side trying to snag the raft. It was a few inches out of reach, and they had to strain to reach it. After a few minutes, Curtis got a hook through a safety line and began to reel it in. Roy quickly got his boathook attached too, and the life raft was drawn up close to the trawler.

"Anyone in there?" shouted Hamish. There was no response. "Come on, we're going to have to get in there."

Curtis and Roy dragged the raft around to the rear of the trawler where they frequently landed the fish. Today's haul was a first for the Mary-Jane. The raft was at the stern of the boat now, and all together, they pulled it up onto the deck. They looked at it in awe, as if they had just pulled up an unexploded nuclear bomb.

Hamish approached it, and ignored his father's warnings to be careful. He put one foot on the wet raft and slowly pulled down the zipper that opened up the protective inflatable canopy. He prepared himself, expecting to find at least one person inside, perhaps injured, unconscious, or dead. He parted the curtains and peered inside, holding his breath.

"What is it, son?" Curtis saw Hamish looking around the raft, and then his son let out a gasp of shock. He stepped up into the raft and crawled inside. "Roy, you'd better get onto the Coast Guard and get us headed back. I think we'll call it a day."

Roy ran up top to take the wheel and Curtis joined his son. He rubbed his beard and tried to peer into the interior of the raft. "Hamish, who's in there?"

Hamish's head appeared at the entrance and then he stepped out carrying two handguns. "There's another one in there too." He handed one to his father who looked it over.

"So, there's nobody alive in there? What the hell is this?"

"I'm not too familiar with handguns, Dad, but I can tell you that this is no flare gun. If there was anyone in there, they're long gone."

Curtis examined the chamber and noticed it was empty. He frowned. "This doesn't make sense. If their ship went down, and they had time to get the life raft out, where are they? And if they made it onto the raft, why only take a couple of guns?"

"And what were they used on?" Hamish stood beside the raft examining the gun. "Maybe Roy's theory is right, maybe it was a private yacht? If they had money, they would have Security. That might explain the guns."

Curtis bent down and examined the reflective tape. He ran a finger over it, coming away with salty grime and a reddish-brown stain on his hand. "I don't like this."

The trawler suddenly jolted, as if it had run aground, and lurched to the starboard, sending the raft skidding back into the ocean. Hamish grabbed his father, and together, they managed to stay on their feet. They dropped the guns, which followed the raft into the water.

"What the hell was that?" asked Curtis.

Goose bumps ran up Hamish's arms. He ran over to the side of the ship and saw a body in the water. It was floating face down and naked. The bloated corpse's pale skin was mottled with bruise marks and as it drifted past Hamish, he noticed it was missing a leg. It had been torn off just below the waist. Bare bone was exposed and sinewy muscles followed it in the water like tangled red sea-weed. Hamish felt queasy. He had gutted fish before, watched plenty of horror movies, but he'd never seen a dead body. He put his hand over his mouth and stifled the sickness that was building in his stomach. The body was not what had bumped into the trawler. He ran over to the other side of the boat.

"Oh, my God." Hamish no longer felt nauseous. He felt breathless. He felt like he was nineteen again and losing his virginity in the basement of Daniella Harris' parent's house. His lungs felt too small for his chest, his heart too large as it sped up in excitement. He could practically see Daniella now, her nervousness matching his, and he had to bring himself back to the here and now. Just as he had done when he was nineteen, and kissed Daniella in places no other boy had kissed her, he blushed. His pale face reddened as his cheeks filled out. He exhaled loudly. What he saw in the ocean was not possible, was not real; it could not be real. He turned to his father and beckoned him over.

Curtis looked over the side into the ocean and Hamish saw the look of amazement on his father's face. A creature floated in the water, knocking against the hull. It had to be a good fifty feet long. Its elongated body was the colour of a toad, dark green with patches of brown, yet, with a hint of pinkish white underneath. It was about six feet across in its middle, and the body tapered after its rear legs disappeared under the water, stretching out into a tail covered with spikes. Hamish watched the creature bobbing up and down, just as the raft had done, and looked up the length of it, past its thick neck to its head. That was what disturbed Hamish most. The thing's head was even wider than its body, probably ten feet across, and apparently all teeth. The two eyes perched atop its head were closed, and its jaws were slightly apart, showcasing an array of teeth that even a werewolf would be jealous of. He wasn't sure, but Hamish thought he could see small holes around its jawline: small holes that might be bullet-holes.

"Holy Moses," exclaimed Curtis.

Father and son looked at each other as Roy appeared above them leaning out of the wheelhouse. "I think we hit something. It's not the boat is it? The one the raft came from? I didn't see anything."

"Roy, get down here now, we're gonna need your help," said Curtis, as he grabbed one of the boathooks from the deck.

Hamish grabbed his father's arm. "Dad, it'll never fit on the boat."

"Sure it will. It's dead ain't it? We'll just bend its tail around. It'll fit."

"And then what? If we do get it on, what the hell are you going to do with a...a...a dead dinosaur?"

Curtis picked up the other boathook and handed it to Hamish. "You're the one with a girlfriend at Wild Seas Park. You think she'll be interested in it?"

"Are you kidding me? She would jump me for...I mean, yeah, she would love it." Hamish blushed again. "Amanda could probably spend years examining something like this. She and her friends would study the hell out of it. She would be in her element. I mean this is a...well, whatever it is, I've never seen nothing like it. You?"

"Nope. One of a kind I reckon. Some sort of mutant maybe?" Curtis began to stick the boathook into the monster to keep it close to the boat. "Looks like an alligator on steroids. And I'm willing to bet that Wild Seas place will pay good money for this. More than we'd get for a boatload of Herring and Thresher any day of the week."

"Awesome," said Hamish. "And what if it's carrying some sort of weird disease? Did you think about that?" Hamish stood shoulder to shoulder with his father, easing the monster closer to the rear of the boat where they could drag it up.

Curtis rested on the rails and looked at his son. "Hamish, you worry too much. Just help me get it in. It's dead, isn't it? It'll be fine, you'll see. This is it, son. This is going to bring us *big* bucks."

Curtis grunted as he tried to manoeuvre the weird creature closer. "Relax. Have a beer. Nothing can go wrong."

CHAPTER 3

OCTOBER TUESDAY 15TH 20:16

Sitting down at a corner table, Don ordered two beers. He had parked up in the lot and was enjoying Amanda's company. They had chatted the whole way there, just making small talk about the price of gas and listening to the radio. Don felt good. With Amanda, it felt like he was a part of the human race again.

"Just a light beer for me, please," said Amanda, as the waitress left them. Amanda looked around at the pictures of cops on the walls, the array of medals, batons, police certificates, hats, and black and white photographs. "Remind me again, why do they call this place, the Old Station?"

Don leaned over the table. "You don't like it, there's a Hooters down the road."

Amanda laughed. "I'll pass, thanks."

Don looked around the bar. For a Tuesday, it was fairly busy. There were a few couples around who he recognised from his apartment block, and several old men, probably retired cops, propping up the bar. Sometimes, he joined them, but tonight, he was entertaining Amanda, and eating honest-to-God food that he hadn't just nuked in a microwave.

"So. You and Hamish. What's the deal? You and him gonna get hitched, or what?" asked Don.

Amanda smiled as she shook her head. "Don, you are always fishing. Don't hold back will you? Stop beating around the bush, and just ask me straight." Amanda slid her handbag off her shoulder and hung it over the back of the chair. "Is it me, or is it hot in here?"

"Amanda, you can avoid answering the question as long as possible, but I'm still gonna get an answer from you," said Don smiling.

The waitress brought them two beers and Don signed for them. He ordered two more at the same time, and asked the waitress to keep him topped up.

Don chugged back half of his bottle. "Look, I ask because I care. I've never met the guy, and it seems like it's getting serious. It sounds like *you're* getting serious. I remember some of the jerks you've been out with. Boy, you can really pick 'em."

"Yes, Dad," said Amanda teasingly. "Some guys, I'll admit I could've done without, but what was wrong with Mike? He was sweet."

"Mike? That idiot from last year? The one who crashed your car. *Twice*? Yeah, he was sweet all right, just a shame he had the mental age of a fifteen year old."

"Oh come on, don't be mean. Some guys like to play video games, what's wrong with that? And he didn't mean to crash my car. *Twice*."

They laughed and Don started on his next beer. Amanda was only halfway through her first when the waitress brought the next round.

"So, you gonna answer the question then, or keep me in suspense?" asked Don.

"Honestly, you sound like Curtis, that's Hamish's father. He's always hinting at Hamish to pop the question. Oh, he's really subtle about it, just like you." Amanda took a breath and looked out of the bar, at the setting sun outside. The sidewalk was cast in a reddish glow and long shadows were gradually covering the city. The sun came in through the bar's window and illuminated Amanda, as she sat pensively thinking over her answer. As she thought how to respond, the frowns on her face deepened and the orange glow of the sun made her skin seem soft and warm.

You are one helluva beautiful woman, thought Don. *If I were in Hamish's shoes, I would've popped the question long ago. He is one lucky guy. It is nothing short of amazing that no guy has snapped you up already. If I'd had children, I could only hope to have a daughter like you.*

Don knew if he didn't stop staring at Amanda, she could turn back to him at any moment, and then there would be that moment of awkwardness. That moment when you catch someone looking at you, and you don't know what to say. He forced himself to look away to the bar, and the men supping on cold ale.

I'm one step away from them. I just have to say the wrong thing to the wrong person, and that's it. No more job. Nobody would hire me now. My skills aren't exactly suitable for the modern workplace. Mind you, is sitting at that bar really so bad? As long as you've some good company and a cold beer, that's better than a lot of people have.

"Yes," said Amanda eventually. "Yes, I am serious about him. I can't say if he'll ask me to marry him, but I don't even want to think about that. We're getting on so well, we'll just see what happens. He's...he's pretty special to me though."

"Hmm," said Don. "When do I actually get to meet this *special guy*?"

"You have met him once, actually. I thought you'd forgotten."

"When?" Don finished his beer and the waitress came back with another.

"You want to order any food, honey?" she asked Don.

"I'll take the calamari please, and maybe get us a pitcher?"

"Sure thing." The waitress smiled at Don. "I don't usually see you in here with company. You feel like introducing me to your daughter?"

"Amanda's just a friend." Don sipped on his beer and looked outside at the city as it cooled off.

"Caesar salad, thanks." Amanda watched the waitress leave, her pleasant demeanour suddenly soured by Don's curtness.

"Don, what gives?"

"What's up?"

"That waitress, you totally blew her off. She was looking at you like you were a Christmas present, and tonight was Christmas Eve."

"Eh?" Don finished his beer and started on the last bottle.

"Don, she was looking for an opening. Could you not see the way she was looking at you? That whole time, she never looked at me once."

"I guess not. Look, whatever, back to the story. You said I met Hamish once..."

Don failed to see the annoyance in Amanda's face, only the sparkle in her eyes and the golden lilt to her shoulders as the sun set.

"Jay's party. Last April, we were both there. In fact, you drove us there if I remember rightly. Flannigan's? Does any of this ring a bell? I met Hamish there, and you spoke to him for a few minutes at least."

Don frowned. "Can't say as I remember it. Or Hamish."

Don remembered going to Jay's birthday party, and he remembered waking up on his bedroom floor the next day with his front door wide open. He remembered Mrs Barkley yelling at him as he tried to close the door wearing the same clothes he had gone out in the night before. The part in between, from arriving at the bar until the next morning was a blank though. "Sorry, so many birthday parties, they all blur into one." Don gave Amanda an innocent smile.

"I'm sure they do," said Amanda as she watched Don finish the last bottle. She was still nursing her first.

"What's that supposed to..." Don stopped as the waitress brought over the pitcher of beer and set two glasses on the table. She briskly walked away, leaving Don and Amanda in silence.

Don poured out two glasses of beer and pushed one slowly across the table to Amanda. "I'm sorry, okay, let's start over. Truce?"

Amanda took the glass and raised it. "To good friends."

"Good friends." Don chinked glasses with Amanda, relieved he had avoided a lecture. Every few months, Amanda would give him a stern talking to, about the perils of drinking too much, staying up too late, of not eating well, and generally telling him how to change his life. The problem was that Don didn't want to change it. The way he saw it, everything was as it should be. At least, everything in his power was. You couldn't control your whole life, certainly not your dreams or your past. As for the future, well, he wasn't sure about that.

"Don, tell me something, you come here a lot, I know you do, you live right around the corner."

"Yep?"

"And clearly that waitress was into you. So how come…"

"How come what?"

"Are you being pig-headed on purpose? Why do I never see you with anyone? Why do I never hear about you picking up some *waitress*, or meeting anyone? I mean, even Jay has girlfriends and he's a loser. You're a good-looking guy, Don, and you're not ready to move to Florida yet. So. What gives?"

Don searched around his head for the right answer. It seemed that today he might only be getting half the lecture. "You know how you've got Hamish? You know how perfect it feels, the way you can relax with him? Tell him everything? Well, I've never had that. And I don't want to settle for second best, or sleep around like some dirty, old man. I'm fine on my own. There are a lot of single people out there in the world, Amanda, and they don't all need saving. It's just the way it is. Honestly, I can't see myself getting married, but I'm not a lost cause. I'm not holed up in my apartment right now, stacking newspapers and counting the cockroaches on the walls. I've noticed her, the waitress from before, but she's out of my league. Look, I'm here having a drink with you, in a bar with real, live people, so don't worry."

Don poured more of the beer from the pitcher and waited for Amanda to tell him he was being foolish, that he was missing out when he could be banging waitresses old enough to be his daughter.

"Fine. Don O'Reilly, I am officially not worrying about you anymore. With this beer, I set you free. No more interfering." Amanda polished off her glass of beer. "Where is that food?"

Don's eyes widened. "No more interfering? No more lectures? Damn, I should've been more pig-headed years ago."

"Ha ha," said Amanda plainly. "Say, what happened with your cousin from out east? Taggart or something? I forget. Wasn't he going to stay with you? You never said if he came."

"Taggart's my uncle. It's his son, my cousin, Ryan who was moving down here. He asked if he could stay, but in the end, he didn't need to. Passed his PST and got fast-tracked over to San Clemente. He's there now, in training. I hear good things about him. He's getting into the SEALS."

Amanda looked surprised. "Well, did you help him? You must have stacks of stuff you could tell him about. You were in the SEALS for how long, like five years?"

"Yeah, but he's a smart kid, he didn't need my help. Besides, I left the service a long time ago. Things have changed, moved on. I'm not sure I'd be able to offer him much help. Anyway, it turned out fine. Like I said, he's at the training base on San Clemente Island now."

Their food arrived, and Don drew the pitcher to his side as the plates were put down. He ordered another pitcher from the waitress, and picked up his knife and fork.

"Don, you should ask her out," suggested Amanda.

"Who, the waitress? You're kidding."

"She'll be back in a minute with the drinks." Amanda shoved a forkful of salad into her mouth. "Why not, what have you got to lose? Do it, do it now."

Don's fork and knife hovered over his plate and he stared at his food. His right hand clenched around the knife and he felt hot. His face was burning and his body temperature was suddenly soaring, shimmering in the hazy sunlight as the sand rubbed against his skin. The scar on his head throbbed, and he could hear the screams, the gunfire, and the blood rushing through his veins.

Do it, do it now.

Smoke from the exploded rocket mingled with the freshly cooked bacon on Amanda's dish, and Don closed his eyes.

Burning flesh. Blood trickling down the back of my throat. I need to get out of here. He's waiting for me.

Don squeezed his eyes shut, but still, he could not block out the dazzling sunlight. The man with the yellow shirt was waving at him, chuckling, sneering, and cracking up as if Don was the biggest joke in the world. The chuckle turned to full-blown laughter, and the man's cracking voice joined with the cheer of the crowd on the television set at the bar, as the Padres defeated the Mariners.

Robert, where are you?

"Don, are you okay?" asked Amanda.

Do it now.

The man in the yellow shirt laughed as sand and bullets fizzed around Don's head like a herd of gigantic mosquitos. He looked down at his meal. The calamari on his plate had turned into bloody dead eyes, and the salad had become maggot-infested raw meat. A thin cat ran up to Don and began scratching at his face, tearing away the flesh, raking out his eyeballs and biting his cheeks. His feet were sinking. His body was plummeting down, floating into an eternal oblivion. Hands pulled at him from the dark hole below, thousands of hands tugging at his feet, dragging him further and further down.

Do it now.

"Don!" Amanda grabbed Don's shaking hands and he looked up at her. "Don, what the hell is going on? You spaced out there. You're not having a heart attack on me, are you? If it's that stressful for you, don't ask her out. It was just a suggestion."

Don gave Amanda the most reassuring smile he could muster, and put his knife and fork down. His right hand hurt from gripping the knife so fiercely. "Sorry, I don't know what that was. I just...I haven't eaten much today. Guess I should slow down, huh?" He held his half-empty glass of beer aloft. The amber liquid sloshed around and Don wished he could just swallow it all. He wished he was sat alone at the bar, then he wouldn't have to apologise for wanting to drink it.

Amanda took a small bite of her salad. Her face showed the worry she felt for Don. "You sure you're okay? I know that tomorrow is..."

"I'm fine." Don slammed his glass down on the table. "Leave me be." The sizzling stench of meat reached Don's nostrils from the kitchen and he wanted to puke. He left Amanda at the table, speechless, and marched off to the men's room.

He flung the door back and sat down in one of the stalls. It was cooler in there, and the smell was of a far richer variety. Don didn't really need to go and just sat there holding his head in his hands.

At least it doesn't smell like death. Shit, I shouldn't have spoken to Amanda like that. She was only trying to help. You're a freak, Don O'Reilly, treating her like that. What is wrong with you? You know very well what's wrong. You're going insane, you know. Since when did the dreams come in the daytime, when you're awake for Christ's sake? What was that, some sort of catatonic episode? Doctor Phil would have a field day with your mind.

She started to talk about it: tomorrow. She knows. You told her and now you can't take it back. When you go back out there, she's going to want to talk about it. If she's still out there. I wouldn't want to be friends with me, either. If she is still there, you're going to suck it up, talk about it, and have a nice evening. Tomorrow is just another day. It's like all the other Wednesdays this year, except you have an errand to do in the morning. So get out there and apologise. If you're lucky, she'll still be there. I am such an asshole.

Don left the bathroom and walked slowly back to his table. He was more than uncomfortable. As he walked, he could feel everyone in the bar looking at him. Whether they were or not, he could feel them. There he was: the weird guy who had slammed his beer down.

I'll probably be lucky not to get thrown out.

Amanda slipped out of her chair as Don approached, and when he reached their table, she put her arms around him.

"I'm sorry, Don," she whispered in his ear as they hugged.

Don was so surprised he couldn't speak. He was supposed to be apologising to her, and this amazing woman was apologising to *him*. He gently pushed her away. "No, Amanda, I shouldn't have acted like that. You don't have anything to say sorry for."

They sat down and Amanda took Don's hand in hers across the table. "I spoke to the waitress, it's all fine. I explained you were just upset about something."

"I don't know why you put up with me sometimes. I'm sorry, Amanda, truly I am. It's just stress, thinking about tomorrow. At the very least, let me pay for tonight."

"Hell yeah, you're paying." Amanda let go of Don's hand and beamed. "Tequila?"

He was relieved that Amanda had forgiven him so quickly. He hadn't suffered from anything like that before. Usually, he left his nightmares at home. He couldn't even remember what had set him off now. He pushed his calamari around his plate with his fork. It was distinctly cold and unappetising, so he nibbled at the side salad, sipping slowly at the beer when all he really wanted to do was drink until he couldn't remember his own name. Some equally cold and unappetising song was playing on the radio, and they ate.

When they had finished, Amanda looked at her phone. "I'm going to have to get going. Zola's got me in at eight tomorrow to go over the figures for last month. A working breakfast."

"Sounds thrilling," said Don. "You want a lift home?"

"No, I'll get a cab. You'll be okay won't you?"

"From here to my place, it's seventy-five steps. True story. I counted once. I'll be fine."

"Look, Don, what I said before. I am revoking my earlier statement. I officially *do* worry about you, and that's not going to change." Amanda picked up her handbag, and lent over the table. She spoke in a hushed tone, as if she was divulging the whereabouts of the President. "I put a good word in for you with Meghan."

"Meghan?" Don took Amanda's glass. His mood had definitely softened and he felt himself finally beginning to relax. A few more drinks and he would be fine.

"The waitress. The size ten who looks like she wants to eat you for breakfast? It would do you good not to be on your own for once. Just think it over. Being close to someone really helps, Don. When was the last time you were close to someone? So close, you knew each other's thoughts? Have you really never had that?"

"I have. I did, once."

Shut up.

"Not how you're talking about exactly, but something similar." Don said. "There was a time when we were happy. My brother was a year younger than I was. We were only a year apart at school and always got on. We would spend so much time

36

together that people thought we were twins." Don chuckled. *"Not like the movie."*

What are you doing? Just shut up now. She doesn't need to hear this.

"So every day, we would walk down and catch the school bus together. We played football together. He was always better at it than I was, but I always aced him at chess. I used to play with my Dad too, but he always beat me."

"Chess? Don O'Reilly, were you a secret nerd?"

"We both were. Dad taught us how to play. My brother and I used to read about Gladiators, Romans, and all that stuff. We loved it. I remember when we would go out into the backyard. I would wear my mother's apron, and we would make swords out of cardboard. We pretended we were fighting lions in the backyard. I gave him a bloody nose once. It was just an accident, but my mother grounded me for weeks. She was...strict, I think is the word."

"What about your brother, didn't he get grounded too?"

The man in the yellow shirt grinned maliciously. You've not got long left. Do it.

Don smirked. "My brother, no way. He was the golden child. We cut each other's hair once. I was ten, eleven maybe? We got home from school and just decided we wanted to, so we found the kitchen scissors and sat in the den chopping bits off each other. It was freaking hilarious. We looked like deranged scarecrows after. I got a good hiding for that. I remember my brother explaining to Mom how we had done it together, but it didn't matter. I was the eldest, therefore it was my fault. I can clearly remember he got a double scoop of ice-cream for being honest. I got six from the belt."

"Is your mother still..."

Don shook his head. "She's not in the picture anymore."

"And your father?"

Don shook his head again. "He's been dead a long time." He didn't want to continue this morbid conversation. His eyes were glazing and Don knew it was time to go. He looked outside. The night had come and stolen the sun for another day.

Amanda looked at her phone again. "Don, I hate to do this to you, but I really do have to get going. Look, I can come with you tomorrow if you want? To the…"

"No." Don suddenly perked up. "Just go. I'll settle up, and then I'm going home. The fresh air will sober me up. You should get going while you can still get a cab."

Amanda hugged Don again. "Take care and call me if you need anything."

"See you tomorrow." Don watched Amanda leave as he put his jacket on. She got into a cab and waved goodbye through the bar's window. Don took a swig of beer and looked around the bar. The couples had all gone home, and the only people left were two old men at one end of the bar and the hot waitress, Meghan, serving them. The radio was still playing soft rock ballads and he saw the football game had finished. The news was on and the banner at the bottom of the screen was something about a missing ocean liner in The Pacific with hundreds feared dead. No doubt that was the result of Al Qaeda too, along with crop circles and global warming. Don wandered over to the bar and held out his wallet.

"Are you doing okay, honey?" asked the waitress, as she rang up the final bill.

Don slumped into a bar stool. "Long day." He looked longingly at the beer pumps lined up in front of him. He had drunk just enough to get a buzz on, but not quite enough to know when to say no.

"Your friend was nice. She just a work friend?" asked Meghan.

Don looked at Meghan. She had soft, brown eyes, and hair to match. "Yep. Just a friend." He looked at Meghan and her hands held out the cheque to him. As he reached for it, she took it back. Her face was kind and her skin was golden and tanned, much like Amanda's.

"Don, right? Meghan McCabe, at your service. If you're not in any rush, you want another drink?"

"You're not from around here, are you?" asked Don as he sized her up.

Meghan shook her head. "Canada originally. Came down a couple of months back. Bit warmer down here," she said winking. "I could use some friends myself."

Don eased off his jacket and decided which one of the tap beers to try next. "Maybe just one more drink then."

CHAPTER 4

OCTOBER WEDNESDAY 16TH 09:44

"O'Reilly, get over there, now. We're moving on this. You've got a green light."

Don clambered up the side of the bank and the gritty sand stuck to his body. As he nestled low into the dirty shoreline, he tried to ignore the stench that pervaded the air. There was a strong fishy smell mingling with what he could only assume was human excrement. It was familiar to him, as though he had been here already. He looked through his goggles and checked that Pozden was on his left flank, Carter to his right. They signalled back that they had heard the directive. Although it was dawn, Don felt the warmth on his back of the strong East African sun.

With a quick flick of his hand, Don motioned for the others to follow him, and he crept up the sandbank, still hidden from view by the town just ahead. Tufts of coarse Psamma scratched at his legs and arms as he climbed. The men behind him were depending on him. Their lives depended on him; the hostage's lives depended on him. Don saw the target and was struck again, by how familiar it was. That dome on top of the mosque, that faded green door - he recognised them as easily as his own face. He had seen grainy satellite images of the target only ninety minutes ago, but the smell, the heat, was all too real. He had a strong sense of déjà vu.

He knew what he was going to see when he advanced over the sandbank. He could see it already. There would be a stray cat between two parked cars. There would be a trailer full of dead rotting sharks to the west, and a boatyard just off to the east. He knew what was coming, but was utterly powerless to stop it.

Do it, do it now.

Don gave the signal. Robert and Wilson went over the top silently, creeping through the tall sand reeds as they had done a thousand times before. As expected, he saw two slumped figures on the ground by the main doors. The reeds rustled as Pozden went past, crouching low as he approached the main entrance to the target building. This wasn't right. A voice in his head screamed at him: *STOP IT, STOP IT, STOP IT!*

Don reached for his Heckler and Koch MP5K. Shouting voices. Urgent screams. A woman crying. Children wailing. A dog barked in the distance. Dust rose from the ground and hung suspended in the air. Don felt himself raise his weapon, his hands acting of their own accord. His knees bent and then he found himself crouching. It was as if he was not in control of his body anymore. This time, everything happened fast. Three men ran toward him brandishing AKM's, firing their weapons. Wilson sprayed the advancing men with a hail of bullets. Don watched calmly, knowing they were dead before they hit the ground.

Suddenly, the mayhem spread, and the doors to the mosque burst outwards. Hostages began pouring out, running in all directions. Don saw the man on the roof of the mosque, instantly recognising the yellow polo shirt and red bandana. Don knew he had to be quick. He fired and the stone walls began to rip and splinter, shards of brittle stone raining down on the hostages. The top of the building was lost in a mist of exploding masonry. The man in the yellow polo shirt crumpled, but Don was too late. The rocket had already been fired.

He tried to shout, tried to warn Wilson, but his voice was lost in the cacophony of screams and gunfire. Don took a step back and felt his legs giving way as he stumbled down the sandbank. In the doorway of the mosque, Robert's left knee came apart. Don yelled at him to get out, but Robert was already being dragged inside the mosque by two of the terrorists.

It was the same, but different. He had seen this before. He tried changing it, tried to intervene, but whatever he did, it kept happening. The explosion from the rocket launched Don into the air, but he was protected from the blast by the sandbank. A rush of wind enveloped him, and then the very air seemed to be on fire. As he twisted and turned, he squeezed his eyes shut, the image of Robert being shot in the leg fresh in his mind. His body smashed into the beach and he rolled over. The sound of the battle was dull, a mere distant refrain to the thrumming in his ears. He reached up to his head and felt fresh blood. The hair there had been singed and his left arm hung limply, broken in three places. Don lifted himself to his feet and saw the mosque through a thick billowing smoke. There was a hole in the ground where Wilson had been standing. Burning, charred bodies littered the ground, and then a figure came through the sizzling black haze.

Carter fell at Don's feet. "Blow it, Don, blow it now." Carter was covered in blood and Don had no idea whose it was.

Don crouched down as more bullets sailed over his head. He pulled the detonator from his pocket, thankfully intact. He held it in his hand and looked at Carter. "The hostages. What about the fucking hostages?"

Carter lay still, his blood seeping into the sand, and looked at Don with dark eyes. He swallowed and then whispered. "All gone. Do it, do it now, and take those bastards down. They're all inside." Carter coughed and spat bloody phlegm into his hand. "I saw them. They think it's a full-blown war. When the rocket went up, they ran inside the mosque."

Don looked at the detonator and then back at Carter. "Wilson?"

Carter shook his head and his eyes glazed over.

Don knelt down and gripped Carter's hand. "Robert? Where's Robert?"

Carter didn't respond and Don felt the man's hand slip from his. A final breath whistled through Carter's teeth, and then he was dead. Don felt nothing. Carter had died next to him so many times now, it was like watching a play he had seen a thousand times before. Don looked back up at the mosque. Two men stood on the roof firing blindly. The smoke had cleared a little, but they could not see Don.

The CRRC was still there, a few feet away. He could still make it, back to the USNS Arctic. He had to. The Evac' Chopper could not come in, *would* not come in while the shit was still falling. How had it gone so wrong? There had been so many of them, far more than should have been there. He looked at the detonator in his hand again. *Press it. Fuck, Robert, where are you? Do it now. FUCK, FUCK, FUCK!* Carter's words rang around his aching head.

Do it, do it now.

Don squeezed his eyes shut. Bullets ripped into the beach, spraying him with dirt and sending mushroom clouds of gritty sand into him. Carter's body twitched as more rounds tore through him, and Don was sprayed with warm blood.

Do it, do it now.

Don felt the burning anger and shame rip through his soul. He was seething, shaking, his head spinning. Blood trickled down his cheek from his head wound, and he wanted to be somewhere else, anywhere but here. A dog barked again, closer, its frantic barking louder than the gunfire that surrounded him. The sun was scorching now, a fireball pressing down on him, lighting up the oxygen he was painfully trying to suck into his lungs.

Press the button. Blow the bastards to kingdom come. Robert, where are you? I've lost the others, you're all I have left.

Don saw Robert's prostrate body being dragged inside the mosque. He saw the stray cat stare at him as it crossed the road. He saw a man with a yellow polo shirt smiling at him. He looked up and saw the sun, a golden orb burning into his eyes, tearing at his soul. He saw the detonator in his hand. He knew what he had to do. Don closed his eyes and the world went black.

Do it, do it now.

An insistent, repetitive banging on the front door interrupted his nightmare, and Don awoke sharply. His head throbbed and he threw back the covers, exposing his sweaty body to the frigid air. His forehead was coated with a sheen of perspiration, and he groaned. Shouting, urgent voices, dog's barking, and more banging on his front door all colluded to heighten his burgeoning headache.

"All right, I'm coming!" he called out picking up a shirt from the floor. Putting it on, he recognised the faint odour of smoke and beer coming from it. He quickly pulled on his creased jeans and staggered from the room. As he passed into the lounge, he paused and put his hands on the doorframe. His legs wanted to give way, and his head was spinning. Ignoring the dizzy spell that threatened to take him down, he staggered over to the kitchen sink and stuck his head under the tap, letting the cool water fill his mouth. He gulped it down, desperate to take away the taste of blood. His tongue was dry, and at some point in the night, he must've bitten his lip. He turned the tap off and stayed there a moment. Goddamn, why couldn't he sleep? The dreams had been getting worse lately, much worse. The banging started up again on his door.

"All right, Jesus, I'm coming." Don looked at his apartment. It was a mess. He hadn't cleared up the empties from the weekend, and he really needed to open a window. He wasn't used to guests. Well, they would just have to take it as they found it. He opened the door to find Amanda standing there.

"Don, you look like shit," she said pushing past him into the dingy apartment. "Man, it stinks in here." She leant over the sink and pulled up the blinds, then cracked the window open an inch.

"Pleased to see you too," said Don shutting the front door before collapsing on the sofa.

"I tried calling, but you didn't answer," said Amanda looking at him with her hands on her hips.

Don felt in his jeans and pulled his phone out of a pocket. "Sorry, it was off." He turned it on and rubbed his chin.

"I thought you said you were going home last night when I left?" Amanda began picking up empty bottles from the coffee table and taking them over to the trash bin. She found a black garbage bag and began to fill it.

"I was. I did. I mean I was going to, but then Meghan asked me for another drink and…"

What had happened next? They had talked. He had drunk a couple more as she'd closed up and then? He poked around in his mind, trying to find the missing piece of information. Meghan had locked up. He had walked home *alone*. Thank God, he hadn't done anything stupid. He had opened a bottle of something though, something with a bit more kick to it than beer. Don looked at the coffee table and saw the empty bottle of Captain Morgan in the middle. Amanda hadn't gotten to it yet.

"Okay, I confess, I had another couple of drinks with Meghan, and maybe a few more beers when I got home. You know what it's like, one always leads to another." Don got up and swiftly picked up the rum when Amanda had her back turned. He rolled it under the sofa. "I know, I know, but...shit, what time is it? I thought you were supposed to be having a breakfast meeting with Zola today?"

"I did. That was nearly two hours ago, Don." Amanda put the black bag down and walked over to him. Her brusque attitude had softened. "I thought I would come by and check that you were okay. Today's important for you and I didn't want you to be on your own this morning."

Don stiffened up. "I don't need a nanny. I'll be in to work later."

"Yeah, but..."

Don's headache was about to blossom into a mushroom cloud of pain, and he couldn't deal with Amanda right now. "No. This is me, saying thank you, but no. Don't push it, Amanda. I appreciate you coming round to check on me." He heard his phone beep indicating he had missed calls. It beeped four times in his pocket. "That all you?"

"I was worried."

Don looked at his phone. It was nearly ten. If he was going to make it to the office by noon, he was going to have to get moving. It would be difficult now. He put an arm around Amanda and ushered her to the front door. "Do me a favour? Cover for me if I'm late. Tell Zola I'm held up in traffic or something."

"You sure you don't want me to help you clean up?" asked Amanda.

"I'm good. Want to go for a bite to eat after work?" He knew he shouldn't take up too much of Amanda's free time, but he knew he would want the company later. It was the one day of the year he was pretty much guaranteed to get Amanda to come out with him.

"Don, I can't tonight. Hamish is back later today. Maybe just a quick drink?"

Don felt like he'd been punched in the side of the head. This thing with Hamish really must be serious. "I thought Hamish wasn't due back until the weekend?"

"He wasn't. I got a text this morning saying he was on his way back and had a surprise for me."

"A surprise?"

"He said it was big, real big, and I would never guess what it was."

"Interesting." Don had no idea what Amanda was looking so excited about, but suspected he would find out later. At this point, he needed to wash away last night's indulgences and hit the road. "You can fill me in over that drink tonight?" he said closing the door.

"Okay, bye."

Don went back to his room and flopped onto the bed. It was still warm.

Just another five minutes. It'll take the edge off. No, you have to get up now; you can't put it off any longer. You don't need any more sleep; you need something hardier than that to take the edge off.

Don felt around under his bed and found the bottle of white rum he saved for special occasions. If today didn't count, then nothing did. He unscrewed the cap and took a long gulp as he lay on the bed. As the burning sensation in his throat subsided, he put the bottle back on his bedside table and got up. He showered, shaved, and slowly the maelstrom in his head thinned out. When he had cleaned up, he put on a black suit with a dark grey tie over a crisp white shirt. It was the only thing in his wardrobe that didn't need ironing, and he only wore it once a year. After he'd dressed, he grabbed his car keys and left the apartment.

"What do you think, Don?"

Don locked his front door to find Mrs Barkley sweeping her balcony.

Probably been waiting all morning for me to come out, he thought.

"I hope it's a big diamond ring," she cackled. "That girl deserves it, don't you think?"

"What's that, Mrs Barkley?"

"Your friend? Such a nice young lady. I was saying that maybe her boyfriend's surprise is a ring. It wouldn't surprise me. You know, I think number six is moving out soon if they need someplace of their own."

As Mrs Barkley continued her speculation, Don did the only thing he knew how, to get out of her way, and left.

"I've still got some apple pie put aside for you! I think I put a little too much cinnamon in, but you can be the judge," continued Mrs Barkley as Don headed out of the apartment block.

He walked back past the Old Station, which was still closed, and got into his car. The coolness of the morning had given way to another fine day, and his first port of call was the bank.

"Your regular deposit, Mr O'Reilly?" asked the cashier.

"Yes, please. Another thousand. Actually, make it fifteen hundred this month," Don said.

"Certainly, sir." The young man behind the counter processed the transaction. "If I could make a suggestion, if you and Mrs O'Reilly were to open a joint account, you could make some substantial savings in your fees, and it would save you the hassle of coming in to see us every month. I can set it up for you right now?"

"No, Mrs O'Reilly and I need separate accounts. Thank you anyway. Just put the money into her account and we're done."

"That's all done for you now. Have a nice day."

Don left the bank and made his second call of the day. He drove out of Mama Kitty's Coffee Shack armed with a Danish pastry and a latte. His third call of the day was seven Collwood Lane. He parked up outside as he had done yesterday, and tucked into his breakfast. The buzz of Captain Morgan's white rum was wearing off and Don wolfed down his pastry. As he ate, he monitored the house. The window shades were pulled open, and it looked unoccupied. The silver car was gone from the driveway too.

Damn it, I'm too late. Now she'll be there too.

Don drove away, leaving the house behind, but unable to escape the memories it dredged up. Years ago, he had poured over textbooks in the upstairs front room, and cried himself to sleep after getting the belt in the back room. Not all of his memories were bad though, and there had been plenty of summer nights spent playing games in the back yard. It was a good area, and he had to be grateful for the start he'd had in life. Back then, the Old Station had been a real cop station, and Mama Kitty's had been a discount clothing store. Right around the corner from there, was the Holy Spirit Anglican Church, where he had been dragged religiously every Sunday. That had changed too, having undergone a facelift some years back. Don might have left home, but he still kept tabs on what was going on in the area. He was pleased to know it had not degenerated like so many areas. Even the house had aged well. The letterbox had changed over the years from blue to red, and there was a new garage, but otherwise, it looked largely the same. There was the front porch where his father had taught him how to tie his laces, the two rusted spots on the side of the house where his old basketball net had been, and the bedroom where he had invested so much time reading about military history. Don's eyes rested upon the wooden front door. That front door hadn't changed since he had found his father dead of a heart attack when he was only nine. Trips to church had increased for a while after that, and then they'd stopped. Not a lot had changed to the house since Don had last stepped foot inside. It was the people who had changed.

His final stop that morning was further out of the city, a twenty minute drive south. The Martin Luther King Junior Freeway was snarled up by an accident that Don couldn't quite see, and he hoped it would be clear by the time he had to leave. He took a turn down Market Street, and then Imperial Avenue, before bringing the car to a halt underneath a Norfolk Island pine. There were a few other cars parked up too, and as he got out, he saw the silver Ford Escort three down from his. Don's mood was already turning sour, and the sight of the car only added to his sagging spirit. He walked up to the gates of the cemetery and let a crying elderly couple go ahead of him. Should he go in, or wait?

Every year he visited, the place looked immaculate. The gravestones were clean, there were fresh flowers dotted about the place, and the grass was cut, always one inch high. He rubbed his bottom lip. She was there; he could see her, bent down at the grave. She wore black, of course, and a hat, always a hat. He was impressed she could still bend at her age. Maybe he should wait a bit longer. She had probably been there for a couple of hours already. A house finch flew overhead, and a black sedan drove slowly past, its engine purring. Don watched the elderly couple reach an unmarked grave. The earth was freshly dug and the woman was sobbing into her husband's shoulder. He watched the old man take a red kerchief from a pocket and pass it to his wife. Had they just lost a child? The woman kneeled down and placed a bouquet of pink roses on the mound of dirt. She then reached into a pocket and took something else out. It twinkled in the sunlight and Don could only see that it was some sort of jewellery. The woman put it next to the flowers.

A daughter? No parent should lose their child. That's not fair. It's bad enough to lose friends, or a sibling. But a child is not fair.

Don watched as the woman stood and the husband put his arm around her. He looked back at the gates and Don caught his eye. The man looked placid and calm, yet, his eyes betrayed his true thoughts. Don felt guilty for watching them grieve.

He's being strong for his wife, and he's sad, but he's angry. There's anger and hatred in those eyes. Hatred for whoever caused the death of his daughter. I don't blame you. Not at all. If He had anything to do with it, then I'm with you on that one. I hope you get your justice one day.

Don used the old man's energy and walked through the gates into the cemetery. He felt anger too, but not for the dead, and not for Him. He felt anger that he had even hesitated. He had a duty to perform, and he was letting her get in the way again.

You don't have a monopoly on grief, you know. You can't hog him forever. I have every right to be here, as much as you do, if not more. Deal with it.

Don walked up to the grave. The woman in black heard him approach and stood up. When she turned to face him, Don could see tears streaming down her face. Her weary old face was wrinkly, and her slender frame too thin. A silver cross hung around her neck and nestled into the folds of skin. A tissue fell from her pocket onto the freshly mown grass, as her red, puffy eyes looked him up and down.

"I wondered when you'd show your face," she said blankly.

"I was giving you some space." Suddenly, Don felt cold and tucked his hands into his suit pockets. "How have you been?"

The woman snorted. "If you ever stopped by, you'd know. Is it too much to ask? But I don't expect I'll see *you* anytime soon. You'd have to face up to what you did then, instead of running..."

"Do we have to? Here? Now? Can't we just...can't we just come and see him in peace? We used to..."

The woman laughed, and her eyes creased together. There was no lightness or joy in the laugh. It was a laugh to sign off the end of the world. "What would your father think of you, Don? God rest his soul. He tried to teach you right and wrong. He tried and look what happened, dead before his time. Oh, I know that it must all be a part of His plan, but I don't know what He was thinking when He took him away from me and left me with you. Look at you, bold as brass. You think if you put on a smart suit and turn up here once a year, you'll be forgiven? Well not by me, and certainly not by Him. God is waiting for you, Don."

"Jesus Christ, give it a rest!" Don was aware he had raised his voice, and remembered the elderly couple at their child's grave. He went closer to the woman in black, so he could speak in a more reverent tone, more appropriate to the setting. "When are you going to accept it? What happened, happened, and it was *not* my fault. I seem to remember forgiveness and respect playing a big part in our Sunday school classes. You should know - you dragged me there every week. Yet, you seem to have forgotten that part. Why is it all wickedness and sin? Why is it you can't..."

The woman drew her jacket together as more tears fell. She brushed past Don without looking at him. "Save it. Until you face up to your responsibilities, you're as dead to me as he is. One day, you'll wind up in Heaven or Hell, there's no escaping that. Which one you'll end up in is up to you. All I can do is pray for your redemption, and hope you find the way."

Don stared at the grave. He didn't want it to go that way. He wanted this to be a chance to move on, for reuniting, not pushing her further away. He tried to pretend he wasn't affected, but he was. It wasn't fair. All he wanted to do was pay his respects, and she had ruined it. Again.

"Goodbye, Mom," he said.

The woman in black didn't answer and kept walking.

CHAPTER 5

OCTOBER WEDNESDAY 16TH 15:04

"When you said you had a surprise for me, this isn't exactly what I was hoping for."

Hamish grinned at Amanda as the truck pulled out of the maintenance gates, finally leaving them alone. He pulled her close and hugged her. "God, I've missed you."

Amanda laughed, pushing him away. "I missed you too, but you stink. You should know that. You stink, like *really* bad."

"Yeah, well, I didn't have time for a shower. We came straight here." Hamish took her hand and they began walking back to the holding pens. "So what do you think? Is it a breed of shark? A whale? I haven't seen Dad so excited about anything in a long time. He thinks he's going to get rich and famous."

"He could be right about that one. Zola is bouncing off the walls. I don't even know where to start, Hamish. I'm going to have to do a lot of tests, but right now, I have no idea. It's not a shark or a whale. I can tell you that for free."

Amanda heard a cheer come from over a fenced wall and knew it was for Pete and Poppy. Jay was taking the afternoon show for her, so she could meet Hamish and their new guest. She reached for the door, entered the code for the keypad, and together they entered a bare corridor. It was cold and their footsteps echoed as they walked.

"So how much do you think Zola will pay for it? You've told me she's a hard-ass, but we're not going to sell it cheaply. Dad will be back soon to talk money, so I figured I'd get a head start, try and butter her up." Hamish squeezed Amanda's hand. "You realise this could set us up. I mean, if this is worth what we think, we are looking at a potential lottery win here. We could do so much with that money. Buy a house, invest in the business. I could upgrade the trawler and Dad wouldn't have to worry about his retirement anymore."

"Retirement?" Amanda looked worried. "Since when was Curtis retiring? He's not...ill, is he?"

"Heck no, he's fitter than me. He'll live to be one hundred. No, I have more news."

They stopped outside the door to the holding pen. Splashing sounds came from behind the closed door and Hamish looked at Amanda in the dull light of the corridor. Even with the rank smell of fish around, the damp air and the monster only a few feet away, she still looked beautiful. "Dad's retiring and giving me the trawler. He wants me to run the business."

Amanda's eyes widened and she embraced Hamish. "I'm so pleased. I'm proud of you! No wonder he's excited. Hamish, things are looking up. This find, this animal, is amazing, absolutely amazing. Now, the business too? Heck, if I can get you into a shower, I might even contemplate kissing you."

Hamish kissed her and she kissed him back. It wasn't the most romantic of places to kiss, but he didn't care. It had been too long since he had tasted Amanda's sweet lips. "Maybe later, you can join me for that shower?"

"You can count on it," said Amanda, as she opened the door and held it open for Hamish.

The room was colder than the corridor, and Hamish felt himself shiver as he walked up the narrow gangway over the pool. With one hand in Amanda's, he carefully placed the other on the handrail as he walked. The cavernous room was filled with the splashing sounds of the creature that swam below them. It moved from side to side, barely able to run in the confines of the pool, even though it was fifty feet long and as far wide.

"This was the best we could do at short notice," said Zola noticing Hamish approach. "I wish you'd rung ahead."

"Sorry, we were a bit busy," answered Hamish. "We kind of had our hands full."

"So I see." Zola looked down at the creature beneath her. "It's breath-taking. Where do you even find something like this?"

Hamish looked at Amanda, and then back to Zola. "Well, Mrs Bertoni, you are not going to find anything else out there like this. We were out in the Pacific and headed for where we'd got a big catch of Herring last week. We're not really sure what happened, but there was some debris in the water, and a life raft, but no sign of life. We thought maybe another trawler or a private yacht had gone down, so we were poking around, but like I said, there was no one around, and just as we were about to leave, this thing appeared.

"It was just floating on the water, so we hooked it in and pulled it up onto deck. It was a bit of a struggle I can tell you. It took all three of us to reel it in and it barely fit. Roy had to get hold of its tail and curve it right from the stern to the bow. He wasn't too happy about having to touch it either."

"I can well imagine," said Amanda.

Hamish stole a glance at Amanda and fought the urge to laugh, remembering how Roy had been loath to get near the animal, least of all, touch it.

"But how did you get it on board? I mean, it's thrashing around now, and there is no way you could handle it with just the three of you," said Zola.

"When we hauled it aboard, we thought it was dead. It wasn't moving at all, and with all the debris in the water, we assumed something had happened to kill it. We lugged it onto the deck and we just supposed we were bringing back a dead animal. Dad thought you would like it as a specimen, something a bit different to showcase. He knew it was different."

"It's that all right," said Zola. "Look at those teeth. Magnificent. So how on earth *did* you get it back? I mean, even if it was 'dead' when you found it, what brought it back to life?"

"We got lucky really. Dad was worried that if another storm came up while we were coming back, that it might fall off the boat and we'd lose it for good. So we tethered it down real tight. He and Roy lashed it to the deck so there was no way we could lose it. Bloody good job too, or I wouldn't be stood here now. It seemed to wake up this morning. Came as quite a shock."

"Who woke it?" asked Amanda.

"That would be Roy," said Hamish, once again stifling a laugh. "He was poking around with it, sticking the boathooks into it, when all of a sudden, it just jerked to life. Roy practically had a heart attack. He fell over and I helped him up. He was fine, but his pride has taken a bashing in the last twenty four hours."

"Hamish, you should've been more careful, what if you hadn't come back to me?" Amanda looked down at the creature beneath her in the tank. It was more docile now, just treading water near the top of the water.

"Anyway, then it quietened down again, thankfully, and we had no trouble out of it. I don't know if it was sleeping, but it didn't move an inch. It was only when we got it to the pool here that it seemed to wake up again," said Hamish. "So, you interested in taking this off my hands?" he asked Zola.

"Well, with Amanda working here I was hoping you might consider donating it, in the interests of scientific research, of course." Zola put on her best plastic smile.

Hamish grunted. "Mrs Bertoni, I love Amanda, but not that much."

Amanda gave him a playful punch on the arm as the smile fell from Zola's face.

"I tell you what, Mrs Bertoni, you come up with a figure. Then add a zero. I'm sure we can work something out. I would hate to have to take this *magnificent* creature back or find a zoo for it. I mean it's up to you, but Animal World up in Vallejo would be fascinated to see what we got here."

Zola put her hand over Hamish's. "Hamish, darling, don't worry, there's no need to be so hasty. I will sort this out with you and your father. There's no need to speak to anyone else. Why don't you come back to my office now, and we can see what we can do. You must be starving after your trip, why don't I order us some afternoon tea and we can hammer out a deal. What do you say?"

"Honey, you mind if I disappear for a bit?" Hamish knew he had Zola right where he wanted her. Whatever figure she suggested, he was going to make sure he got double. His father had worked hard his whole life, and he deserved a big payday.

Amanda nodded and looked at the clock on the wall. "Go ahead. I'm just going to start having a look at our new friend and then I've got the dolphin show at four. I'll see you later. I finish at six. Meet you then?"

"Oh, and Amanda, can you get me a report by six?" asked Zola. "I want to know what this thing is. Jay can take your shows for the rest of the day."

Hamish kissed Amanda and then followed Zola out of the room, leaving Amanda alone.

"Now then," said Amanda, "just what *are* you exactly." She climbed down to the water's edge and peered in at the monster. It was impressive, truly like nothing else she had ever seen. Its basic physical structure was reminiscent of an alligator, but the head was shaped differently, and overall, it just wasn't the same. She noticed the creature was quiet now. Its tail was languid and even its eyes looked like they were closing. If it were going to sleep, it would make her job easier. She had two hours to come up with what this thing was. "Right, you and I have work to do."

OCTOBER WEDNESDAY 16TH 18:17

Don slipped into the boardroom quietly, hoping he wouldn't be noticed. He arrived at the park late, well after the start of his shift, and so hoped to avoid Zola for the rest of the day. Unfortunately, he hadn't factored in the arrival of a giant sea monster, and so, when he had finally arrived at the park several hours late, Zola had been on the war path looking for him.

After she had done balling him out in the privacy of her office, she softened. Apparently, Amanda had tried to cover for him, and had let it out that today was a special anniversary. He was a bit annoyed that Amanda had let slip, but he knew he couldn't blame her. He was the one who had decided to go to the Old Station after the cemetery, instead of work. He had been the only one drinking instead of working, and he had been the only one who had decided it was better to get drunk than to turn on his phone. If he had, he would've come across the ten voicemails and texts a lot sooner than he had. He also would've arrived at work in a far more sober, fresher mood than he was in right now.

Once Zola brought him up to date, Don quickly organised the monster's removal from the temporary holding pen, and had it transferred to a larger tank. He reasoned that if they didn't know what they were dealing with, they needed to take precautions. The tank where the Orcas were kept for monitoring when they showed signs of ill health was the largest they had, other than Shakti Stadium itself. The last hour had been a bit of a blur, and he hadn't found time to catch up with Amanda yet. He was intrigued to know what was going on, and after finally organising night shifts to watch the new arrival, he surreptitiously sneaked into the meeting late.

"Right on time, Don, as expected," said Zola. She was stood at the front of the room with Amanda. In front of her were three rows of chairs. Only half of them were being used, filled by essential members of the park staff for this urgent meeting: Marketing, Advertising, Accounts, and Security.

Don saw Amanda wink at him and knew he might be in the doghouse with Zola, but Amanda hadn't a cruel bone in her body.

"Amanda was about to tell us what she has found out. I'm sure we're all waiting with baited breath, so I'll let her get on with it. I don't need to remind all of you here that this is completely confidential. What is said tonight stays in this room." Zola sat down in the front row. On her left was Jay, Amanda's co-worker, and to Zola's right, Don saw a young man. He didn't recognise him, but had an idea it could be Hamish.

"Well, I haven't had long to examine it, so I am not fully prepared. What was delivered to us this afternoon is nothing short of a miracle. If you thought Jay's four p.m. dolphin show was impressive, then hold onto your seats, 'cause you haven't seen anything yet."

Amanda held up six large prints she had made up of some photographs she had taken. The first one was a close up of the creature's head. "See here, the ridge-line of the jaw goes all the way back. Its mouth is larger than an alligator's. It also has more teeth. Your average 'gator has twenty-four teeth. Our guest has, by my count, about sixty. It also has four elongated incisors, two on each side, so we can safely assume it is a carnivore."

Amanda proceeded to hold up five more photographs, each one showing more of the creature: its body, legs, and tail. She then stuck each one up on the wall behind her, making a crude mosaic of the photographs. "See how its tail is almost as long as its body? I would say it could move through the ocean extremely well. We don't have the space to see it in action, but I would say we are looking at a predator here, one that is highly capable, adept at manoeuvring through the water at speed, and has incredibly powerful jaws. Its feet suggest it is amphibious in nature, and it has a strong spine to support its body weight. We know it survived several hours out of the water on the trawler that brought it here."

"What about its vision?" asked Jay. "Could you ascertain how it tracks its prey? If it only has a single long-wavelength-sensitive cone type in the retina, it may be…"

"What does it eat? Fish? Seals?" asked another voice.

"Is it male or female?" asked another.

"Were you able to classify it yet?" asked Zola.

Amanda looked at Hamish in the front row for reassurance. He nodded back at her.

"I'll be able to tell you more tomorrow. I hope. The reality is that it could take weeks to figure it out. Based on what limited knowledge I have so far, my best guess is that this is a throwback, a relative of the dinosaurs that has so far, evaded any interaction with man."

"A dinosaur?" asked Zola.

Don could see that her face showed traces of incredulity, but her eyes were alive. He didn't doubt that her brain was running a million miles per hour.

"Primitive amphibians died out in the late Triassic through Cretaceous period," said Jay. "Amanda, you're not suggesting we have a live dinosaur are you?"

"It's at least a close relative. Perhaps a descendant of Metoposaurus or Eryops?"

"Thanks, Amanda," said Zola as she got up. "Amanda, you sit down now, thank you. Everyone, please remember that what we have here is something unique. I do not expect any of you to discuss this outside of the people you see in this room. I have made a few decisions, which I will share with you in a moment.

Let me first of all thank Mr Williams for bringing it to us." Zola pointed out Hamish to the room, and there was a smattering of applause.

He looked around the room, blushing at the attention. Leaning over to Amanda, he whispered in her ear. "And I'd like to thank your boss for giving me the biggest cheque I've seen in my life."

"Right, to business." Zola picked up her notebook and began tapping into it as she spoke. "We are pushing this forward, and we have no time to waste. The longer this dinosaur sits in our tanks, the more chance there is of what we have leaking out. On Friday, we are going to host the biggest event in the history of California, if not the US. We have a bona fide star here people, and I want the whole world to know that Wild Seas Park San Diego is the *only* place it can be seen. That means we have less than forty-eight hours to get organised. Shakti Stadium is getting a makeover. People will be fighting each other for tickets.

"Jay, work with Susan and get Shakti moved on. Animal World will probably take him. We need the stadium and his time is up anyway. I need him gone by Friday morning. I don't care if you have to chop him up into pieces and mail him to Vallejo, just make it happen. John, Fiona, I want you to come up with a marketing plan. I need it on my desk by noon tomorrow. In exactly two days' time, at six p.m., I am going to let the whole world in on our secret. We'll hold press briefings tomorrow at eleven and five. We'll get them excited. Come up with something juicy for me. Tantalise them. *Tease* them. It's date night and you're wearing edible panties, got it?"

John and Fiona looked at each other nervously.

"Tate, get hold of the media, use everyone you've got. I want CNN, Fox, the BBC, freaking Al-Jazeera for all I care. Get me the best price for the best exposure. Get me a statement I can read tomorrow too at the briefing. Make it snappy. Give it *teeth*."

Tate laughed to hide the anxious nausea stirring up his bowels. Half of the room followed him with light laughter. Don could tell it was a response borne from fear, rather than humour. Zola was going to milk this cow until it bled dollars.

"Don, I don't need to tell you how important it is that this is kept under wraps. Double your guards, do whatever it takes to keep our new friend under wraps. Your budget has no ceiling for the rest of the year. Our dinosaur is now Wild Sea's number one asset. I am investing *a lot* in this, and it needs to work.

"Everyone, listen up. We need TV, newspapers, the whole show. Geographic will suck my balls to get exclusive access on this. Get ET on the phone for me first thing tomorrow, Fiona. Who said celebrities have to be human? Friday night is going to go off. I want red carpets and champagne. I want lights and fireworks. Most of all, I want everyone watching to know this is Wild Seas. I want A-list celebrities right in the front row when we unveil our latest exhibit. I want a camera shoved in their faces when I bring out our big-toothed man-eating monster, so we can see them shit themselves on live television.

"Jay, Amanda, you've got contacts in the neighbourhood. I want the local press and schools involved with this, too. You know, to show we haven't lost that community spirit bullshit. Get some little kids in, maybe some retards, it looks good. Give them free passes. Everyone else pays through the nose. Accounts, get me a draft of what we can charge for this thing. Book deals, magazine shoots, interviews, whatever else you can come up, I want it all on my desk tomorrow morning. Marketing, we need to update the kiosks and souvenir shops with dinosaur stuff: cuddly toys, posters, badges, T-shirts. If you can stick a price tag on it, I want it in my shops by Friday.

"I need one more thing. By eleven tomorrow, we need a name. We can't keep calling it a dinosaur. We need something they'll remember. John, Tate, Fiona, and Don, think on it tonight and I'll see you back here tomorrow at eight for brainstorming. Everyone, let's get to work."

Zola snapped her notebook shut and slammed the door on her way out, leaving the room to fill with excited conversations. Slowly, the people dispersed, leaving Don to wait until he could get to Amanda. He found her talking to the young man he assumed was Hamish.

"How heartless can you be? Shakti's been here for years. Suddenly, it's 'oh well, who's next?'" Amanda looked angry. She was constantly tugging at the hair back behind her ears.

"Susan will arrange it with Animal World. You said yourself Susan wouldn't let anything bad happen. There's an opportunity here and you have to be in on it, Amanda. If you walk away from this, you'll regret it," said Hamish.

"He's right," said Don, "if you let Zola walk all over this, it'll end in disaster. You might not like it, but work with her. Make sure that whatever that creature is out there, you look out for its best interests. Don't let Zola get to you. There are a lot of animals in the park who rely on you. A lot of people too."

"Hey, Don," said Amanda, "this is Hamish, as you probably guessed."

Don shook hands with Hamish. "Don. Pleased to meet you at last, Hamish. Amanda never stops talking about you."

"Is that so?"

"Very funny, Mr O'Reilly," said Amanda.

"Hamish, what do you say we take this girl of yours for a beer? I think we could all do with a drink. I have a feeling tomorrow is going to be a long day."

"I'm with you on that one," said Hamish. "I just need to call my father and let him know what's going on, but I can call him from the car."

Amanda sighed. "Urgh, I am so fed up with that woman. Who does she think she is? She can't just *decide* like that, it's ridiculous. Wild Seas Park isn't some carnival for curiosities. This isn't Ripley's. We're here to educate people, to show people how to treat animals and how amazing life is. She just wants to turn it into a circus."

"Amanda, chill. We'll figure it out. There's nothing we can do now except go find a cold beer and a plate of ribs." Don didn't want to go home alone, not tonight. After the day he'd had, the last thing he needed was to go back to his apartment and watch yet another reality show. He knew he'd just end up tossing things over in his mind about the confrontation at the cemetery earlier in the day. "Hamish, it's my shout. I think you've brought home the catch of the *year*."

"Lead the way, Don. Although, with the cheque I've got in my pocket, *I'm* paying tonight."

"All right, boys, it's only ribs and a beer, not three weeks in Bora Bora," said Amanda.

"Hamish, just one thing before we go," said Don. "Do you think you could have a shower?"

Laughing, they left the meeting room. Don couldn't help but glance back at the photographs Amanda had stuck on the wall as he left. He wasn't convinced it was such a good idea to put a monster like that out there for the whole world to see either. He and Amanda were going to have to watch Zola like a hawk. He had a feeling his crappy day was about to turn into a crappy week.

CHAPTER 6

OCTOBER WEDNESDAY 16TH 20:48

"So, what can you tell me? Other than that it's clearly related to the Ugly fish. I mean, it's that or Zola's twin sister, right?"

Hamish and Amanda laughed at Don's joke, yet, he instantly felt a pang of guilt. Why should he be in a nice bar making jokes, eating and drinking when others were cold in the ground? He couldn't think about that now. There was plenty of time for that in his sleep.

Stop over-thinking things and relax for once. He's waiting. Where are you?

Those old Sunday school lessons had taught him to be careful and respectful. Old lessons were hard to unlearn, especially when they had been beaten into you. He watched Amanda laugh and pretended to smile too, hiding his mood behind a large gulp of beer.

They had eaten quickly, and only Hamish and Don were drinking. Amanda wanted to keep a clear head for the next day, whilst Hamish wanted to celebrate. Don liked Hamish, as he seemed very down to earth, reliable, and content within himself. He was just what Amanda needed. Don was pleased to see her looking so happy. He noticed how they kept holding hands and touching each other under the table too. He realised he was keeping them from each other, but he was hoping the evening might last a little bit longer. He wasn't tired, and his apartment beckoned him like a sore rash.

The day will soon be over. Then the nightmares will fade and she'll forget she saw me until this time next year. I've got twelve months to forget her. Just keep depositing the cheques. Take care of her. Dad isn't here anymore, so you're the man now. Just do it.

Amanda leant back in her chair. She didn't need to worry about anyone eavesdropping in the bar. The volume of the music and people's conversations would easily drown out what she was about to say.

"Well, number one it's amphibious. It hasn't shown any sign of wanting to get out of the tank since we put it in there, but it has webbed feet. It also spent several hours out of the water on Hamish's trawler. If it is amphibious though, I'm surprised we haven't come across it before."

"How do you mean?" asked Hamish.

"Well, it's not uncommon for species to disappear only to reappear again years later, when we thought they were extinct. Look at the Coelacanth. Everyone knew they were extinct, *knew it*, period; they were wiped out sometime around the end of the Cretaceous period, until a fisherman randomly caught one, around 1930 something, and boom, they're back. The oceans are massive and there are lots of places to hide."

"Especially if you don't want to be found. I heard they found sea slugs in the bottom of some trench near, um, Indonesia I think, that were twice as large as any others they had seen before," said Hamish. "Imagine a giant sea slug. Yeesh."

"A dinosaur though?" Don finished the pitcher of Bud' and looked out for the waitress so he could order another. "You're the expert, Amanda, but you'd better get this right. If Zola puts herself out there on Friday, and announces to the whole world that we've caught a dinosaur, and you're wrong...I wouldn't want to be in your shoes."

"I know it's quite similar in appearance to an alligator, but its genealogy is different. It's more like a shark with legs, than a croc' or an alligator," said Amanda.

"A shark with legs? You sure you want another one of these?" asked the waitress as she took away the empty pitcher.

"Thanks, Meghan," said Don chuckling.

"We'd better keep it down," said Amanda. "I wouldn't want our little secret to come out too soon. Or I wouldn't want to be in *your* shoes, Don."

"So, what else? Did you look at the wounds on its head?" asked Hamish.

"What wounds?" Don idly lifted his glass to his lips before realising it was empty.

"Hamish thinks they're from a gun. I couldn't get close enough to examine them properly, but it's possible. There are several around its head and neck, and a few more on the body too. They look like puncture holes, but without a thorough examination, I couldn't say for sure."

"Bullet holes? That doesn't sound good," said Don. "How thick is its skin if it can take a bullet?"

"When we found it, it was alone. But I did find a gun on a raft close by. It might also explain why we thought it was dead. Maybe it was just unconscious? The bullets can't have done much damage if it was just knocked out."

The waitress appeared at Don's side and put the pitcher of beer down on the table. "How're you tonight, honey?"

"I'm doing fine thanks, Meghan." Don didn't like lying, but he wasn't about to tell his new friend his sordid life story, or how he spent half the day in a cemetery. Besides, Hamish and Amanda were taking his mind off the thing he didn't want to think about.

Meghan put her hand on his arm. "Well, you want anything, you just holler. I mean it."

Don looked into Meghan's eyes and saw a warmness he hadn't seen in many people. He was tempted to believe she meant it, but wasn't that what all waitresses did? They were all sweetness and light until they saw the tip. That was how it worked, right? Except last night, she had chatted to him for hours and it had felt good. It had felt like a normal conversation between two normal people. Outside of Amanda, Don hadn't found anyone like that he could talk to.

"Don't go far, I may take you up on that," said Don as Meghan left.

"Hey, Don, we may get going. Sorry to leave you with all that, buddy," said Hamish as he got up looking at the pitcher.

"You're leaving? I thought we might celebrate. With the result you had today, I thought I'd have to *drag* you out of here," said Don. He looked at his watch and knew he wouldn't be able to go home yet.

Amanda was getting up too. "Sorry, Don. I'm tired and I have to be at work early. You do too, so take it easy, okay?" She was looking at the pitcher as she spoke and Don knew what she was saying. He was also going to choose to ignore it.

"Nice to meet you, Don. I'll pick up the tab on our way out. See you soon." Hamish went off to the bar and Amanda hung back.

"Don, I know what today is, but I haven't seen Hamish in a few days, and we've a lot to talk about. I'll see you early tomorrow morning. Take care of yourself. Call me if you need me." Amanda gave Don a quick kiss on the cheek and then hurried to catch up to Hamish.

Don knew he wouldn't call Amanda, not tonight. He had to leave her out of his problems; it was unfair to expect her to pick him up all the time. She had her own life to lead. He watched her and Hamish jump into their car outside. She flashed the lights and beeped once to say goodbye, and then they were gone. Don looked around the bar. Evidently, the Old Station didn't draw as good a crowd on Wednesdays as it did on Tuesdays. Other than a family in the far corner tucking into a huge ice-cream sundae, he was alone. Not even the old men who usually propped up the bar were there. He poured himself a drink, and then swivelled around to face the television above the bar. There was no football tonight, no music on the jukebox, and just CNN on to push the silence and dark thoughts away. Don walked over to the bar and pulled up a stool so he could sit closer and listen. He watched the screen as he drank.

"The search for the missing ocean cruise liner, 'Tranquilla,' continues tonight as we enter the second day. A number of planes and ships are now searching for it, and experts are questioning just how a large ship could simply disappear. Relatives are gathered at the Hilton Honolulu anxiously waiting for news, and desperately hoping something will be found today, as fears are raised, the liner may *never* be found. Our Hawaii correspondent, Josh Hall, is outside the hotel now with the latest."

"Thanks, Cindy. It has been another devastating day for the relatives of those aboard the Tranquilla. Of course, most are US citizens, as the ship was en route from Honolulu to San Francisco when it disappeared. The owners of the ship have said there was no mechanical fault with the ship, and it was serviced as recently as February this year. All search efforts have so far drawn a blank, and questions are being asked now just *how* can a cruise ship sink without trace? I spoke to one of the dockworkers here who preferred to stay anonymous, and he told me there are rumours that there was some sort of underwater earthquake, which may have triggered a whirlpool. Even if something catastrophic happened, it doesn't explain why there was no emergency call made. Cindy, as the days go on with no success, there are only more questions."

"Josh, have they widened the search area? We were told there was a narrow path that the ship was on, yet, surely if nothing has come up, they must look further afield."

"Yes, in fact, the planes are now looking over such a wide area of ocean that it could take weeks to find anything. Millions of square meters of ocean have to be covered, as there are indications the ship may have gone off course. How, or why, is open to suggestion, and terrorism has not been ruled out at this stage. No one person or group has claimed responsibility yet, and the authorities are keeping all options open until they find some concrete evidence of what has happened to the nearly five hundred people aboard."

"Josh, thank you. We will, of course, keep you updated as the story continues. In other news…"

Don's mobile buzzed in his pocket and he plucked it out.

Private number calling. Who the hell is this?

"Don speaking."

There was silence on the other end of the phone.

"This is Don, can I help you?"

"Don, it's me."

He finished his beer and put the empty glass down so as not to break it. His mother hadn't called him in years. What did she want now? They hadn't parted on very amicable terms, which actually was not unusual. Still, she never called him, *ever*. Suddenly, the CNN anchor wasn't there, the bar wasn't there, and he was at home, bending over the kitchen table as his mother raised a brown leather belt in the air.

Get a grip, Don told himself. *You've nothing to feel guilty for. She can't punish you anymore. She's fallen over and broken a leg. She's crashed her car. She's been mugged and now she needs you. She's...*

"I'm fine. Are you? I just thought..." She trailed off and nobody spoke.

Don broke the awkward silence. "I'm sorry I got angry earlier. I shouldn't have. Maybe us meeting today wasn't such a good idea? Not on his anniversary. You need anything?"

"No, I just stopped by the Holy Spirit afterwards and stayed there a while. I got to thinking how I'm not so young anymore. You're not either, Donald. Time creeps up on you. I don't know, I think perhaps I'll see him again soon."

"Mom, you're stronger than most people I know. Don't go talking like that." Don picked up his wallet. He should go round and check on her. "I can be round in a few minutes if you like?" He was nervous asking and wanted to burst out laughing. Nervous about asking his mother if he could come home? What a joke. "Mom, you hear me?"

"Like I said, I was at the Holy Spirit today. It got me thinking about a lot of things. How short this life is. How we need salvation before we meet Him. I wanted to ask if you'd come with me on Sunday. I think it would do you good."

Don didn't feel like laughing anymore. "Mom, you know I don't go anymore. I don't need to. I know that..."

"You don't *need* to? Don, you more than anyone *need* to go. I thought I could help you. There are a lot of good people at the church, people who you can talk to about it. They can help you realise what you did, so you can seek forgiveness from Him. I could..."

"Jesus, are you for real? Forgiveness? I thought you were calling to talk to me like a regular person. Huh, what was I thinking? You know what, Mom, forget it. You go to your church and pray for me. I'm already at mine, and I'm going to drown in holy water tonight."

Don hung up and about two seconds later, he knew he was going to get drunk. Damn Zola and her pet dinosaur. He set his phone alarm for seven thirty, giving himself just enough time to shower and get to the park for eight, and shoved the phone in his pocket.

Meghan was drying glasses and he called her over. "Fill her up," he said with a scowl on his face.

Meghan poured him a beer and handed it to him. "Want to talk about it?"

Don downed it and shook his head. "Another, please."

Meghan handed him another beer and watched him down that too. She wrestled the empty glass from his hand and held onto him. "Don, you don't have to be like that around me. I'm your friendly waitress, remember?"

Don't drag her into it. Look at those eyes, so warm and kind, even now, when you're acting like a jerkoff.

Don smiled humbly. "You're right. Sorry, just had a thing with someone."

"Anyone important?"

"No. It's nothing." Don looked around the bar and realised it was deserted. The family in the corner had finished and left, leaving the bar empty. He glanced up at the TV and saw it was getting late. "Sorry, you must want to close up. I'll get going."

Meghan bit her lip and kept her hand on Don's. "You live round here, don't you? You know, I should really make sure you get home. I can't have my best patrons walking these streets late at night when they've drunk as much as you. What do you say? I'll lock up and meet you out front in five minutes? Or if you're busy, I'm off Friday night. We could hang out then."

Don thought about his apartment and how dirty it was. He still hadn't thrown out the empties, or the dishes in the sink. Meghan was probably half his age, yet, when she looked at him, he forgot his sadness. "Sure, I've got something a little stronger at home if you're keen for a night-cap?"

Meghan smiled. "Now you're talking."

She clicked off the television set and Don wandered over to the door, leaving her to lock up. He waited outside in the fresh air as the lights flicked off behind him. The evening air was comfortable and still. The faintest breeze was coming from the south, bringing warm air with it. Standing outside the bar, under a cluster of palm trees, he was pleased he didn't have the smog of LA to contend with. He had tried living there for four months and hated every second. When he had left the SEALS, he hadn't really known where to go, or what to do, and so had tried LA first of all. It was too big, too industrious, and cluttered with people everywhere. Eventually, he had wound his way back down to San Diego. He knew deep down that he had come back to make sure his mother was all right, even if they didn't see one another. He told himself he had come for the diving though, and for a long time, he had enjoyed it.

There were so many spots to visit, and he had enjoyed the solitude he found underwater. Coral grew in abundance off the coast, and if you knew where to look, there were shipwrecks and caverns to explore. There were so many you could go diving every day and not have to go to the same spot twice. On the boats that took them out, he frequently met a few other guys who had been in the SEALS too. He made small talk with them, and they were pleasant enough, but he didn't want to get close. Friends like that were not what he needed. If he'd wanted to hang out with people like that, he would have never quit in the first place.

"Ready?"

Meghan was locking the door and wore a leather jacket over tight jeans. He took her arm and began walking back to his apartment. "I have to warn you now - my neighbour is a terrible gossip. If she sees you, I won't hear the end of it for weeks."

"Well that's okay. We'll have to make sure we give her something to gossip about."

Don looked at Meghan and wondered why she was drawn to him. It was obvious why he was drawn to her. Any man with two eyes would be. Don couldn't understand what she saw in him, but he went with it. He'd had the perfect amount of beers not to question everything, and just to go with the flow right now.

"I have to warn you about something else," Don added as he led her up the steps to his apartment. "I might not have cleaned up for a while. I wasn't expecting company."

"Trust me, it's got to be better than the place I'm renting. Honestly, I share with two men, sorry *boys*, and they are pigs. I can handle a few empty pizza boxes, but do you think they ever clean the bathroom? Do you think they ever empty the dishwasher or... Forget it. I didn't come here to moan about those two."

Don put the key into his front door and hoped Mrs Barkley was asleep. He hadn't been kidding when he'd told Meghan she would gossip about him for weeks if she saw him coming home with someone.

"So, what did you come here for?" asked Don, as they stood in the doorway. The night was dark, and Meghan's face was lit only by the moon that hid over the top of the apartment building. He couldn't help but smile as he asked her.

Don heard the creaking of her leather jacket as she slowly reached up and kissed him. Her lips were so delicate and fresh. The warm breeze carried her scent to him and sweet perfume mixed with the delicate citrus smell from the orange trees nearby. Slim, cold fingers wrapped around his neck and then withdrew as their lips parted.

Don went into the apartment and switched on the lights. "Drink?"

Meghan saw the coffee table and black bag that had fallen over, spilling a dozen beer bottles over the floor. There was a musty smell and she cracked the kitchen window open wider. "You weren't kidding, were you?"

Don ignored her and went into his bedroom to find the white rum. He didn't feel like beer anymore. He wanted more, more of everything. He sank down onto his bed, kicked off his shoes, reached for the rum on the bedside table, and took off the cap. The bedroom was bigger than the lounge, and whilst just as cluttered, far more comfortable. He had no interest in watching television, in cleaning up, or even talking. He embraced the rum, drinking long and hard. A meagre light shone through the blinds, making him look like a ghostly zebra-man as he sat on his bed drinking.

What right had his mother calling him like that? She was as bad as Mrs Barkley, interfering in his life when he hadn't asked her to. When had he ever asked his mother for anything? Her and her church could go to hell. As if today wasn't hard enough, he didn't need to listen to any sermons from her. He knew he should check on Meghan, yet, was all of a sudden shy. He drank more of the rum for courage.

Where are you? Where am I?

Meghan walked into the room and stood in front of Don. "You gonna share?"

Don handed her the bottle and Meghan took three large gulps. She handed the bottle back to Don and walked closer to him in the darkness.

Don watched in a haze as Meghan cast off her leather jacket, and began unbuttoning her blouse. He drank more as she slipped it off and unhooked her bra, releasing her breasts. In the dim light, Don could see the outline of her nipples and he passed her the bottle. As she drank, he drew her to him, and she wrapped herself around him on the bed. He opened his mouth to speak, but she put a finger on his lips.

"Shh, Don. We don't need to talk anymore."

Meghan pushed Don onto his back and began to unzip his jeans. And that night, Don did not dream of anything.

CHAPTER 7

OCTOBER THURSDAY 17TH 07:54

As Don drove to work, he felt different. He knew he was the same person, but something inside him had changed. When he had woken this morning, his head still hurt and his mouth was dry. That was a common occurrence. There were still empty beer bottles strewn around his apartment, and the place needed a good clean. It had only occurred to him as he brushed his teeth, but he had been woken up by his alarm. He had woken without bullets, sand, and blood on his mind. In fact, the first thing he had thought of when he'd woken was Meghan. He remembered how she looked, still sleeping soundly when he'd got out of bed. Her body was warm and he had been tempted to get back in, but he knew he couldn't skip school today. If he didn't show for Zola's meeting, he would get more than detention.

Meghan had been slow to rise, and promised to lock up when she left, so Don left her in bed with a kiss and a promise to call her soon. He wasn't sure if there would be more nights like last night with her, but he sure wasn't ashamed about it. Why should he be? He had nothing to feel bad about, he had not cheated on anyone or forced her into anything. Yesterday had been and gone, and no doubt, there would be more days like it in the future. But as of now, he almost felt good about himself. He had connected with a real person instead of Jack Daniels and Captain Morgan. He wondered if Meghan had left yet. She worked late nights at the bar and tended to sleep in the morning, so he doubted it. Clearly, she wasn't as used to the hard stuff, and it was going to take more than a quick shower to bring her round.

As he pulled into the staff parking zone, he thought about the creature that was locked up inside. It was something different all right. He would never have believed such a thing existed if he hadn't seen it for himself. He had to admit, it was quite incredible. Just the size of it would be enough to give people nightmares. If it was a fifty foot high rabbit, that would be scary enough, but this thing had a mouthful of teeth to go with it. Cuddly, it was not.

There had been no phone calls or messages, so he trusted there had been no problems last night, got out of the car, and headed straight on over to the meeting room.

Once inside, he saw Zola and John already in discussion. Tate was reading through some notes whilst noisily slurping a mug of coffee. Don pulled up a seat at the large table next to a woman he recognised, but couldn't quite remember. He thought her name was Fiona, but couldn't be sure, so he just smiled politely as he sat down next to her. It was as if she was actively trying to slip unnoticed into the background. When she said hi, her voice was not strong, and she dressed plainly, in a dark grey business suit. Her brown hair was tied back and she wore little to no make-up.

"Don, thanks for coming," said Zola. "Let's get started shall we? I've been over to see our little friend this morning, and he, or she, is doing fine. Amanda and Jay are trying to get a closer look, but I understand their reluctance to get too close to those teeth."

Don wished he had stopped for a coffee too, but there hadn't been time this morning and he settled for getting one from the security room shortly.

Please let this meeting be over quickly, he thought.

"We need a catchy name, something that will really stand out. I want people to be in awe of this thing when they haven't even seen it. I want kids to demand their parents bring them here. I want this to reverberate around the whole freaking world. So let's go. What have we got? John, why don't you kick off?"

Don knew John was one of Zola's favourites, a marketing man who had dreamt up the 'snappy meal' concept last year, which meant giving away a free plastic turtle with all kid's meals bought on site. Business increased by fifteen percent in the cafes as a result of the promotion, and those crappy little plastic turtles had brought in an extra hundred grand to the bottom line last summer. Don knew they had been shipped in from Panama at a cost of sixty cents per toy. They had ramped up the prices of children's meals by a dollar over the promotion. John was young, energetic, bright, and an absolute ass-kisser. Thankfully, Don had little need to get involved with marketing or advertising most of the time, and knew even if he came up with the best name in the meeting, he would be shot down. The suits would never give him the time of day. That was one thing Zola did have going for her. She usually listened to Don and clearly respected his opinions.

John smiled and stood up. He flattened down his tie, adjusted his cufflinks and then addressed the table. "Thanks, Zola. What we have here is, as Zola said, is something really unique, and the name we attach to this new product needs to reflect that."

Don contemplated leaving as they discussed the new 'product.' He watched John walk up and down, throwing around generic marketing terms like 'consumption audience,' 'intangibility,' and 'product lifecycle.' At no point did he mention the animal's welfare, or if what they were doing was in the animal's best interests. He could've been talking about a new car, not a breathing animal.

Don looked at his watch. How long was he going to ramble on? Twenty minutes later, and John was still droning on in that monotone voice of his about 'nano-campaigning.' He hadn't even mentioned having an idea for a name yet. Don let his mind wander as the executives carried on with their mindless suggestions. Now and again, he heard a crazy name thrown out by Tate and Fiona, but John shot them down every time. He kept the room, pacing up and down, leading the gathered suits as if he was the conductor in a choir.

"Tate. Any other suggestions?"

Don finally watched John sit down, a smug look on his face, as if he had just won a prize Christmas Hamper in the office sweepstake. John had sweat circles under his armpits that were spreading slowly, and Don audibly sighed, resisting the urge to look at his watch. Why had Zola wanted him along?

"I was thinking," said Tate, "that as Zola said, there is predominantly going to be interest from children and teenagers about this. We need something trendy and quirky, something catchy. All kids like sharks, right? So I'm thinking, 'Super-shark.' No, I think 'Mega-shark' is better. Don't you?"

His suggestions drew withered looks from everyone, and even Don cringed.

"Um…"

Tate was floundering and Fiona tried to help him out. Don had only met her once, but she had been pleasant enough to him, far more than Tate or John had ever been.

"You're on the right lines, Tate, but it's not a shark is it? I mean, we can't be too specific when we don't really know what it is. Mega-fish, super-fish, I don't know, just keep going."

John snorted. "Super-fish? What are you, five? Err yeah, that's real *dynamic* Fiona." He and Zola snickered and then fell into silence.

Fiona quietened down as John took over. He rifled through some papers before him. "I don't know what your vet's and trainers are doing, Zola, but we could do with some more information. If I was them, I would've pulled an all-nighter, but hey, we all have different priorities, right? Now, according to our best guess this is a…Metoposaurus Rex, or some bullshit like that."

"Metoposaurus," said Don. Until then he had not spoken, preferring to watch the developments instead of getting sucked into a meeting he had no intention of taking part in. How they marketed the creature bore little relevance to his job. "And it's *not* bullshit. The park's best marine-life veterinarian worked on that report. Do I need to remind you that nobody has *ever* come across one before?"

John stared at Don and shrugged his shoulders. "Whatever. As I was saying, Metoposaurus is too clumsy. We can't call it that, but we could shorten it. The name just needs to fizz. I think…"

"Supersaurus?" suggested Fiona. She looked at Tate for support, but he kept his eyes straight ahead fixed on John and didn't acknowledge her.

John waved her down and scrunched up his face. "Fiona, isn't it? You're new so we'll give you the benefit of the doubt. I'm sure

you'll come in useful later. I have a stack of paperwork to be done."

Don could feel the woman's anguish, and wondered what would happen if John were accidentally to get hot coffee thrown in his face.

Let it go. This buffoon is clearly building up to something. Probably has a name already planned out and has been letting the others struggle. Jerk.

"Zola, I'm not sure we should push the whole dinosaur angle. I was watching my kid this morning, and you know what he was watching on TV? Barney. We don't want to associate what we have with a friendly purple dinosaur, or we'll come across as a joke. We have to get the branding right from day one. There was something my maid said to me when I left today. She wanted me to pick my kid up from school. Can you believe it? When I told her I expected her to do what she was paid to do, she spouted some garbage that I didn't understand. Hello, do I look Mexican? Who cares what the help has to say as long as they can cook and fuck, am I right?"

A sexist and racist joke in one? You really are a jerk.

Don looked at his watch. How much longer was he going to have to listen to this moron?

Nobody responded to John, and he carried on. "Anyway, one word that she said resonated: Diablo. I think what we have here is a dangerous animal. It's a killer. It's something mysterious, from the dark side. I think our pet dinosaur is...'Diablo.'"

Tate and Fiona said nothing, and Don waited to see what Zola's response would be. Depending on her mood, she would either kiss John or fire him for talking like that. She might be a ball-breaker, but she knew where to draw the line. Usually.

"Diablo. The Diablo. Diablo of the Deep. That's not half bad," said Zola. "I think we can use this. Di-ab-lo." The word came out as a whisper and as she said it again, she drew her hands out in the air horizontally, as if putting the word onto an imaginary banner, and smiled.

Don rolled his eyes in the back of his head. Of course, if Zola liked it, then everyone liked it. Chatter grew around the room and he knew that they had found what they wanted. Pleased he hadn't had to get involved, or punch out John's teeth, Don stood up and looked at his watch.

That's an hour of my life I won't get back.

Don watched Fiona and Tate file out, congratulating each other and slapping John on the back. They left with smiles on their faces, but Don knew they had been crushed. Zola hung back and caught Don as he was about to lock the door behind them.

"Don, thanks for coming, I appreciate it." She rested her hand on his arm as he reached for the door. "I needed a clear head on this. They're a bunch of ass-kissers and you're..."

"Not?"

"No, you're too pig-headed for that, Don. I could've fired you on the spot yesterday. The last person who turned up four hours late for work cleans my pool for a living now. Once a week it gets a thorough seeing to." Zola lent in closer to Don. "You know what else they see to?" she asked suggestively.

"Mrs Bertoni, I really have to get going. There's a whole heap of stuff I have to organise for Diablo's party tomorrow."

"Party? I think that's an understatement, don't you? I've heard expectations upwards of a hundred million viewers, Don. *Upwards.*"

"Hope you've got a nice dress picked out," said Don sarcastically.

A look of shock crept over Zola's face. "My God, I nearly forgot! I'd better get something new. See, you've got your head screwed on. What would I do without you? So what do you think of the name? I mean, we can't keep calling it 'it.'"

"Yeah, well I think it's fine. Its got a certain ring to it. Go for it. Like you said, there's a lot you can do with it."

"Honestly, you like it? I need some perspective on this; I've been up all night thinking about it."

Don edged towards the door. "I think Diablo is perfect. Now I really have to hustle."

Zola let Don pass. "Make sure you come by my office later. I'm going to be in there all day up to my neck in it. Maybe after the press briefing you can stop by. I need to run the logistics by you. We're going to have a full house tomorrow and on top of all that, there'll be cameras, photographers, celebrities. Ooh, that reminds me, I need to get hold of Brad's agent. I think he's in Mexico shooting right now, and I might be able to persuade him to come see our dino'...I mean, come see *Diablo*."

"Good luck!" Don escaped Zola's clutches and wandered off to the security room. It was starting to hit him now, just how much work there was to do. They were used to staging shows and events at the park. Shakti Stadium was often full, and thousands of people came through the park gates every day. To get everything set up for tomorrow was a tall order though and he hurried to the office. He knew he would have to catch up with Zola later. He just hoped she had calmed down by then. When work excited her, she got all hyped up and threw herself at him. He could fend for himself, but still, he'd rather keep out of her way if he could.

OCTOBER THURSDAY 17TH 11:49

Don watched Amanda walk toward him by the pool. Her wet hair slicked back over her shoulders and the black wetsuit clung to her body. Sometimes, he wished he could cling to a body like that. Then he remembered last night with Meghan. He had been out of the game too long. He hadn't planned for anything to happen; never thought a bit of flirting would lead anywhere, or be anything more than playful banter. When he thought about it, Meghan and Amanda were completely different. Yet, he had a connection with them both, and for the first time in a long time, he wasn't so worried about the future.

As Amanda walked up to him smiling, her feet padding quietly around the edge of the pool, he gave her a wink. "How's Diablo?"

"Well, he prefers David, but the boss says it's Diablo or nothing."

"Zola told you?"

"Yeah, she flew past on her broom a while ago, on her way to the press briefing. Told me the grand plan. It's top secret, of course."

"Of course." Don looked at Diablo lurking in the tank. He was not really moving, just floating on the surface. Yet, he was very much alive, and his eyes were fully open. Don hadn't seen them so wide before, and could see the dark yellow iris around the jet black pupil. It felt like the monster was watching them talk.

"Did you go to the briefing? How did it go?" asked Amanda as she wrung the water from her hair.

Don realised Amanda was wet, and yet couldn't believe she would've got into the water with Diablo. "You didn't get in there with it, did you?"

"With that monster? Are you nuts? No, I just had to go check on Poppy and Pete. Jay took my dolphin shows yesterday, so I wanted to check on them. They missed me."

"Oh, *they* missed *you*? Right. Anyway, the media room was chaos. I hung out at the back of the room. I don't want my face on the news, thank you. Zola was in her element."

"I bet. Did she do that thing where she wags her finger when she wants someone to listen to her and they keep talking?"

"Yeah, but only like a hundred times. Anyway, she's got everyone curious to see Diablo. She showed them one of those photographs from yesterday. It just gives a glimpse of the neck and face, so you can't really see much, but you can tell it's not just another shark or whale. I think she stirred them up well. There's another briefing tomorrow and she's going to accidentally 'leak' it out between now and then that we may have a dinosaur on our hands. Then when they start asking questions, she can deny everything and tell them to get tickets for the unveiling tomorrow night."

"She mentioned that to me. She's actually closing the park tomorrow, so we can get ready. I've got to get Diablo here moved into Shakti Stadium, and somehow make him perform on demand. She's treating it like a piece of meat. Bless Susan, she's got Animal World to take Shakti off our hands."

Don looked at the monster that was perfectly still and quiet. There was a guard outside the room, but it was unnerving. If anything were to happen unexpectedly, he wasn't sure what good a guard with a walkie-talkie was going to be. They didn't know what this thing was thinking. They didn't know if it thought at all, but the way it was looking at Don now, he was quite sure something was ticking over inside that big head. He walked towards the exit, and the orange eyes followed him.

"How is Diablo? Healthy? Behaving?" Don asked.

"I would say he's under a lot of stress. He hasn't moved much since yesterday. He just sits there. I tried feeding him earlier, but he wouldn't eat anything. I'm worried if he doesn't perk up, that Zola's show is going to be a let-down. And we both know whose fault that will be."

"Don't worry, even if he just swims around on the surface like this, the whole world will still be amazed. Amanda, why did you call it a 'he'?"

"Just a feeling more than anything. Look at it. He looks like a 'he, don't you think?"

Don thought it looked like it belonged stuffed in a museum, but no matter what animal she was presented with, Amanda always treated it with respect, that was just who she was. If he let her, she might end up getting too close and then Diablo might not be so hungry anymore. "I'm going to talk to Zola. I don't like it. We need more guards. I'm not happy with you being in here alone with it."

"Don, you don't have to look out for me all the time. I can handle myself."

"It's not just you, Amanda. I wouldn't trust Diablo to be around anyone right now."

Those eyes are still watching me. I wonder if it can hear me. Does it know I want to see it gone? Does it know what we've lined up for it tomorrow? One minute you're swimming around the ocean, the next, you're an international star. International freak is more like it.

"You got time for lunch today?" asked Don.

"No, I need to go see Susan and then I need to catch up with Jay. I can't expect him to run everything out there while I work on our new project."

"Dinner tonight?"

"I promised Hamish I'd cook. He's picking me up if you want to grab a quick cold one though?"

"Maybe. I'll check in on you later."

Don left and could feel the monster's cold stare on his back as he left. Zola would agree to almost anything right now, and he knew exactly what he wanted. Diablo was starting to sound about right. There was nothing natural about those eyes. Don made his way to Zola's office and knocked before entering.

Once more into the fray.

CHAPTER 8

OCTOBER THURSDAY 17TH 18:58

Don entered through a narrow doorway into one of the sick bays they kept empty for when one of the park's animals required treatment. The room was fully enclosed, decked out with CCTV and panic buttons, a first aid kit, and pin-encoded access was required, limiting entry to only those who truly needed to get in. The room was cool, but illuminated well by several lights overhead. Around the long pool was non-slip tiling and a hydraulic lift, for when animals were so sick they had to be sedated and lifted in and out of the pool. The last time Don had been in here was six months ago when Poppy, one of the female dolphins, had fallen sick.

Don raised his hand as Amanda saw him come in. Immediately though, Don's eyes were drawn to the pool and the beast within it. Water splashed over the lip of the tiles as it swam back and forth. Don walked a couple of feet further into the room, closing the door behind him. The animal nearly filled the pool's length and every time it turned, it splashed more water over the side. It swam close to the surface, but its body was submerged. Normally, the smell in the room was a mixture of disinfectant and fish. Today was quite different. A dirty smell reached Don's nostrils, one that hinted at putrescent meat. It was so overpowering that Don couldn't help but wince, as he watched the animal with fascination. Here in the larger room, its size was even more evident. Its body was thick and scaly, long, yet with short front legs and feet that could only surely lift it inches above ground. There was no way this had been flushed down some rich kid's toilet in Florida. The head was wide and flat, easily as wide as its body, and its jaws were slightly parted, revealing a stunning row of sharp teeth. There were more teeth than Don could count. The incisors at the front were elongated, and the two on the upper and lower jaws looked razor-sharp. Don didn't want to think about what it would feel like to be snapped between the thing's jaws. Any fish would stand no chance.

As Don watched it swim, he realised dead fish floated around it. The monster was ignoring them. It couldn't have eaten for a few days, so Don was surprised it hadn't gobbled them down instantly. The animal was clearly agitated, and its eyes darted back and forth as Amanda kept throwing it more dead Herring. It refused to eat a single one and just swam up and down the holding pool. Only its head remained above the water line, making Don uncomfortable. The way it was moving reminded him of a lion in a cage, pacing up and down, unable to vent its frustration, its anger, or express its true feelings. A deadly beast reduced by man to a sideshow, its killer instincts now impotent.

Those damn eyes are watching me again.

Don had stationed two guards on duty at the pool, insisting on it until they knew fully what they were dealing with. Without knowing how it might react to captivity, or interaction with humans, he had to put safety first. Ultimately, that was why he did this job. He was convinced that given the chance, Diablo would only too happily snack on any one of the people working at the park. This was quite unlike anything they had dealt with before, in fact, unlike anything *anyone* had dealt with.

After his short meeting with Zola earlier, he had equipped both guards on duty with ASM-DT Amphibious Rifles, an expensive, but necessary addition to the security outfit he had made Zola invest in. He had only managed to get hold of two at short notice, courtesy of a contact at the Naval Amphibious Base at Coronado and Don's past, but more were arriving tomorrow. The guards of course, had never fired one, never had cause to, and he hoped they weren't going to have to. Don had told the guards that if there was any sign of a breach, any indication that the animal was posing a real and genuine threat to human life, that they were to shoot first and ask questions later. Of course, Zola had no idea he had put such a policy in place. He had told her the guards were there to protect the animal; to ensure nobody tried to steal it from them. There was also the legitimate threat of eco-terrorism, something that had so far avoided the park, but nonetheless, was always possible. With that in mind, Zola had allowed Don to upgrade his security forces and weaponry. It was convenient that she was being distracted at the time by a call from Fox, asking if they could get first rights on the as yet undetermined creature. None of the park or security staff was allowed to carry weapons during opening hours. This was a family park, Zola had reminded him, not a school in the Bronx.

"What's wrong?" Don asked Amanda, nodding a courteous hello to his guards as he walked past them to the top of the pool where Amanda stood. "Why's it not eating?"

Amanda dropped the bucket at her feet and Don saw it was still two-thirds full.

"I don't know," Amanda shook her head and sighed. "It won't touch anything. Nothing yesterday, or this morning. There's no doubt it's carnivorous, and wherever it lived out in the ocean, its diet must've been predominantly fish, at the very least marine-life. With those teeth, it wasn't living off plankton. I'm at a loss what else to try. I mean, I'm not about to throw it a penguin."

"What about one of the dolphins?" asked Don.

Amanda looked at Don in horror, her mouth agape. "How the hell can you even…"

"Joke, joke!" Don held his hands up defensively and laughed as Amanda relaxed. "Look, if it's hungry, it'll eat. I wouldn't worry about it too much. It's probably nervous. It's been taken out of its natural habitat, it doesn't know what's going on, and we don't even know what type of fish it likes to eat. For all we know, this is the first human contact it's ever had and it's probably freaked the hell out right now." Don wasn't trying to defend the animal, just put Amanda at ease. He was trying to put himself at ease.

"Yeah, you're right," agreed Amanda. "It's been swimming up and down like that for hours. I'm worried we might push it too far. If we stress it out, it could die, especially, as it's not eating. Maybe we should give it a break. I've been working in shifts with Jay trying to study it. We've been running tests all day. Perhaps it needs a rest."

Maybe you need a rest, thought Don, noticing Amanda stifle a yawn. "Look, why don't you knock off now? Hamish will be here any minute, and I could use a drink. I know, I know, you said just a quick one, but perhaps you can tell me what this thing is?"

Amanda rubbed her eyes and then picked up the fish-bucket. "Sure. Let me get washed up. Just one though, okay? Hamish wants to talk to me over dinner. I think he's booked somewhere fancy. I've hardly seen him in the last week."

Don's mind was already at the bar, and he could taste the beer on his tongue. He just had to lock up, and he would be on his way.

OCTOBER THURSDAY 17TH 21:20

When Amanda said it could only be a quick drink, she hadn't been joking. They had gone to the Waterfront Grill, where Hamish and Amada had first met, and talked briefly. Hamish told them how his father had already put a deposit down on a new house. Curtis had spent half the money before the cheque had even cleared. Hamish was being more cautious with his share. He wanted to invest in the business, get some new equipment for the trawler. He was also in need of a new first mate. Roy had officially quit yesterday, and Hamish knew he couldn't talk him around. He wasn't even sure if he should.

The conversation had quickly moved onto Friday night. Don had seen Tate leaving and rumour had it that there was a major movie star confirmed, as was the mayor. Tate had also heard that the USDA, Marine Mammal Commission and NSA were sniffing around. The rumours about a terrifying new species emerging had apparently been taken quite seriously. He had it on good authority that the Pentagon was sending someone down to see what the fuss was about. Don wasn't sure if Tate was yanking his chain, but he had been quite serious about it. He'd told Don that marketing had been following the social media feeds and news stations, and talk of Diablo had gone global. Zola had got maximum coverage, just what she'd wanted.

At this, Amanda had wanted to run home crying in despair. The pressure was on to really deliver, but Diablo had so far shown no interest in anything. Don and Hamish had reassured her they had her back, but it was enough to put a dampener on the mood. Amanda and Hamish had swiftly left, leaving Don to contemplate the day on his own. He had arranged passes for the media and booked an extra marquee. There were always more turning up to these events than were supposed to, and Zola didn't want to piss anyone off, so they had agreed to erect an extra tent. All leave had been cancelled for the next week, and Don had secured a special license for his guards to carry weapons. Zola still insisted they were not allowed to carry them around the park, and Don had been forced to compromise. The guards could be armed, but they were to hang back out of sight, and only react to an emergency if she, or Don himself called it.

After leaving the Grill, Don had headed home, but didn't feel like a frozen pizza, and so looked for somewhere to eat. As he settled into his booth at the Korean restaurant around the corner from his flat, he felt rueful. At tables all around him, were couples and families. He had chosen to come here, telling himself on the way that it was because he needed to try something new, to break his routine. Now that he was here, he wished he had simply gone back to the Old Station. Meghan would be there. He didn't really know what he would say to her when he saw her, and that was half the reason why he was now choosing between the Kimchi Deopbap or Bibim noodles, when he should be sat at the bar talking to her and nursing a beer.

He looked through the menu as the waiter approached, confounded by the list of wines. "You have any beer?"

"Yes sir, we have Cass or Hite if you would like to try a Korean style beer? Of course, we have the regular beers as well."

Don ordered a Cass with a Kimchi stew. The restaurant was a short walk from home, yet, he had never been here before. Tonight he saw a smattering of diners, barely enough to pay the rent, but enough to mean it didn't look weird and empty from the street. There was something a little too formal and awkward about dining in a restaurant alone. He wished again he was at the Old Station, listening to some old Springsteen while drinking a good old fashioned American beer.

What are you doing drinking something called Cass in a family restaurant? Coward. It's not the frozen pizza you're scared of, it's the reality that this thing with Meghan might actually lead to something.

Whilst he ate his meal, his phone rang. It was another unknown number. The last phone call he'd taken hadn't gone so well and he was wary of answering it without knowing who was calling.

"Don here."

"Don, hi, it's Taggart. Not interrupting, I hope?"

Don literally breathed a sigh of relief. He hadn't really expected his mother to call again, certainly not in the next ten years, and he half expected it to be a hospital telling him there had been an accident. He had spoken to his uncle a few times in the last few weeks, what with his cousin moving down to the area, but certainly wasn't expecting to hear from him now.

"No, I'm not doing anything. What's up?"

"Just wanted to know if you'd heard from Ryan? I asked him to give you a call when he got settled in."

"Can't say that I've heard anything. You want me to check up on him? I know a few people at the base I could contact." Don hoped he wouldn't have to. He did know people there, but he kept them at a distance. It was a life he didn't particularly want to return to.

Taggart laughed down the phone. "I'm not surprised. No, don't worry about it. I gave him your number though, so let me know if he gets in touch."

"Sure." Don buried a fork full of pork and rice into his mouth. Taggart didn't respond straight away, and it was unlike his uncle to be short of a few words. There was clearly something else on his mind. "You okay? Look, if you want me to check on Ryan I can, it's no problem."

"No, it's not that. I was just watching the news, and well, you work at Wild Seas so you must know what's going on. What's this Diablo thing? The station up here says it's probably a giant squid, but I was talking to Jim next door, and he says it's Chimera. He always was short of a fruit loop though, so I don't take much heed of what he says. I got the Bugle spread out in front of me with a picture of something. I can't tell what the heck it is. Looks like it's got some teeth on it. What you got yourselves down there, bigfoot?"

"Uncle Taggart, if I told you, I'd have to kill you."

Laughter echoed through the phone to Don's ears, only this time it was not so genial. "You take care, Don. Sometimes, things are best left alone. Don't go messing around with things you don't understand. I don't know about bigfoot, but we don't have to be able to explain everything away with science. Something with teeth like that? I'm just saying I hope its bark is worse than its bite."

"Thanks, Taggart, I'll be fine. We've got more guns trained on it right now than the Middle East."

Another laugh from his uncle, but Don could hear the nervousness too. His uncle had twenty years on him, yet, he sounded like he was twenty years his junior. "Well, I've held you up long enough. You and your mother doing okay?"

Don scraped together the last of his meal and balanced it on his fork. "We're fine. Goodbye, Taggart." Don ended the call and ate his last mouthful. He washed it down with the Cass and then decided to call it a night. The phone call had set him on edge. Was it the talk of Diablo? It was true, they were going out on a limb; they were exposing thousands of people to it, and they didn't know anything about it. The stadium held five thousand people and there would be more than that at the park that night. Zola was having a special stage erected so she could stand directly above the tank and do a presentation with Diablo right beneath her. If all went well, she was going to invite the mayor, and anyone else who was brave enough, to come and get a close up look at the new species that only Wild Seas had. She was also going to charge fifty dollars to anyone who had their photo taken with it. Don knew they were likely to make more money tomorrow night than they had in the whole of the summer season.

Don paid and left the restaurant. The streets were quiet in this part of town and he had a choice to make. Go left and go home, or go right, and go to the Old Station. Tempting though it was, he wasn't in the mood for company anymore. Taggart had lifted the scab, and now he needed to scratch it.

Don crossed the street and walked a few blocks as the evening turned to full dark. He knew the way by instinct, he had walked it so many times, yet, he couldn't recall the names of the streets he walked down, or the shops he passed if his life depended on it. He wanted a drink, but Mama Kitty's was dark and closed up for the night. A bum on the street corner looked up as Don passed and waived a book in his hands. "Repent. Seek His forgiveness. God is waiting for you!" Don ignored the ramblings of the homeless man and pressed on. He had no time for Bible stories today, any more than when he'd left home.

Soon the coffee shops and chain stores gave way to 7-Elevens and garages. He stopped to buy a bottle of Stolichnaya from an Indian grocery that had more stains on the ceiling than the floor. From what, he couldn't tell, and didn't want to know. The large man who served him wrapped the vodka in a paper bag, wished him a good evening, and Don carried on down increasingly smaller roads.

Large houses with green lawns gave way to smaller houses with concreted driveways and six by six patches of mud that passed as gardens. There was a chill in the air, and he turned up his collar before shoving his hands into his pockets. He found himself on a familiar street and rested on a red letterbox. The streetlights were on, but he didn't need light for what he wanted to see. Don huddled under a palm tree and sipped from a brown paper bag. The house at the end of the driveway was asleep, its lights out, curtains closed, standing immense and proud, protecting its only occupant.

Where are you?

Don let the vodka take the chill away and he decided to check the letterbox. There was nothing but junk mail: flyers for the local churches 'kitten-adoption day' and invitations to 'earn $1000's working from home at your own pace.' He took another cautious sip and ventured up the driveway. Nobody was around, he was quite sure of that. The driveway was sheltered on one side by a row of trees, and they gave Don the perfect hiding place should anyone question him. As he made his way up to the front door, each step slower than the last, he became aware that he had no idea what he would do when he got there. Was he supposed to knock? Was he going to stand there and just stare at it? Like a zombie, Don slowed to a shuffle and his feet scuffed the ground until he came to a complete stop, six feet from the door.

What are you doing? She doesn't want you here. The house doesn't want you here. Can't you feel it? Leave her alone.

"I want to go home," he said quietly. "I want…" Don guzzled down more vodka and stood swaying in the driveway of his old home as crickets jumped around him and flies swarmed to the streetlights.

I want to make it right. I want him back. I want to see him again and say sorry. I want…

Don looked at the spot where he had found his dead father almost forty years ago and a tear fell down his cheek. It hadn't changed in all that time. He bent down and traced his fingers along the asphalt.

Where are you? I want…

Don felt in his back pocket and pulled out his wallet. He grabbed a fistful of twenties and went back down the driveway, away from the house and its memories. He stuffed the money into the red letterbox and left.

OCTOBER THURSDAY 18TH 23:41

As Don relaxed on the couch with a cold beer, the vodka bottle half empty at his feet, he tried to focus on the television. A cop was kneeling on the back of a youth whilst locking him in handcuffs. Bored, Don flicked through the channels aimlessly. He skipped over another reality show, a police drama, a game show, a makeover show, another reality cop show, a hospital drama, and a bunch of teenagers grinding to something on MTV. He let the dross sink into oblivion until he found something interesting and paused over CNN. The pictures were blurry and the newsreader's voice kept fading away, but it caught his attention.

"Speculation is rife…San Diego's most…experts… do we even know if Diablo…discovery is…" The programme was abruptly interrupted for an advert for a new Chrysler, before the anchorwoman returned. She was accompanied by an image of carnage that carried a warning that the images were not suitable for younger viewers.

"If there are any young viewers in the room, please look away now," Don said before turning up the volume. He yawned, getting bored. The attractive anchorwoman was holding his attention, even if the news was getting tiresome.

"Harold Wintermeyer reports on the mystery of Seal Island. This was recorded just a couple of hours ago from Ucluelet, British Columbia."

"This grisly discovery has only just come to light, and so the timeline of events has not been established yet. A colony of seals appears to have been wiped out, with *no* sign of any survivors. The small island they inhabited, near the quiet town of Ucluelet, is desolate now, decorated only with the bodies of the seals that once lived here so peacefully. A town spokesperson said they had no reason to believe anyone would intentionally harm these normally placid creatures. The town is in shock tonight. You can see from the amount of blood on the rocks here that something terrible has happened. These seals did not just get up and leave, but something forcibly removed them. Just what, remains to be seen."

"Harold Wintermeyer there with that report."

Don gulped down a beer as the blonde woman with dark eye shadow and too much blusher, fluttered her eyelash extensions at the camera.

"Whilst large migrations are not uncommon, Seal Island is a permanent colony, and the tragic events we are learning of are estimated to have taken place sometime in the last twenty-four hours. The colony is not monitored, and it was only when a tourist boat visited the island today that the grisly discovery was made. Horrified tourists were quick to tell us their stories and theories, as Judy Budett now explains."

Don tuned the television off and yawned.

"You want to play now? It's getting kind of late, you know."

Don's apartment was drenched in silence. The clock on the wall ticked, oblivious to Don's statement.

"Okay, um, right, here's one." Don stood up unsteadily. "Somewhere out there is the beast, and he's hungry tonight." Don closed his eyes. "Yeah, I know, too easy. Well shit, it's my favourite war film. Don't try to tell me it's not yours. Fine, think you can out-quote me, go head. Make my day."

Don laughed and picked up a beer. He cracked the top off it on the chipped coffee table and slumped down into the sofa.

Go to bed. Put the bottle down and go to bed. You don't need this.

"Your turn." Don rested his head back on the sofa and then spoke. "My name is Maximus Decimus Meridius. I am...I am..." He frowned and took a gulp of beer. "I am commander of..."

Don stood up again. "Okay, okay, you got me. He kept his eyes closed as he spoke. "Look, we can't play games all night. It's been a big week, you know, don't you think we should talk about it? You know, it's just, what? No, I didn't mean that. Yeah, well, it's a pretty big fucking monster. Did you see it? Jesus, I nearly crapped myself. I thought Amanda was exaggerating when she told me about it." Don spread his arms apart. "It was this big, man."

He laughed again and chugged back the rest of the beer before helping himself to another. The bottle cap flew off into the TV and the coffee table scored another hit. "Yeah, she is. I know. Well, you can't, she's spoken for. Spo-ken for." He drew the last words out slowly.

Go to bed. What would Meghan think of you now? She hates you. She knows what you did. Everyone knows what you did.

"Plus, you just can't. You know why. You know why, don't you?"

The clock kept ticking, and nobody answered Don.

"Shut up. You know why. You fucking know. Don't be... You know. YOU KNOW! YOU FUCKING KNOW WHY, BECAUSE YOU'RE DEAD. YOU'RE FUCKING DEAD!"

Don threw the bottle against the wall and it smashed, showering the floor with broken glass. He collapsed down onto the sofa and stayed there until his mind swam out into unconsciousness.

CHAPTER 9

OCTOBER FRIDAY 18TH 08:34

Warm sand flooded into his mouth, choking him, stifling his cries, and filling his lungs. The sand burned in his throat, scratched his oesophagus, and Don couldn't breathe anymore. His arms tried to grab the last of the harsh sand reeds as he sunk, but they slipped from his grasp, cutting and slicing through his palms. Choking on the burning sand, Don closed his eyes and the world turned a hellish, fiery black.

"Who..."

Thumping sounds from the front door disturbed Don's dreams and he was pleased they had woken him. He didn't want to know what came after the blackness. He peeled himself up off the sofa and looked at the time. "Shit, I'm gonna be late," he mumbled.

As he shuffled over to the door, he trod broken glass into the carpet. He still wore yesterday's clothes, and pulled a sharp wedge of glass from his shoes. He discarded it on the coffee table and pulled open the front door.

"Mrs Barkley?" Don kept one eye closed and the other squinted, as he looked at the stern face of his neighbour through the doorway. Brilliant sunlight streamed over her head and burnt through his retina to his brain. She wore a light grey cardigan and shawl, and despite it still being early, the temperature was already easily in the nineties. "Everything all right?"

Mrs Barkley tried to look past Don into his apartment as she spoke. "No, Mr O'Reilly, it is not. Are you okay? You're not hurt are you?"

"No, why would I…"

"There was quite a party going on last night. I heard shouting and glass breaking. I thought you might have had trouble. Are you quite sure everything is all right? I didn't know if I should call the police."

"Oh, that. I'm sorry, Mrs Barkley, it was just a movie, and…I dropped a bottle of wine. I hope you got some sleep. Really, really sorry about all the noise."

"Don, you don't look well. And might I say you don't smell too well?" She turned up her nose and tried once more to look past him into his apartment. Luckily for Don, she had not brought her glasses with her.

Don could smell himself and it wasn't an agreeable odour that he was giving off. The alcohol was coming out of his pores, and he knew he was going to have to shower quickly. "Mrs Barkley, I have to get to work. Was there anything else, or…"

She presented him with a small plate wrapped on foil. "I know you're a busy man, Don, so I brought you a piece. I was saving it for you. I confess I've had the rest myself, it was too good to waste."

He peeled back the lip of the foil and peered inside at the large slice of apple pie. He smiled, knowing that once he closed the door he was going to eat it in three seconds flat. Her baking was almost as good as her nosiness. "Thanks, Mrs Barkley, you're a life saver. I could kiss you."

Mrs Barkley raised her eyebrows and looked at Don disapprovingly. "You'll need some mouthwash before I stick *my* tongue in your mouth."

Don watched her turn around and she left using her walker for support. Had she just said that, or had he imagined it? He smiled wryly as he closed the door.

Without bothering to sit down, he ripped off the foil and ate the apple pie, still cold. His stomach had been growling and turning over since he'd woken, and he was beginning to feel a bit better already. What Mrs Barkley had said about the noise last night was worrying. He did remember breaking the bottle, but shouting? Who had he been shouting at? He remembered watching the news, but little else. If she had called the police, it would've been embarrassing to say the least.

You were wrong, Mrs Barkley, there's not too much cinnamon in it at all.

Don showered and jumped into some fresh clothes. As he ran outside and down to his car, he bumped into Amanda coming the other way. She wore a white Wild Seas polo over a navy skirt and sandals.

"Hey, good looking, what are you doing here?" he asked her.

"Coming to find you. I overslept and figured we could drive in together. I'm parked right downstairs. You're ready I take it?"

"Perfect. Let's go."

Amanda explained as she drove. "I stayed at Hamish's parent's house last night. We had a big family dinner thing, a bit of a celebration. You should see Curtis' new car! Oh my gosh, it is a work of art. And he wants to get a Harley, although Hamish said he's too old. I don't know. It's good to see them happy." Amanda groaned and rubbed her stomach. "I am so full. We had rack of lamb last night, and it was *so* good. For dessert, his mother made a New York style cheesecake. I think I put on ten pounds since I saw you last."

Don listened to Amanda as they sped down Mission Valley Freeway, watching the stores and cafes zip by. He contemplated asking her to call at Mama Kitty's, but they didn't really have the time, plus he didn't want to interrupt her talking. It was like listening to soothing music, just letting her voice fill the car as they drove.

"Hamish has gone out to the trawler this morning, but he'll be back this afternoon. He just wanted to fix up a few things first. I'm kind of nervous about later. What if something goes wrong? What if Diablo turns out to be a dead fish? What if…"

"It'll be fine," said Don. "If anything goes wrong, it won't be on you. Zola has rushed this. She should've given us more time to prepare and find out what we're dealing with."

"Jay didn't call. He was going to check in last night, make sure Diablo was tucked up safe and sound, and let me know if there were any issues. I didn't get a text or anything. I even checked my emails."

"Well, there you go then. He only said he'd call you if there was a problem, so stop worrying. I've got guards posted all around the place, so we've got all our bases covered. There are plenty of other things to worry about. You see the news? It's pretty bad about that liner."

"I know, isn't it awful? They still haven't found it. Those poor people, what must their families be thinking?"

"It's an odd one, I'll grant you. Some fluke that is, an ocean liner just disappearing into thin air. It's like when those planes and ships disappeared in the Bermuda Triangle. Then there's that Seal Island thing. There's been a few odd things lately."

"Seal Island? I didn't hear about that."

Don had a hazy recollection of the previous night's events, and was less sure of the story about Seal Island. He filled Amanda in as best he could.

"Crazy. Who would want to hurt them? If anyone tried to attack them, they would defend their territory. I hope they catch whoever did it. Bastards."

"I read one of the theories about the disappearance of the cruise ship was an earthquake. You know, one out in the seabed that created a whirlpool, and they all got sucked down into the ocean. You don't think something like that could've drawn the seals away do you?"

"I'm not so sure about that. You said there was blood on the rocks, which suggests some asshole with a gun probably took them out."

"Maybe it was a virus? Maybe they all got sick and died, and someone tried to cover it up by removing the bodies. You're right, it doesn't make sense. Nothing does. Something weird is going on, for sure, but I can't figure it out. I'm getting a headache. I need a coffee," said Don. He pressed his forehead against the cold passenger window and the smoothness of the glass felt good.

"We're nearly there," said Amanda, as they pulled into Cove Drive. "You'll have to make do with a coffee from the canteen. So who are you bringing tonight?"

Don looked at Amanda puzzled. "Who am I bringing?"

"To the show. Didn't you read Zola's email? You made the list. You get one ticket to the show. Strictly one, she said, and don't even bother asking for more. I was going to bring Hamish, of course, but he's got a special invite anyway, so I gave mine to Curtis. Have you got someone, 'cause if not, I know plenty of people who would kill for a spare ticket."

Don wondered who on the planet would want to spend Friday night at the Wild Seas Park, and who he could invite. His mother was out of the question, and he didn't really have any close friends, not ones who didn't work at the park anyway. There was always one of the guys at the base, but it would be out of character to ask one of them to come to his work. He could give his ticket away, but then he remembered Meghan. He hadn't seen her all day yesterday, so maybe he should give her a call. Hadn't she said something about being off on Friday night? Fate might just be sending something good his way.

Amanda pulled into her space and turned the car's engine off. "I don't know if I can go through with this, Don."

He looked at her, surprised to see her face set, her brow furrowed in concentration. Was it Hamish, had he said something to her last night? Just when things seemed to be going so well?

"It's this 'Diablo' thing. It's just that...something isn't right. I was with him yesterday afternoon, just making some notes at the side of the pool, and I swear he was looking at me. He has these big yellowy eyes and they follow you around the room wherever you go. It's creepy. We're supposed to be studying it, and yet..."

"I know what you mean. It's like he's watching us instead of the other way round." Don remembered how he'd felt yesterday. So it wasn't just him. "You told anyone else about this?"

"I tried talking to Jay, but he wouldn't listen. He said it was my imagination and we should just do what Zola says. You know what he's like. I mean he knows his stuff, but he sucks up to her big time. Even if he had any concerns, I doubt he'd say anything. I'm worried if we put Diablo on display tonight, what his reaction will be. You heard Zola, she wants fireworks, cameras, the works...if Diablo's already stressed, what's he going to be like under those conditions?"

"I can't say," said Don. "I don't think anyone can answer that question. If you've got doubts, you need to talk to Zola. I'll back you up."

"It's not just that. I actually think we should release him. Strap Diablo to the back of Hamish's trawler, take him back to where they found him, and dump him in the middle of the ocean."

"You want to get rid of it?"

"I don't want to kill him, but it's not natural, Don. There's something about him, something horrible and nasty and vicious. I've worked with animals my whole life, and I can't find any redeeming qualities here. Whoever came up with the name of Diablo, chose it well."

"Fine. We'll suggest it to Zola."

"Really? You don't think I'm mad?"

Don shook his head and smiled. "Amanda, you're not mad, you are the most genuine person I've ever met! There's at least one other person in this car who is crazier than you are. Look, you've spent more time with that creature than anyone else has, so if anyone is qualified to decide what we do with it, then it's you. If you say we get rid of it, we get rid of it. If you say we stick a firework up its ass and fly it to Mars, then I'll light the fuse."

Amanda wiped a tear from her eye. "God, I'm such an idiot. Sorry, Don, I just couldn't talk to Hamish about this. He's so excited about everything. He's got the business to sort out, his family, me...there's so much going on right now that the last thing he needs is me talking about work."

"Amanda, you know you can always talk to me, right? But you should tell Hamish what you're thinking. Don't bottle it up. He's good for you, and he's a good person, I can tell. He would listen to you. He clearly thinks the world of you, so don't hold back, talk to him."

Amanda flipped down the mirror and straightened her hair. She wiped her eyes. "God, I'm a mess. I haven't slept so well these last couple of nights. I keep dreaming about Diablo: every time I see him, his jaws are right there, about to bite me in half."

"We all have our demons and nightmares, Amanda. Come on. Let's get inside," said Don opening his door. "You need to talk to Zola about this."

OCTOBER FRIDAY 18TH 10:42

"This is ridiculous, she can't still be busy."

Don pushed open the office door and saw Zola sat at her desk. Jay was sat in one of the two plush chairs by the mahogany desk, and when Don and Amanda entered, he quickly stuffed a piece of paper into his pocket.

"Mrs Bertoni, we can't wait any longer, we need to see you," said Don. "Sorry, Jay, but this is important."

"I'll go," said Jay standing.

"No, sit down. Let's hear what they've got to say." Zola looked at Don and Amanda calmly.

Don was surprised by Zola's reaction. She was a picture of serenity, and hadn't tried to shoo them away as he had expected. She even let a smile creep across her face. Don was thrown off balance by this as he had prepared himself for an argument.

"Amanda has been telling me some interesting information that I think you should listen to."

Amanda stepped forward and cleared her throat before nervously pushing her hair behind her ears. "Mrs Bertoni, I have spent many hours with the creature, Diablo, in the past two days, and I am not convinced that this show tonight is the best situation for him to be in."

"And why would that be, Miss Tass?" Zola smiled sweetly, but her eyes were looking daggers at Don and Amanda.

"Diablo has not eaten since we got him, so he's not had any sustenance for days. I can't force him to eat. He's clearly suffered from gunshot wounds, and we don't know what else. Physically, we just don't know what state he's in. Mentally, I would say he is stressed, confused, and exhausted. In a nutshell, this is not an animal you want to be putting under the spotlight, expecting it to behave how you want it to behave. He could suffer from a number of reactions, none of them healthy."

"And you agree, Don?"

Don felt Zola's withering stare and knew he had to stand by Amanda. He had not been convinced all along about this whole show, and this was their last chance to put a stop to it. "I do. Amanda's done what she can, but we need more time. Jay, you've seen it. You must agree. Diablo is not like the dolphins, or Shakti, or anything else this park has ever had. If you let the show go ahead tonight, you risk everything we've done, everything this park has ever stood for. The best thing you can do would be to let it go. A creature like this does not belong in a tank or on television. It shouldn't by rights exist, but it does. The best thing for us, and it, would be to send it back to where it came from."

"Really, is that so?" Zola shook her head in disbelief. "You want to let it go? Do you know how much this is worth to the park? I had an email this morning from Modern Science magazine offering me fifty grand for an interview. I had Justin Randall from HBO asking if they could make a mini-series based around the park and our new discovery last night. I can't even begin to tell you what NBC offered me this morning. Don't you see this can secure the long-term future of the park for years? It's not just Diablo, but *all* of the animals in our care who will be better off after tonight. We can finally upgrade the penguin enclosure that you've been asking me about for the last six months, Amanda. And Don, you said you needed to hire more staff, well, this is how we do it. There are so many things I can achieve now, and really make my mark.

"Diablo is history in the flesh, and we are not turning it down on a feeling. Diablo might look dangerous, but he's harmless. I've been talking to Jay and read your reports, Amanda. Since he's been at the park, he's done nothing. I mean, literally, nothing. He hasn't shown any interest in eating, playing, or doing anything remotely alarming. All I need you to do, Amanda, is get him ready for this evening. Try to coax him into doing something. If he just swims around on the surface of the water, it won't make for very exciting television. I would much prefer him to be active, maybe to thrash around a bit. Perhaps you can try and get him to put his head out of the water at least?"

Don picked up a letter on Zola's desk. It was a short offer to buy Diablo from a private collector in Dubai. The cheque stapled to the top corner was blank, for Zola to fill in the figure herself. He whistled and put it down. "Zola, I don't think you are listening to what we're saying. Diablo isn't going to perform tricks or jump through hoops for you tonight. Amanda's been chucking dead fish at it for days and he's not interested. We don't know what it feeds on in its natural habitat. It's lethargic and apathetic, and I don't think now is the right time to shove a camera in its face."

Jay finally spoke up. "You're right. Beneath the water lurks a monster, a prehistoric behemoth that by rights shouldn't even exist. But a predator this size, this lethal, and with so much potential for raw power could destroy marine life as we know it. Fishing stocks would be destroyed. What about the threat to man? You would have to take Diablo a long way out to be sure it wouldn't come back to the beaches of the west coast. Imagine the massive death toll if we let this go. We would be doing more harm than good. The creature needs further study, which is precisely why we can't release it back into the ocean. There is a *huge* amount we could learn from this. The scientific value to this find is immeasurable."

"Scientific value or financial value?" asked Amanda. "Or perhaps you're more concerned with your own career, Jay?"

"You don't know what you're talking about," said Jay. "In fact, Zola agrees with me. We need to change tack, refocus on how we're looking at this."

"What do you mean, *refocus*?" asked Don.

Amanda laughed. "This isn't funny, it's pathetic. I know what he means. He's taking over. Isn't that right, Mrs Bertoni? You're taking this away from me?"

Zola stood up and looked out of her office window, across the lot to the entrance of the park. "Do you know what I see out there, Amanda. I see thousands of people rushing through that gate. I can see excited kids, their faces beaming with happiness. I can see brand new exhibits, interactive shows, expansion; I see the future of Wild Seas Park." Zola turned back to face Amanda. "What do you see? If you get on board with me over this, and get Diablo ready for tonight, then who's to say where this will lead? I could certainly see you having a long and successful future here with all the animals you care so much about. Of course, if you don't share my vision, then…"

Amanda said nothing and stormed out of the office.

"You want me to talk to her?" asked Jay, getting up.

"I'll go," said Don. He looked back at Jay and Zola. There wasn't an ounce of regret on their faces. All they could see were dollar signs. "Amanda's still the best person you have to deal with this, Zola. I'll talk her round. I hope you know what you're doing," he said as he left the office to find Amanda.

OCTOBER FRIDAY 18TH 16:05

Setting up for the showcase event had taken a lot of effort, but the time was almost upon them, and the park's gates were going to be open soon. Security-wise it had been a logistical nightmare. Don had cancelled all vacation, something his crew had not been too happy about. He had twelve full-timers, eight who worked weekends, himself, and three others to man the cameras at the security office. He had called up everyone he could at short notice. Scurrying around the stadium now were caterers, project managers, artists, retailers, park directors, their assistants, their assistant's assistants, and what seemed like more people than they got on July fourth.

As he walked through the park, past the Sea-Lion stadium, Don couldn't help but feel anxious. He tried to make sure everything was on plan, and as much as he didn't like strangers wandering around, he understood it was necessary. There was something else though, something he couldn't put his finger on. It wasn't like any other event they had held at the park, and the media tent being erected was testimony to that. As he made his way to the office, he walked past the huge marquee being erected adjacent to the Skytower. Shakti Stadium seated five thousand people, and they could have sold tickets ten times over. They managed to set up a media area at the front of the stadium, enough for just over forty people. Zola had all the networks prepped, with CNN and the BBC being given prominent positions. Deep pockets opened a lot of doors. There had been so much interest in the new discovery though, that they needed to find somewhere else to put another fifty cameras and journalists from television channels across the world. Don was happy to see that the media tent was almost ready, and could see rows upon rows of chairs being lined up inside. A tangle of cables came out the back, leading into three trucks, which were mounted with a variety of dishes and aerials.

As he passed the children's play area, the Bay of Play, he noticed an array of market stalls and carts being set up. He stopped by one and watched as a young girl carefully arranged the stall full of drinks and snacks. Apart from the usual disposable cameras and park maps, he saw a whole new range of merchandise.

"Base, this is Don, put me through to Zola please," he said into his walkie-talkie. It crackled with static as he waited, watching the girl who could barely be nineteen open a cardboard box and bring out a pile of children's T-shirts. She lined them up on hangers on both sides of the cart and then stopped to check her mobile phone. A beep on his walkie-talkie indicated he had someone on the line.

"Yeah, Zola, what's with the stalls? I'm in the southwest quadrant and the walkway is covered with what, ten, eleven stalls? I wasn't told of...yeah...yeah I know, but...so you want... Fine, I'll see to it. Maybe next time it would be nice to get a heads up?"

Don clicked the walkie back into his belt. The girl continued unloading the stock and piling it up high, unaware Don was watching. There were stuffed toys, posters, key rings, lunch-boxes, caps, candy bars and even romper-suits. He walked over to the stall.

"Hey, how's it going?" he asked.

The girl stopped unpacking a box full of 'Diablo' baseball mitts, and looked him up and down. She shoved her phone back in her pocket and then resumed unpacking. With her back still turned to Don she muttered, "We're not open yet. Come back in an hour."

"I didn't want to buy anything, darling, I'm chief of security here. You got some ID?"

The girl pulled a wallet from her back pocket and held up an ID card with the Wild Seas logo emblazoned across it. "Look, mister, I've got a lot of stuff to sell tonight. I need to get rid of at least half this crap to make my bonus, you understand? So what's up? What did I do wrong?"

Don took the ID card and checked it over. "And you're so busy that you still have time to check your phone?"

The girl shrugged. "It was my friend. They found that missing cruise ship in the middle of the ocean. Reckon some of the bodies might wash up on Pacific Beach. We're gonna check it out later."

"Charming."

The girl reached into her other back pocket and pulled out a packet of cigarettes. As she placed one into her mouth, she grabbed her lighter off the cart and raised it to the unlit cigarette. Don suddenly snatched it from her mouth and grabbed the lighter. It had a picture of naked woman on it, lying on a tropical beach, silhouetted against a setting red sun.

"Hey, that's mine. You can't do that!"

"I think, Stacy Woodman, eighteen years old of Fern Glen, La Jolla that you need to listen up." He handed back her ID card and stuffed her lighter into his pocket. "First of all, this park is no smoking, so you can forget about that until you finish up. Secondly, if me or any of my staff ask you a question, I would request that you answer a little more courteously next time. You're here representing the park and there are going to be little kids around soon. Knock off the attitude, or you'll find yourself on a bus home *without* your bonus. You understand that?"

The girl nodded, suddenly losing her nerve. "I'm sorry, I didn't mean anything. I just really need to make some money tonight."

"Well, by the looks of your stall, you should make plenty. The reason I came over here was to tell you to mark up everything by another ten percent. I just had word from the boss. Can you let the others know for me?" asked Don, looking down the row of stalls that led all the way to the park entrance.

"Sure thing," said the girl sweetly. "I'll do it. I'll do it now."

Don froze and shivered as a blanket of fear wrapped itself around him as he heard those three words.

Do it now.

He was instantly back there. The dirt and the blood and the sand were flying everywhere, his head ringing, and his body aching. Don clenched his right hand into a fist and gritted his teeth. The scar on his head seemed to spring to life, and he wanted to rub it, to touch it to know that it was real and not a figment of his imagination. He wanted to know this was real and not the start of another nightmare.

The girl smiled. "You know, we're going for a drink afterwards. Take a few beers down to Pacific Beach after sunset. You want to come along?" She was so close Don could feel her breath on his face.

Stacy Woodman inched closer to Don and he could smell her perfume, sweet and light on the breeze. He became aware quite suddenly of how close she was, and how young she was. This was a nightmare, but of a different sort to the ones he was used to.

"Sure is hot tonight, ain't it? I can't wait to get my lips around a..." Stacy licked her lips and took a step toward Don. "A nice, cold beer," she said, smirking.

"Here," said Don handing back her ID card, "I've got to go. You have fun tonight and stay out of trouble. And move your cart, you're blocking an exit."

He left the girl by her stall. He didn't know if the girl had seriously been coming onto him, or just trying it on, trying to butter up the chief of security. It wouldn't be the first time. It was usually college graduates trying to impress their friends, trying to see if they could get a visit after hours or a lock-in so they could dare each other to skinny-dip in one of the Aquariums. Don let his tightly balled fist loosen, and put Stacy and her tacky merchandise out of mind as he headed to the office. He didn't hear Stacy whisper "ass-hole" under her breath as he left, or see her sneak a gulp of beer from the six-pack she had hidden underneath the cart's base.

Don checked his watch. He hoped Amanda was getting on with Diablo. He had managed to talk her out of quitting, and made her realise that the best way to ensure the safety of everyone tonight, was to be there. He told her that Jay was competent, but his intentions were unclear. Zola had clouded his judgement, and the lure of promotion was all Jay needed to dance to her tune.

He just had one more job to sort out and took his mobile phone out. He dialled the number and looked up at the blue sky as he waited for her to answer. When she picked up, he smiled. "Hey, Meghan, how are you, it's Don. Look I know that it's late notice, but you said you might be free tonight. I wanted to ask you something. You ever been to Wild Seas?"

CHAPTER 10

OCTOBER 18TH 16:58

The seven men, made up of six cadets and one officer, jogged down the coastal pathway, halfway through a gruelling run. The sun was sapping their strength, and each of the men was determined to not only finish the course, but win it. They were undertaking a series of tasks, each one designed to test their endurance and stamina, both physical and mental. Their Warrant Officer, Bob Hendrickson, had developed a new programme called 'Iron Men,' and he made new recruits start on it the moment they arrived on San Clemente Island. The programme today consisted of two six-mile runs sandwiching an assault course in the middle of the island. At the end of the run, they had to complete another circuit of the island on a cycle followed by a one-mile swim. It was the most demanding thing Ryan had ever done.

Training for the Navy SEALS was more intense than regular military training, and they had already passed several tests just to get this far. The six men had gone through the Physical Screening Test and had been selected to attend the training base on San Clemente. The island was isolated, just under eighty miles from the western coast of the US, and all the more perfect for training because of its isolation. There were no distractions, just the US base purpose-built to enhance and develop every man and woman who resided there.

Ryan Pieters was comfortable in the middle of the pack, aware that the WO at the rear was monitoring his every move. His friends had told him he was lucky to get in. His family had said they couldn't believe little Ryan Pieters had gotten so far. He had always been a slight boy, fair-haired, blue-eyed, and innocent looking, so it had come as a bit of a surprise to everyone when he announced his intention to join the Navy. His father had tried to talk him out of it, assuring him of better trades he could learn. His mother was just worried he would be sent overseas and come back in a body bag. She had cried when he'd left home and his father had shaken his hand, saying nothing. Ryan, however, knew he wasn't merely lucky. He had worked hard to get in and sacrificed a lot. When the boys had started drinking, taking bottles of Rolling Rock back to the clubhouse, he had gone home and worked on his fitness. He had been a slim teenager, but had soon bulked up when he became serious about joining the Navy. He gained muscle and size, but no fat. There had been no late nights or parties for Ryan Pieters. He had even skipped Prom. Sandra Hamilton had virtually guaranteed she would go all the way with him if he took her, but he still refused. He had lost his share of friends too. George Merriweather, his closest friend, had called him for the last time one late night last spring. George had told Ryan he was dreaming if he thought he would ever make the SEALS. Ryan had said something about friends supposedly supporting other friends, and the phone conversation had descended into another argument. It was the last time Ryan had spoken to his once best friend. The last he had heard was that George Merriweather was selling curtains and blinds for his father, working fifty hours a week.

The coastal path was a killer, and they had not done the full circuit before. The stretch of path they were on now was steep and the path itself was stubborn, strewn with small stones that tried to trip him up. The goats who used to inhabit the island had worn their own groove into the path, but they were all gone now, removed for their own protection. Ryan casually wiped the sweat from his forehead and kept focused. Fagan, Dobbs, and Creech were a few feet ahead of him, Crowson and Kelly just behind. After a week on the island, he was just beginning to figure the others out. They had all been welcoming and friendly, with the exception of Fagan who was proving to be more than competitive; he was an animal. He spoke little to the others, really only interacting with them when he absolutely had to. Ryan knew there was more to being a SEAL than fitness though. Being part of a team, trusting who you worked with, and being able to communicate with them, was integral to the success of the role and any mission you were given. Fagan was going to have to join the party sometime, or he would never get through Boot Camp.

As the incline levelled off, Ryan cast a look to his left, down the cliff face to the jagged shoreline. One trip, one foot in the wrong place and it was sayonara. It had to be a hundred feet down, and the coastline was littered with huge boulders and jagged rocks. There was no beach to speak of, and no reason to go down there apart from what could be found underwater. The Pacific was calm this morning, and Ryan could see a tourist's yacht. The Navy allowed boats to moor up close to the shore, in certain designated areas, to allow avid Scuba-divers access to some of the best scuba diving around. Ryan could make out a long yacht today, its white hull reflecting the brilliant sun. On the wooden deck, he could see a lone figure, lying prostrate in the sun, wearing nothing but bikini bottoms and a pair of sunglasses. The woman had wavy brown hair and a perfect body, as far as Ryan could tell from so far away. It had been a long time since he had seen a naked woman. That was something else he had sacrificed in the last few years. When George had been feeling up Libby Tucker in the back of her Dad's Camry, Ryan had been in the basement at home, lifting weights and working up an altogether different kind of sweat.

"Shit!" cried Creech as he stumbled. The athletic man tripped and his ankle went from under him, sending him crashing into the stony ground.

The group slowed, and then stopped as they realised Creech had done some serious damage.

"Creech," said WO Hendrickson, "get your ass up now."

Creech got up and when he tried to put his weight on his ankle, he crumpled back down to the ground again.

"I think it's broken," said Creech, rubbing his ankle and loosening his sneaker. "Fuck."

Hendrickson sighed and crouched down beside Creech. "God damn it, Creech, you had to do this now?"

Ryan looked at the others. They were all using the time to get in some more oxygen, and stretch their aching limbs.

"Sir, let's roll," said Fagan impatiently. "Creech can hobble back on his own. I want to finish the course. Looks like Creech is more glass than iron, Sir."

Nobody laughed apart from Fagan. Ryan knew the base was halfway across the island, at least five miles away, and it was going to be a long walk back for Creech. As much as he wanted to finish the course, he knew Hendrickson would be looking for volunteers to help.

"Sir, I'll take him if you want. Let Fagan and the others finish the course."

Hendrickson looked up at Ryan. "You sure, soldier? It's a long way home."

The WO appeared to mull the situation over. Ryan could see that Creech was in pain, as much as he didn't want to admit it. Creech was probably going to be out of action for a while, even if it turned out to be nothing more than a strain.

"Sir, tomorrow's a rest day. Perhaps I can complete the course then, on my own? Then nobody misses out and Creech will get back to base to have his ankle looked at before we're all singing carols round the campfire, Sir."

"Dickwad," muttered Fagan from behind Ryan's back.

"Fuck," said Creech again as he stood up using the WO for support.

"Okay, Ryan, try to get back before nightfall. If I have to send out a search party for you girls, you'll find Christmas comes early and Santa's bringing a pink slip." Hendrickson passed Creech over to Ryan. "Okay, ladies, this isn't a Sunday stroll, move it!"

Ryan put an arm around Creech and watched Fagan and the others jog up the path to complete the course.

"Sorry, dude, guess you drew the short straw." Creech was pale and sweating, and not just from the exertions of the run.

Ryan shrugged. "You really think it's broken?"

It was time for Creech to shrug. "Could be. It's starting to go numb."

"I guess we should move out. Hendrickson's right about one thing, if we don't hurry up it'll be dark before we get back."

As Creech began limping along side Ryan, he apologised. "I'm sorry, Ryan, truly I am. I should've looked where I was going."

"Forget it, this path is a bitch," said Ryan kicking a large stone away. "I'm surprised this is the first time anyone's fallen. There's shit everywhere."

"Yeah, but...well, I was kind of distracted. I was looking down there." Creech pointed down the cliff to the yacht Ryan had seen earlier and grinned. "Can you blame me? I haven't seen a nice pair of tits like that since Prom night."

Ryan looked down at the yacht again, anchored by a small cove, and admired the woman's curves. He supposed her to be the wife of a rich tourist, or more likely the mistress. The husband was no doubt under the water right now, swimming amongst the kelp forests and coral. Sometimes, they had famous actors come out. Fagan told them he'd seen Jennifer Lawrence on his first day, putting on snorkel gear at Lark Cove. He had been dismissed and laughed out of the canteen, but now Ryan wondered if there had been some truth in it. He had never seen anyone famous in real life. He squinted and held his hand up to shield his eyes from the sun. Ryan couldn't really make out who the woman was from atop the cliff, so he looked over the yacht for clues as to who the owner might be. Other than the name of the yacht, 'The Mangahoe,' he couldn't see anything. It was just another rich tourist with nothing better to do.

"Let's get moving, Creech, the speed we're going it's got to be a good two hours back." As they trudged down the path, Ryan noticed Creech looking out to sea. After a few minutes, he couldn't ignore it any longer. "Hey, come on, man, you've seen tits before."

"It's not that, it's...there's something else. It's...odd."

They stopped walking and Ryan began to get irritated. "Look, Creech..."

A loud barking noise interrupted him, so loud that it echoed off the cliff walls and reverberated around inside his head. Three short, sharp barks that could only have come from the direction of the ocean.

"What the hell is that?" asked Ryan.

"There's something down there. In the water." Creech pointed, but all Ryan could see was the yacht. The woman was on her feet, apparently looking around for the source of the unusual noise as well. "You see it?"

Ryan shook his head. "What? I don't see..." Then he saw it and his blood froze.

The sunbathing woman was at the stern of the yacht, looking out at the still Pacific Ocean. On the shore, just a few meters from the yacht, was the head of an enormous creature. Its head was almost as large as the yacht itself, and it was stealthily climbing out of the water. Its neck was thick and scaly, and as the creature emerged, Ryan was able to see more. It moved slowly, gallons of water cascading off its back as it came, and it had two front legs that dragged its heavy body along. As it rose, its long body began to brush the yacht, and it tipped up, sending the woman into the ocean with a faint scream. The creature kept climbing, its hideous head getting closer and closer to the top of the cliff.

"Amazing," Ryan said quietly.

He watched as the thing finally dragged itself completely clear of the water. It reached from the base to almost the top of the cliff and had to be nearly a hundred feet in length. Its body was fat, and yet, it heaved itself over the jagged rocks as though they weren't there. Ryan was reminded vaguely of a crocodile, yet this was ten times as big. The creature thrashed its tail around, splitting the yacht in two, and Ryan lost sight of the woman. If she had any sense, she would be swimming away, far away from the sea giant that had materialised from nowhere.

The monster barked again and Ryan put his hands over his ears. The noise was like the combination of a barking dog and a Jackhammer. Ryan stood still, in awe of what he was seeing. The monster kept climbing, over the top of the cliff, across the goat path, until it had finally hauled itself up onto the island top. The monster was so big, it was blocking out the sun, and Ryan was cast into shadow by its head. He saw two rows of teeth with two larger incisors at the front. They dripped with seaweed and the ground beneath his feet trembled when the monster moved.

Ryan crouched down and whispered to Creech. "Is this real? Is this…" He reached out for Creech, but found himself reaching through thin air. Spinning around he saw Creech running across the open ground. Running was not really the correct term, for what Creech was doing was really screaming and hopping on one foot, trying to get away from the monster.

Ryan had doubted the creature could move quickly, such was its width and length, but no sooner had he noticed Creech's screaming, than so too had the monster. In one leap, the monster had jumped fifty feet and planted itself directly in front of the running man. When it landed on the earth, Ryan felt the vibrations course through his body. The thing had to weigh several tonnes and half of it was made up of sharp teeth. Ryan watched as the monster opened its jaws. He could see down its throat at the pink gums and red flesh. There was a small brown tongue, but it moved with such speed that Ryan had no time to take in anything else. The monster's jaws swept up Creech and a mound of earth, and then he was gone. Creech was swallowed whole without even being able to utter a cry for help.

There was shouting, and then Ryan saw Fagan. He was running alongside Hendrickson over the crest of the hill at the centre of the island. Evidently, the others had not reached the assault course before hearing the monster's arrival. Ryan watched in a daze as the monster gave chase, its four legs powerful enough to carry it across the land. He watched as Dobbs, Crowson and Kelly were killed instantly, smashed beneath the thing's jaws and chewed up. Blood spurted out of the things teeth as it crunched on the men's dead bodies. Fagan tried to out-run it, but the monster was too quick and snatched him up. Ryan felt dizzy as he saw his colleague dangling half in and half out of the things jaws. Fagan's torso was pinned between two teeth and his arms flailed uselessly as the monster continued to grind its teeth and bludgeon the life out of him. Hendrickson was hiding behind a rock, and Ryan tried to shout to him, to warn him, but there was no time. The monster raised itself up on its two elongated, stronger, hind legs and then simply smashed its front legs down upon the rock, permanently leaving the WO embedded in the island.

When the monster crashed down on top of Hendrickson, it felt like an earthquake and Ryan stood up unsteadily, unsure what to do next. The monster was picking them off with ease, and he needed to find shelter, to find some way of avoiding becoming just another snack. Creech, Fagan and the others were gone, dead. It had taken the monster all of sixty seconds to devour them. Healthy strong men, reduced to fish food. Yet, Ryan knew he had to get help, and warn the base what was coming. If the monster continued on its current path, the death toll would be terrible. He couldn't let that happen. He had to…

Ryan was terrified as the monster's tail smashed into him. He was suddenly airborne as he was thrown twenty feet up into the air and he was given an opportunity to see the monster in all its glory. Between the blue sky and the wildflowers growing amidst the island's tough grass, the monster looked like an impressive joke. It was a mammoth beast, full of teeth, its hideous brown-green skin still glistening as the sun dried the water off its back. Ryan caught a glimpse of the naval base, low grey and white buildings scattered to the east over the runways, and heard another of those awful barks, before he fell to the ground and he was knocked unconscious. As he slipped away, the barking of the monster faded into silence and the world disappeared.

***

Picking a clump of grass from his hair, Ryan got to his feet. The landing had not been soft, and it had knocked the wind out of him. Thankfully, nothing was broken, and he was able to stand with only a little bruising to show for his encounter with the strange creature. He wasn't sure how long he had been out, but judging from the altitude of the sun, it could only have been an hour. Ryan's shadow walked ahead of him as he made his way back to base. He was taking the most direct route he could, straight across the centre of the island. The coastal path would take too long, and he had to get back as quickly as possible. His gut was sore, and he suspected he was going to arrive too late to be of any use. There was no sign of the monster itself, but plenty of evidence where it had been. It had gouged out a path across the island, a deep track that Ryan could follow precisely. Even in the dim light, there was no way he could get lost now.

As much as he wanted to circumnavigate the place where his team had been killed earlier, he didn't have much choice. Splashes of dark blood gave away where they had died, and it was as if the monster was leaving a trail of breadcrumbs for Ryan to follow. As he walked past the rock where Hendrickson has been hiding, he felt his eyes drawn there. He had expected to see his Warrant Officer's body there, decimated and bloody, but there was little to see. The body was mostly buried beneath the giant rock, and all Ryan could see of his former WO was an arm and hand, the fingers rigidly stuck up and pointed to the sky.

Plenty of blood had pooled around the base of the rock, and Ryan broke into a jog. He had been incredibly lucky, twice. The monster had somehow missed him as it had eaten its way through his team, and then when it had accidentally thrown him into the air, he had landed on the ground. If he had been thrown any further, he would most likely have ended up in the ocean or halfway down the cliffs. Either way, he was fortunate still to be here. He picked up the pace, wondering how far the monster had gone. He couldn't hear anything and was worried. If it was still around, shouldn't there be gunfire, noise of some sort indicating they were taking the thing on? Equally, there were no more of those barking sounds, which simultaneously filled him with terror and relief. If the monster was quiet, then either it was dead or gone, and Ryan was grateful he wouldn't have to face it again. The other reason for the absence of noise though, was too horrible to think about. If the monster had come upon the base unprepared, there might not be much left to go back to.

Finally, Ryan reached the border of the base and stood at the edge of the runways. Two small strips of land had been concreted over, and on the other side of them were the collection of buildings he had begun his training in and now called home. He could see the officer's quarters, the mess hall, the training rooms, two jeeps and one plane. All of them had been destroyed.

Ryan walked across the runway, confused. How could a beast just climb from the ocean like that and tear its way through a naval base? How could they not have known about it? Was it some sort of mutant aberration, or an escapee from a private enclosure somewhere? Was it a freak of nature that had come up from a deep-sea abyss? Ryan realised he was focussing on the wrong thing. It didn't matter right now where it had come from, only that it was here. And it clearly ate a lot more than plankton.

As he neared the base, he noticed bodies on the runway, the clothing torn, and the limbs twisted at unnatural angles. There were hunks of meat too, arms and legs missing their owners. As he got closer, he saw the people were all dead. Nothing moved. The features on the few faces he dared to look at were unrecognisable. It looked like they had been literally torn apart. He remembered how easily the thing had scooped up Creech and could imagine how the animal tore through the base just as easily. They would have been running for their lives, and the beasts' jaws would've scythed through them like a combine harvesting a field of corn.

Usually the base was full of activity, but now it was eerie. To walk through the deserted streets, amongst the burning buildings, was disconcerting. Ryan felt very alone right then.

"Anyone here? Anyone at all?" Ryan had reached the mess hall and the door was open. Inside, it was deserted too. Broken chairs and food scattered the floor, and from the kitchen, a radio played quietly in the background. Ryan listened to the song as he stared into the vacant room. It was something about fish not having feelings, and caused an old rhyme to pop into his head. It darted around his head as he searched for any sign he was not alone.

"And once I caught a fish alive...Jesus, this isn't happening," he said as he turned about and ran over to the main office. The building had been obliterated. The walls had caved in and smoke was pouring out, obscuring the interior from Ryan's view. He tried again.

"Is there anyone there? Hello?"

A resounding silence met his questions, and Ryan looked around for help. More blood was splashed over the ground as he ran from building to building, looking for something, anyone, just any sign that someone had made it. As he ran, he felt the evening drawing in. The sun was low and shadows loomed over Ryan as he ran. He sped up, getting more and more desperate to find someone.

He rounded a corner and tripped over something on the ground, sprawling over the harsh tarmac.

"Are you…" Ryan stopped when he saw that the person he had tripped over was most definitely dead. The woman was one of the mess hall staff, an elderly Spanish speaking woman he recalled serving him with a chorizo pasta only last night. She had been decapitated at the knees, and had bled out. Her face was pale and tight, her eyes wide with fear at the moment of death. Ryan turned away on all fours, and dragged himself across the ground, away from the dead woman. His hands and knees slipped through oily puddles of thick, black blood. He crawled over another body, then another, and finally came to a rest by the wheel of a truck. He sat upright, drawing in gasps of breath. His head was light, and as he looked around at the carnage, he knew then he was the only one on the island alive.

There had been over two hundred people on the island. Was he truly the last one alive on the island? Had *anyone* else made it? He didn't feel like a man anymore, didn't feel like a soldier either. He felt like he was that slight, fair-haired boy from Ramona again. He wished he had drunk too much Rolling Rock with George Merriweather. He wished he had gone to Prom and screwed Sandra Hamilton in his basement. He wished he had smoked too much, bunked off class more, and listened to his father. Selling curtains for a living suddenly didn't seem like such a bad option. Then as panic threatened to swallow him up completely, a sense of responsibility washed over him. He might be the last one left alive on San Clemente, but…

"Oh God, no." Ryan jumped up and ran through the broken buildings, running toward the east of the island, to where his thoughts were now headed. The monster's path was easy to follow once he cleared the base, and the deep trench left behind by the thing's tail was like an arrow, headlining where it had come from. More importantly, it showed exactly where it was headed. Ryan stopped running and looked out across the ocean. The lights of San Diego were too far to see, but the outline of the coast was just visible in the dusk. The Californian shore was dead ahead. Ryan forgot about Sandra Hamilton, assault courses and chorizo pasta. He knew he had to find a working radio, and fast.

CHAPTER 11

OCTOBER 18TH 16:48

"Come on," hissed Amanda. "Get your ass up here." She was lying at the back of the stage, her arms over the water and hidden from the growing crowd in the stadium, trying to coax Diablo up to the surface. If the star of the show didn't turn up to the party, the evening would be disastrous, and Amanda knew just who Zola would blame. The stage was currently hidden from view of the public, shielded by a huge curtain that would only be pulled back when they were ready to start the show and unveil Diablo. Amanda could hear the volume of the crowd on the other side of the curtain, and was beginning to feel the pressure. Nervous energy twisted around her gut and she hadn't eaten all day.

Still lying submerged at the bottom of the pool, Diablo was like a mirage, constantly shimmering in and out of view. The creature was stubbornly refusing to join in, and Amanda was running out of ideas. They'd shot it full of tranquiliser earlier so they could transport it safely to Shakti Stadium. Now that it was here though, it was even more inactive than before. It was as if it had taken one look at the stadium and decided to give up. Amanda had hoped that with the extra space to swim around in, Diablo might perk up. An hour earlier, he had swum to the bottom of the pool and stayed there ever since.

With the lack of food the most likely cause for the creature's lack of animation, she had tried to slip it vitamins and supplements to give it some energy. Even when she had forcibly dropped a large dead tuna into the poor animal's mouth, it had refused to swallow it and regurgitated the fish, vitamins and all.

Zola had wanted to give it a stimulant, just something to give it a boost before the show, to make sure the paying guests got what they'd come for. Jay had agreed, but Amanda wouldn't let them. They had absolutely no clue as to what the drugs might do to it. Its metabolism and nervous system was like nothing they had ever studied, and a stimulant could cause it to react in a number of ways, including a heart attack.

"Come on, please," whispered Amanda again, as she drew her arms across the surface of the pool. She actually felt sorry for it. It was an ugly son-of-a-bitch, but it looked one step closer to death every day. It was no way to die, plucked from the freedom and space of the open ocean, only to die of starvation in captivity.

"Well?" Zola appeared on the stage behind Amanda, causing her to jump.

"Mrs Bertoni, you startled me," said Amanda getting to her feet. "I was just trying to get your star ready. Apparently, he's a bit shy. As you can see," she said, pointing to the pool.

Zola stood with her arms crossed and her face set. She wore a sparkling dress for the occasion, red fuck-me heels, and more make-up than Amanda had ever seen her wear in her life. Mr Bertoni had spared no expense tonight on his wife. Amanda was impressed at how good Zola actually looked. It was a shame she was such a bitch.

"Miss Tass, I don't have time for any more excuses," said Zola walking toward Amanda. "I have to go out there in ten minutes, and present this to an audience of millions. *Millions*. I've got CNN out there going crazy and offers from all of the dailies wanting an exclusive. There are about fifty reporters down there, not to mention the Governor of California and some suits just showed up from the NTSC. A major movie star is arriving in exactly seven minutes and twenty-three seconds. I spent more money on this dress than you earn in a year. I have planned this down to *the* last detail. I have got the whole world watching, and now you're telling me it's *shy*?"

Amanda offered Zola a timid smile and looked at the maroon curtain that was obscuring them both from the awaiting audience beyond the stage. She could probably lay a drop on Zola now, hold her head under the water until her Botox-riddled body went limp, and be out of the state before anyone figured it out. She took a step forward. "I did try to tell you. He's not a performing monkey. Your new pet is not like Poppy or Pete. He's not going to jump through hoops or do back-flips just because you *want* him to. I mean for Christ's sake, he hasn't eaten in almost a week. What do you expect?"

"I should've done this already. I don't know what I was thinking trusting you with this, Amanda. For some God damn reason I listened to Don when I should've gone with my gut all along." Zola turned her back on Amanda and spoke into the wireless headset she wore discreetly beneath her lush brown hair. "Don, can you hear me? Don? Yes, get me Jay right now. Tell him to bring the Methylmethcathinone. Actually, tell him to bring the Mephedrone that we got in last week too. And tell him I need it down here right now, he's on." Zola paused. She tapped her headpiece. "You got all that? Tell Jay if he's not here in four minutes, he can look for another job in the morning." She turned around to Amanda.

"It's your choice, Amanda. You can help Jay, or you can join him at the social welfare office tomorrow morning. What's it to be?"

"Seriously? Are you fucking joking? You can't do this, it is *way* too risky. You have no idea what will happen." Amanda strode up to Zola and jammed a finger in her face. "I *won't* let you do this."

Zola was unfazed by Amanda's outburst. "Actually, I have a pretty good idea what will happen. It will wake up at last. Our superstar is the hottest thing on the planet right now and I need a performance tonight, Amanda, not a wet fish. Excuse the pun. If you won't help Jay, then you know where the exit is. Thank you for your work. I'll have your things sent to you."

Zola walked away leaving Amanda stunned. How could she do this? The animal didn't need a stimulant, particularly a dangerous one if delivered in the wrong doses. She looked back at the pool, at the unmoving form deep in the water. Her heart began racing, as she heard the compere on the other side of the curtain announce the arrival of yet another celebrity and the noise of the crowd went up a notch.

"Zola, wait." Amanda raced to catch up to her boss. "Zola, please, just listen to me. I'm sorry. I'm just concerned, okay? Just put it off for another day or two. Let's study Diablo a bit more, get him ready, and back to good health. I can figure it out. Just give me a little more time? You can use the underwater viewing area for now, just give the media a glimpse, get them interested and they'll come back for more. What do you say?"

From a side-door below the stage, Amanda heard footsteps and then Jay's head appeared. She looked back to Zola imploringly.

Jay came over to them both, sweaty and dishevelled. He was out of breath, and carrying a small briefcase. "I got here as fast as I could, Mrs Bertoni," he panted.

"Jay," said Zola looking at Amanda, "pump Diablo full of drugs, whatever you've got. I want it thrashing around in five minutes like a wild fucking banshee in the middle of Hurricane Irene."

Zola disappeared down the side steps, whilst Jay rushed over to the edge of the stage. He proceeded to bring a tranquiliser gun out from the briefcase, and a set of vials. He loaded the gun and stood with it facing down into the water.

"Jay, stop, think about this." Amanda put an arm on Jay's and tried to get him to look at her. "I know you. You know better than this."

"Let it go, Amanda, it's too late. You really think you can stop this now? If I don't do it, she'll just find someone else." Jay squinted as he trained his sights on Diablo. "Now, come here you overgrown lizard, I'm gonna make you famous."

The dart exploded through the water and Jay was sure he had hit Diablo. There was a slight movement from the creature, but then nothing. The animal's hide was so tough, he had to be sure at least one of the darts penetrated its skin.

Amanda recoiled and shivered, despite the warmth of the evening sun. "Jay, no more. One is enough. Please." She could see Diablo wasn't moving and it crossed her mind that maybe he had died already. Perhaps he had just swum to the bottom of the tank and drowned.

Jay reloaded and fired again. He reloaded, and then fired a third time and a fourth time. "In one minute that curtain is coming back, Amanda, and Diablo had better show up or we're all finished."

"How much did you give him, Jay? How much?" Amanda watched as Jay packed up the briefcase. He closed it and then headed toward the side steps that led to the underground passageway, away from the stadium. Amanda ran after him and grabbed his arm. He shrugged her off and she slipped backward, falling awkwardly on the steps. "Tell me how much you gave him!"

Jay hesitated. "Enough." He gave Amanda an apologetic look. "Enough to give her what she wants."

Amanda watched Jay leave and she scrambled to her feet. She heard the clamour of the crowd behind the red curtain and didn't know what to do next. She was supposed to be at Zola's side for the presentation, the on-hand expert to answer any questions. Did Zola even want her around anymore? Was she supposed to stand there smiling, having her photograph taken as Diablo lay dead at the bottom of the tank? Amanda stood and looked around. She felt utterly hopeless. In what should be the biggest night of her life, she wanted to cry.

As the curtain began to pull back, revealing thousands and thousands of cheering people, she knew she had left it too late to do anything else. There was Zola at the front, beaming, and the flashes of cameras going off were almost blinding. Amanda stood to the side of the stage and forced a smile. The show must go on.

***

"James, Terrick, you in position? Any problems?"

Don saw them give him a thumbs up on camera twelve, and settled into his chair. He was going to watch the event from the security office, so that he could monitor the whole thing. The rest of the park was quiet now, as almost everyone was watching the unveiling. The concourses, pathways, cafes and stalls were all empty, save for a few employees who were waiting for the exodus at the end. In the stadium, there were officially five thousand people. Unofficially, it was closer to six. He turned to the main screen, and watched Zola begin. She walked up and down the stage, telling the crowd that what they were about to see was a miracle of nature. He could see Amanda at the sidelines and was impressed that she was still there. He didn't know if he would've quit by now.

He focussed camera three on the front rows of the stadium in the splash-zone, and saw Hamish and Curtis side by side. A few seats down from them, he recognised the state governor, and finally, he saw Meghan. He just got her into her seat in time, and even though she'd complained about not having enough time to get ready, he still thought she looked hot. She wore a simple floral blouse over jeans, and she had curled her hair. Even though her presence reminded him of the Old Station, he didn't feel like a beer. Maybe he would take her out afterwards and go easy for a change. This time, he wanted to remember everything about her.

As he panned the camera out to take in the whole stage, the phone in his pocket vibrated. Who would be calling at a time like this? He drew the camera back to the water, and saw Diablo there. The creature had sat quietly in the pool since arriving, and showed no sign yet of waking up. Zola was going to have to keep talking a while longer if she wanted to show them a bit of animation.

The vibrating continued and reluctantly Don drew it out; he didn't know the number displayed on the screen, but there was a chance it could be important. One day, he was bound to get the call; his mother couldn't keep living by herself for much longer, and he knew he was going to have to answer it, just in case. If it was an offer to buy a timeshare in the Bahamas, they would receive some choice words about where they could stick their offer.

"Don speaking."

"Don, is that you? Thank God. You have to help me. You've got to do something. It was huge, just so big we couldn't stop it."

"Who is this?" asked Don. The voice sounded young, and he didn't recognise it. "If this is some sort of a joke, then…"

"No, don't hang up! It's Ryan, Taggart's son. I tried dad, but he didn't answer, and I don't know who else to call. I phoned the authorities, but they didn't believe me. It's coming, Don, it's heading your way. Oh, Jesus, it was big."

"Ryan? Hold on." Don told another guard to watch the cameras and then went to the back of the room. "Ryan, what's going on? You in some sort of trouble?" It occurred to Don that he didn't really know his cousin. Taggart had always said good things about the boy though, so Don had to take him at his word. It was inconvenient timing though, to call right now.

"Don, listen. We were attacked."

"Attacked? Taggart said you were still in training. I didn't think you'd be on active duty yet. Am I missing something?"

"I *am* still in training. That's where we were attacked, on San Clemente Island. I was running the course and then it came up out of the ocean. It climbed up the cliffs and it...it ate them, all of them. This thing, Don, it must be a hundred feet long at least. It killed everyone. I've been trying to find someone alive, but there's nobody left."

Don instinctively wanted to help Ryan, but he could not believe what he was hearing. "Ryan, I'm going to ask you something and you have to be honest with me. Your Dad asked me to look out for you, and that's what I'll do. Tell me now - are you being straight with me? Have you been drinking or smoking? Are you on the level?"

"Don, I promise I'm telling the truth. I was going to radio NAB Coronado, but it's all smashed. I couldn't find a working unit anywhere. The monster destroyed nearly everything. I managed to find a phone, and I called 911, but they thought it was a prank. To be fair, gigantic monsters don't exist, right?"

Don looked at the monitors. Zola was walking toward the back of the stage and waving her arms around animatedly. Without sound, he didn't know what she was saying, but he knew it was something about Diablo. Something about a gigantic monster that came from the ocean and was now under her control. "Ryan, what did you see? Tell me." Don left the office and slipped into a corridor. He began walking toward the stadium with a sinking feeling in his stomach.

"It was like, a hundred feet tall. I was standing right there when it tore them apart. It just picked them up in its mouth and..."

Don heard Ryan sigh. "Go on, son. Tell me what you can." Don stopped by a locked room and punched in the entry code quickly. He went into the arsenal and picked up an ASM-DT Amphibious Rifle, hoping he was wrong.

"I got knocked out. Its tail struck me and I was out for a while. It was like being hit by a truck. When I came to, I followed its path over the island. It took apart the base and killed everyone. Don, with all the firepower we have here, it should be dead, but it's like we didn't even scratch it. This thing was hideous. Its skin was dark and it had teeth, oh fuck, did it have some teeth. It had these horrible, big yellow eyes and…"

"Hang on," said Don as he loaded the rifle, "did you say yellow eyes?"

"Yeah, but what does it matter what colour its eyes are. It reminded me a little bit of a crocodile, but it wasn't a croc'. I'm not crazy, Don, and I'm not lying to you. This thing was standing up, like a freaking Tyrannosaurus or something. Don, it's heading straight towards you. I figure it's headed somewhere. I mean it crossed the island in no time, and judging by the tracks it left behind, it was going in a straight line. If it hasn't changed direction, it could get to you anytime. I'd hate to think what will happen if it gets to San Diego. I'm hoping it will surface around Camp Pendleton and the marines can blast it to hell. That fucker killed my friends, my instructor…it was relentless, Don, fucking relentless. I promise, I'm not lying about this."

Don was halfway to Shakti Stadium, and he crossed down into the underground corridor that led right around it and came up by the staging area. He didn't want to be seen walking around with a rifle. Zola wanted publicity tonight, but not that kind of publicity. Besides, he wasn't convinced he was right. There was a chance he was completely wrong about this.

Please, God, let me be wrong. Don't let it happen. Just let me be wrong. This is all a big misunderstanding. Ryan's freaked out about something, but it's not what you think. It can't be.

"Ryan, listen to me. Stay where you are and call 911 again. Ask them to put you through to Commander Ravensbrook at NAB Coronado. Tell him that Don O'Reilly asked you to call. First of all, they need to get you out of there, so ask him to pick you up. Secondly, tell him to call me. He's an old friend of mine. He'll listen to me. You did the right thing, Ryan. I'm glad you're okay."

The phone crackled and Don knew the reception was beginning to cut out. Down by the tank under street level, the phones often failed. "Ryan, if you can hear me, make yourself useful and gather up anything that still works. I'll try to get the troops ready at this end. Ryan?"

He had gone and Don shoved his phone away. He grabbed his walkie-talkie and called the main office. "Sam, I want the park put on high alert, copy? Tell James and Terrick to meet me at...Sam, you copy?"

There was no answer from the other end. "God damn cheap..." The first thing Don wanted Zola to get with her new found wealth, was a decent communication system that wouldn't cut out every time they went through the underground corridors. Don broke into a sprint and he passed Jay running the other way. A minute later, and he was at the bottom of the steps to the stage. He was still out of sight of the crowd, but he could feel the excitement and hear Zola.

"As you can see, Diablo is an immense creature, coming in at sixty feet in length, and around two thousand pounds of pure muscle."

Don advanced up the steps, just so he could see the top of the stage. Amanda was there, but the look on her face was not one of happiness or pride. She was pale, and nervous. Don could see her hands shaking, and wondered what had spooked her. Then he saw Diablo.

The creature was swimming up and down the length of the pool wildly, its wide body twisting and turning, and its tail gracefully arching as it flew through the water. It wasn't exactly jumping out of the water, but it was close. Clearly, it was agitated, and Don had never seen it so alive. How had Amanda managed it? Had it finally begun eating? Diablo reached the stage and poked its head above the water, showing off an array of pointed teeth. At this, the crowd gasped and Don saw more flashes of light, as a thousand cameras went off at the same time. Then the monster slipped back beneath the water, only to resume gliding through the cool water back and forth, back and forth. It was almost as if it was waiting for something.

Like rolling thunder, a boom echoed across the stadium, shattering the ambience, and sending a ripple of giddy excitement amongst the already over-stimulated audience. Don saw Zola look at Amanda, an expression of confusion drawn on her heavily made-up face. She and Amanda looked around for the source of the noise, as did Don, but there was nothing. The sound was deep and low, like the boom a sonic jet makes when it flies low over the ground. Don felt like the sound was sad. It was like the plaintive calling of a cow that has had her calf taken away. Yet, it was so much louder than a cow that Don could not help but feel he was right. He couldn't risk leaving it any longer.

"Amanda, I think you should get off the stage. Zola, you too," said Don. He climbed up onto stage, still carrying the rifle, and saw Zola's mouth drop open in shock.

"Don, what are you doing here?" asked Amanda. "What was that noise?"

A murmur rose from the spectators, many of whom still seemed unsure if this was a part of the show, or not. Some cheered when Don walked out, some went quiet. The mood of the night was changing.

"Amanda, get over here," hissed Don.

"Don, you can't..." Amanda stopped, as the stage began vibrating.

The ground seemed to be shaking all around them, and clearly, the crowd was feeling it too. A spotlight crashed onto the ground as the stadium shook. Don felt his blood turn to ice, as he saw it. At first, it was just a head, but then the enormous body followed. The monster was even bigger than Ryan had described. It came from the west, crashing through buildings, trampling over the Rescue Centre, and barging through the animal house as if it wasn't there. With a terrible roar, the monster bellowed again, the sound this time echoing not just around the stadium, but the whole park. It approached the stadium, and the terrible sound filled Don's ears. Its open jaws revealed a plethora of teeth, each one as big as a man was. As it roared, its whole body trembled, and drops of saliva fell from giant teeth onto the shaking ground. Huge eyes looked around hungrily, and Don knew then that this thing was looking for Diablo. The monster reared up on its extended hind legs, and the stadium was cast under a shadow, as the setting sun was blotted out. Standing easily over a hundred feet tall, the watching crowd was stunned into silence. The belly of the creature was pink and white, covered in molluscs and barnacles. As it roared, the monster's body quivered, and Don was fascinated by the colour of its skin. Dark and green, it was also covered in patches of maroon and purples. The ragged spots seemed to change colour as he stared at it, as though the monster was trying to blend into the background by changing colour. It was as if a shimmering film had stretched across his eyes, blocking out the truth, hiding the hideous animal.

It crashed down to the ground, and the stage shook again with so much force that Amanda was knocked to the floor. Don reached out for her. He was worried that if the creature lashed out, she would be first to feel the strength of the brute. Zola stared, astounded, and Amanda took Don's hand as they slowly crawled away.

"Um, folks, please stay calm," said Zola, "just stay in your seats and..." She trailed off as the monster took a step forward. The crowd was silent, struck dumb by the awesome sight standing and breathing right before them. It made Diablo look like a child's toy.

Don saw a lone figure walk from the front row out into the middle of the concourse. The man was dressed in a smart suit and suede brogues. He clapped his hands together and then laughed. "Wow, what a show!" The man turned around and laughed once more, emitting a throaty guffaw that reminded Don of sitting with his father, and both of them laughing as they watched Cheers.

Playing to the cameras, the man turned back and looked up at the giant beast. "Wow. Who needs Godzilla, huh? It's genuinely amazing what you can do with a few pyrotechnics and mechanics these days. How lifelike is this? Am I being filmed right now? Am I going to be in the Jurassic Park remake?"

When the crowd failed to acknowledge he had spoken, the man turned his back towards them and Don could see it was a movie star. Zola had invited several celebrities to boost the show's profile, and he was undoubtedly the biggest name to come.

A photographer crept closer to the tank and took a snap of the monster up close, although twenty feet away was as close as he dared. The movie star smiled broadly, and Don watched as with one lightning-quick movement, the monster flicked its front leg forward and the actor was sent hurtling back into the stadium headfirst. He splatted against the stadium roof like a bug on a windshield, and blood splattered everywhere as his body came apart. Another quick kick followed, and the photographer followed him into the mosh pit of other journalists. A scream came from the crowd and Don's legs turned to jelly, as the behemoth took a step forward, now ignoring the buzzing photographers and paparazzi. Instead of pushing and shoving to get to the front for the best shots, they were pushing backwards, trying to get away from the advancing monster.

It let out a low grunt, then a series of noises that sounded like the bark of a rabid dog. Its cruel bark seemed to tease, and was certainly intimidating, even more than the bellowing it had produced previously. The rough barks resonated with Don at the back of his mind. He was reminded of how a vicious dog barks at intruders, both as a warning and an invitation to a fight you could never hope to win. Don grit his teeth and held onto Amanda tighter, as he listened to the primordial noises echoing through the park.

The titan turned its short neck slightly and seemed to look straight at Don. Large yellow eyes narrowed and then its neck twisted around, its flesh wrinkling up as it kept its feet firmly planted on the ground. It scanned around the stadium, at the people frozen in awe, at the photographers and media who were embarking on a frenzy below, and finally at the tank where Diablo was being held captive. As those huge, dark golden eyes went past Don, he shuddered. This was no base creature, without feeling, without conscience or consciousness. It knew exactly what it was doing. It looked mad and there was an unrestrained wrath and evil behind those yellow eyes.

The short, sharp barking stopped, and then a terrifying noise erupted from the belly of the creature, a roar so brittle and deep that it set Don's teeth on edge. His stomach squirmed and writhed as he tensed, and he knew it was inevitable now. The creature was not going to slink off, back to the depths of the ocean. It wanted its family back, and it was not going to disappear quietly. Don looked over at Diablo who was still swimming up and down, only with more urgency.

Zola sank to her knees and let the microphone tumble from her hands. It rolled across the stage and a whistling echo came from the overhead speakers, the painful sound distorting as it rang around the stadium. She looked around at the stadium that was threatening to become a morgue. Somebody had laid a blanket over the famous movie star's prostrate body, and people around him were crying and holding each other. The photographer who had been so casually brushed aside was surrounded by paramedics. His colleagues were moving up into the grandstand seats, trying to get away, whilst the people in the stadium seemed oblivious to the immediate danger. Some were calling 911, some shouting and gesturing, not knowing what to do or where to turn. Some were headed for the exits, only to find them blocked as more and more people tried to cram through. Some sat in their seats expectantly, as if waiting for the show to continue. Nobody was being told what to do, and Zola was in a daze, as her expensive world collapsed around her.

Don saw the microphone tumble over the side of the stage and into the tank, as it sank into the water out of view. This couldn't be happening. He could see Zola on her knees now, her mouth agape and her eyes just staring into space. It was as if her mind had been wiped. He wanted to tell her to do something, to call the police, to order an evacuation of the stadium, to do *anything* instead of sitting there like a dummy. But he couldn't. Amanda was clinging to him tightly. Don was absorbed like everyone else at the sheer size of the thing that had gate-crashed the party. It was almost as tall as the stadium itself, certainly much longer. Its head was flat and oblong, and its skin was thick and oily. Its rubbery hide reminded Don of a snake, and Diablo.

Don reached around for his radio, wanting to alert security to the situation. Although, if they hadn't already heard or seen what was happening by now, then half of America had. He knew the event was being screened live on CNN. Well, they were certainly getting a show. Like fifty million Americans, Don felt powerless to take his eyes off the monstrosity that was standing between the tank and the seats of Shakti Stadium.

A series of vibrations shot up Don's body and he saw a shadow flash over the concourse. There was a splashing sound, a frisson of excitement from the crowd, and suddenly, a tremendous surge of water spilled over the lip of the tank, drenching both Amanda and him. He grabbed her to him as Diablo leapt from the tank. When Don looked up again, he could see Diablo in the stadium. Don knew he was only looking at a baby. Maybe that explained why it had been so quiet these last couple of days. It hadn't known what to do, yet, now that it had its mother or father nearby, its confidence had grown. Maybe the barks were their way of communicating. Don could think of no other explanation. Somehow, the adult of the species had found its way here.

Don had no time to piece it all together, as Diablo was now free. A mere two thousand pounds, the infant crashed into the lower half of the stands, instantly crushing most of the assembled media, two teachers, and a dozen school children. In the water, it moved swiftly, silently, and with precision. Out of water, it was ungainly and it crashed around noisily, as it began to snap its jaws at the screaming audience.

Don was reminded of an image from an old history book. Roman gladiators in the Coliseum with people cheering and baying for blood. The blood of the beasts mingled with the sand in the arena, and the crowd went wild. He used to love pouring over the pictures and imagining he was there. The crowd today though, was screaming in terror and fear. The gladiators were absent, and the beasts were hungry.

"Oh, God, no," was all Don could mutter as the scene began to play out. As the infant began to feast on the abundance of humans laid out before it, as if on a platter, the other monster, the newcomer, turned away, content to let its child devour as many people as possible. Don watched the carnage, terrified as the monster turned its misshapen head to face the stage where Zola still sat. Don wanted to keep Amanda close to him, to shield her from the horrible terror that was opening up before his eyes. Nobody should have to witness the ruin he was seeing. Amanda, however, was only too aware of what was happening. She could hear the screaming of petrified children, the anguished cries for help, and the incessant crunching of bones as Diablo finally filled his empty belly. The screams for help were almost drowned out by the sickening sound of people being scooped up in the monster's jaws and eaten alive. With the reassuring presence of its parent, it was showing no fear, and whipping its snarling teeth back and forth, as it greedily took more and more fresh food.

That's why it wouldn't eat, thought Don. *It wouldn't touch the dead meat. It wants fresh meat. And now, we've given it a five-star banquet to tuck into.*

A magnificent roar from the larger creature briefly drowned out everything else, even Don's thoughts, and then the infant began to work on the crowd with almost a childish glee. Like a frenzied dog attack, its salivating jaws scissored through people of all ages, as they ran aimlessly, stumbling over chairs and bags in a desperate attempt to exit the stadium. An obese man with a goatee that only covered one of his chins made a break for it, pushing through a school group and knocking children to the ground. Diablo jumped up and snatched the obese man into his mouth. The man's guts spurted out over the running children, as Diablo chomped through him. A little girl in a chequered blue and white pinafore smock broke away from the others and tried to climb upwards, clambering over the seats to get away.

"Look out!" Don shouted at her, but in a flash, Diablo had swallowed the man and taken the girl too. A ripped shred of blue cloth caught on one of its incisors was all that remained of the girl. Diablo crawled higher, its vicious jaws snapping eagerly. Limbs flew through the air, as it mangled and crushed the desperate people beneath its feet.

"Don, look." Amanda pointed at the stage. Zola was getting to her feet slowly, to face the monster. She held her hands up in front of her, her palms raised in defence.

"Zola!" shouted Don. "Zola, get out of there!" Don saw Diablo's parent approach the stage.

If Zola heard him, then she didn't show it. There was no sign of understanding on her face, not a twitch of an eyebrow or a flicker of movement from any part of her body. She faced the creature stoically as it bore down on her.

"I...I'm sorry. I didn't...," she whispered. Zola stumbled backwards as the monster unleashed a nerve-shredding bark and drowned out her words.

The monster lunged at Zola, and with a flick of its head, launched her high up into the air. It took a step forward onto the stage, which creaked under the weight. Zola screamed and a shoe flew off as she zipped high into the warm air above the tank. The monster looked up at her, opened its jaws, and snapped them shut just as Zola plummeted down. It caught her in its sharp teeth, so her lower body was inside its mouth and her torso was caught between its teeth. Zola screamed again as the teeth ripped into her and the monster flung her ragged body from side to side. Don saw beads of blood fly from Zola into the pool, and waited for the thing to swallow her. Instead, he was amazed to see the monster release her and drop her back onto the stage. It stepped back and emitted three short barks.

Zola lay on the stage, her body broken, her spine crushed, and her wounds bleeding profusely. She lay at such an angle that her face was turned toward Don, and he was helpless to do anything but watch, as the life began to ooze out of her.

Responding to the barks, Diablo abruptly left the stadium and raced up to the stage. Cautiously, it placed its feet on the sodden stage and then approached Zola. Its face was covered in blood and gore. It snorted once and looked up at its parent. One short bark was all it required, and then it grabbed Zola's feet in its jaws. With a sickening crunch, Don saw Diablo bite off Zola's legs and gulp them back down its gullet. Then it moved further up her body and took the rest of her in its mouth. Zola screwed up her face and tried to scream, but could only spurt a mouthful of blood out, as Diablo began to chew on her body, its sharp teeth grinding through her and ripping her apart. Its tremendous jaws tore through Zola as if she was nothing more solid than cotton candy, and Diablo swallowed her piece by piece. The once glamorous stage was now covered in bone, tissue, and a solitary red high-heeled Manolo Blahnik shoe, the only proof left behind that Zola was ever there at all.

Don looked back at the stadium. People were running amok, desperately trying to find loved ones or a way out of the stadium.

"Amanda, we have to go, we have to get out of here." Don couldn't help anyone now. He had to get back to the office and call for help. "We need help. We need to call the police, the army...fucking anybody."

Amanda felt like a doll in his hands. As he got up and pulled her with him, she felt so light that he was scared she would blow away. He gripped one hand and pulled her back into the tunnel beside the tank, away from the monsters above. Now there were two of them. One had been bad enough, but two?

"We should get Zola," said Amanda. She looked comatose, her eyes glazed, and her speech slow. "She...she..."

"She's gone, Amanda," said Don slowly. "She's gone, and we're next if we don't make a move now."

Amanda turned to look at the stadium. The crescent-shaped roof was still in place, but beneath the shining lights, it was utter carnage. It looked like a slaughterhouse, as dead bodies and blood covered the concourse and the smashed seats. Most of the spectators had now escaped the stadium and only a few remained; those who were unable to comprehend what was going on, and those who were cradling their loved ones, simply unable to leave them behind. Amanda raised a hand to her mouth, and then looked at the two monsters that were ambling toward the stadium to pick off the stragglers. She turned back to Don.

"It's our fault, Don, we did this. We should've let it go. We shouldn't have listened to her. Oh, Jesus, what do we do now?"

CHAPTER 12

OCTOBER FRIDAY 18TH 18:39

Meghan was out there, somewhere. Had she made it? Don had seen a few people escape, but in the chaos, he hadn't seen her. He had to trust she had. He had to believe she had made it out alive.

She's waiting for me to get her. I need to find her. I need her. If I hadn't asked her along, she wouldn't be here, so she's my responsibility. The whole park is my responsibility. I have to do something. Why didn't I shoot? I've got the rifle, but I couldn't. There was no time. It was too big. What could I have done?

"Amanda, listen to me, we *have* to go. We have to go get help." Don tried pulling her with him, but Amanda was not moving.

"Oh, Jesus, what are we going to do?" Amanda looked back at the monsters again. "Diablo. What a joke. Look at the size of it. Look at the other one. It must be three or four times the size of the one we had. What if we only had a baby version? I think we just had an infant, Don. Oh Jesus, I can't…"

Amanda's knees buckled and Don put his arms around her, letting her sink slowly to the floor. They were beside the tank, just under the shelter of the tunnel that led back to the control room. The monsters out there hadn't seen them yet, but he didn't want to wait much longer. Amanda was losing it, and he couldn't blame her. How many people had just been killed; a hundred, a thousand, more? If Don and Amanda were spotted, they would be dessert. He had to make her move.

Don cupped Amanda's face in his hand. "Listen to me good, Amanda, 'cause I'm only saying this once more," he said sternly. "Unless you want to be a snack for a giant fucking sea monster, then you need to get up and out of here. We have a slim chance if we go now. You ever tried killing a mouse with a tank? Well, those things are bigger than tanks, and we're the mice. We can get past them, we just have to be smarter than them. Now get off your ass and move!" He literally pulled Amanda up onto her feet, and together, they began walking quietly down the tunnel.

Don kept them as close to the tank as he could, hoping it would provide them with cover. The tunnel was dim, but they only needed to get as far as the security control room. He couldn't hear any noises behind them and chanced a look over his shoulder. The monsters were well behind them now, and he let out a breath. His heart was pounding. He had thought he was going to have to drag Amanda out of there by her hair, like some prehistoric caveman. He looked at her and his heart reached out. She was broken. The shock was subsiding and reality was setting in; tears were streaming down her face and the hand he held was starting to tremble. She coughed and then tripped, holding herself up by leaning against the tank's walls.

"Don, just a second. Please?"

He let her go and watched her recline against the tank. He nervously looked back to where they had come from. He could no longer see the stadium, and he was pleased to see nothing was following them. The newcomer wouldn't fit down here in the tunnel, but Diablo certainly would. Don nodded and let Amanda gather herself together. He wanted to get back upstairs as quickly as possible, to make sure the authorities were on their way. He also wanted to get Amanda out of her wetsuit and into some dry clothes. He could do with something dry to put on himself, and felt a shiver run down his back. It was a mixture of cold and fear.

Don knelt down beside Amanda. "I don't know what the hell happened back there, but I can tell you this, my guys know what they're doing. I'm sure the police and paramedics are on their way right now. We need to get you someplace safe, okay?" Don was aware that so far, Amanda hadn't thought about Hamish. He had been out there to watch the show with his father. There was no way of telling what had happened to him, and if Amanda picked up that thread, it could lead anywhere. Don really hoped he could get Amanda out of harm's way first.

"Someplace safe? Where the hell is safe anymore?" Amanda hissed. With shaking hands, she swept her hair back behind her shoulders. "It's got to be its mother. What else could it be?"

Don shrugged. "What does it matter? We've got to kill it. Kill them both."

Amanda looked at Don and nodded her head. "What if they head further inland? What if they head for the city? What if...oh God, what about Hamish, he was there!" Amanda jumped to her feet and looked down the tunnel.

Before she could make a run for it, Don grabbed her arm. "There's nothing you can do about it now. Either he got away or..."

"Or what? I have to find him. He and Curtis might still be out there, in trouble. You saw what Diablo was doing, what he did to Zola." Amanda tugged her arm from Don's grasp.

They were interrupted by more barking noises from outside that echoed down the tunnel and stung their ears.

Don lowered his voice. He couldn't fight her anymore. "Amanda, if you go back out there, you're as good as dead. Hamish isn't stupid, he would've made it. He was with his father wasn't he? At the first sign of trouble, I bet they bolted. He's probably waiting up in the staff room for you now, wondering where the hell *you* are." Don took a step back, away from the stadium, and held out his hand. "Please, Amanda, come with me. We'll find him, I promise."

Don watched as Amanda thought it over. He genuinely didn't know which way she was going to turn. He hoped that reason would win over emotion, but such was the expression of worry and fear on her face that he was expecting her to run away from him. His heart stopped pounding a little as soon as she took his hand.

"Fine. Let's get upstairs. Then I'm going to get Hamish, with or without you."

Amanda started running away from the tank and the stadium with Don, when a tremendous crash brought them to a stop, and natural daylight blinded their vision as a section of the roof above them was lifted off. Chunks of masonry fell around them, and then water swirled around their feet as the tunnel began to fill. The Ocean King was standing above them, and his tail had crashed through the roof. Large cracks appeared in the glass wall on their right, and then they saw Diablo swimming toward them through the water at speed.

"Run!" shouted Don as concrete and dust fell around them. Sprinting down the corridor, he heard more barks from the two monsters. The Ocean King was tearing the park apart above them, whilst Diablo chased after them. This was no random attack anymore; Diablo was going after them all. The vindictive Ocean King was urging its infant on a rampage, and Don's pulse soared as he sensed Diablo's approach. A sickening, crashing sound indicated the tanks walls had given way, and Don felt more cold water surging past his feet. "In here!"

Don opened a doorway and shoved Amanda through. She was immediately faced with a set of steps leading upward. "Go, go, go! It leads up to the janitor's room. We can get out that way."

The very building seemed to shake as they ran upwards, water filling the stairwell as they climbed. At the top, Amanda burst through another door and encountered a large room stocked with cleaning materials. She tried the door that led to the park, but it was locked.

"Don, I can't open it."

There was another bellow as the monsters destroyed the building. It was as if Diablo was specifically hunting for Amanda. Having killed and eaten Zola, was it now looking for her too? The room trembled and splintering sounds suggested the doorway below had finally given in to the pressure of the water. From beyond the door, Don heard screaming and the very ground shook, as the Ocean King began marauding through the park for more victims, leaving Diablo to finish the job at Shakti Stadium.

"Stand back," said Don. He fired his rifle at the door, shredding it under a hail of bullets. The door flung open and Don and Amanda rushed outside.

Don heard the sirens before he saw help arriving. They had surfaced near Dolphin Point, and he saw a giant tail swing around and smash into the structure, causing the roof to cave in.

"No!" screamed Amanda as the dolphin enclosure was buried beneath a mountain of rubble.

Don saw people running everywhere, hopelessly lost. People with missing limbs, covered in blood, ran for their lives. A man collapsed at Don's feet, his neck torn open and bleeding. Many of the retail carts were toppled over, and the Ocean King was there, its massive jaws swinging around and around as it scooped people up and ate them alive. A crush of around two hundred people had amassed by the park exit. Two stalls had been set up right outside, narrowing the access to single file, and the crowd had no chance. A dark shadow flitted overhead, as Diablo's parent reared up and then landed on the pile of men, women, and children. Most were crushed instantly beneath its swollen belly, and the rest were killed in its jaws.

"Where's Diablo?" asked Amanda. "Where did he go?"

"Who cares," said Don. "Let's move."

With Amanda in one hand and the rifle in his other, Don scurried through the park toward the staff entrance, away from the normal public one that was now blocked by the sea creature. Its tail curled around the toilet block and restaurant, so he had to take them the long way round, past the Bay of Play. It used to be a colourful array of children's rides and games, but now it was a mangled mess, destroyed when the beast had simply walked over it and crushed it.

As terrorised people criss-crossed the path in front of them, Don saw a screaming toddler was stood alone just a few feet up ahead. No more than three or four years old, the boy wore a light blue T-shirt that read, 'I met Diablo.' Holding a stuffed toy, the boy was terrified and his parents were nowhere to be seen. Don saw the monster's tail flick out and threaten to crush the boy, so he fired his rifle, sending round after round of explosives into the beast's meaty tail. It was just enough to cause the monster to deflect the tail's path, and it ended up swiping away a hot dog cart. Don fired again and reached for his walkie. "Terrick, where the hell are you? James? Sam? Someone answer me."

"Terrick here, Don. I'm by the Reef gift shop. There was a stampede to get out and I got swarmed. I can see it now. Christ, it's eating them. What the hell is happening?"

"Terrick, just tell me someone made the call?"

"Yes, sir. Sam called for help as soon as we saw it arrive."

"Good. Where's James? We need all the firepower we can get."

"He didn't make it. He was trying to help the crowd get through the exit. Some idiot blocked it. I just saw that monster land on them. He was right in the middle of it. I don't think anyone could have survived."

Please don't let Meghan or Hamish be in that pile of dead bodies. They have to be all right, they have *to be.*

"Terrick, if you can, try and shoot it. Keep back, but if you get a shot, take it. I'll join you at the exit in a minute."

Amanda had taken the crying boy's hand and was trying to comfort him. As night swept over the park, it brought with it the stench of death. The screams and cries were fading, but the monster was still there, and feeding on the bodies.

"Amanda, get out of here and take the kid with you. We'll worry about finding his parents later. Take the staff entrance, it's clear. I have to help Terrick. I can't let this thing get out of the park. I don't know how, but I have to try to stop it."

Amanda nodded as tears fell down her face. "Be careful."

Don knew the kid was most likely an orphan, and he didn't like to let them go, but he had a duty to everyone in the park. How could he have been so stupid? He should've made Zola listen to Amanda, not the other way around.

Don ran toward the monster, dodging the dead bodies on the ground and searching for Terrick. With the two of them armed, maybe they could at least scare it enough to retreat. He ran fast, passed the tail and the hideous dark green body, until finally he arrived at the park gates. He found the monster feasting upon so many people he wanted to be sick. Little was left in the pile of meat that resembled a human anymore.

"You sick fucker." Don started firing at the creature, aiming for those large eyes on its head. He sprayed the monster with bullets, and it writhed around before arching its back and scuttling backwards. As the monster raised its head, ready to strike, Don saw Terrick appear. He unleashed more firepower and the monster shook its head from side to side, bellowing and roaring furiously. Its jaw's quivered, and bloody saliva dripped onto the ground.

Don kept firing as he crept toward Terrick. He noticed a SWAT team swoop in through the narrow entrance, and they immediately joined him and Terrick in shooting at the monster. The giant bounced up and down, and it felt like the earth was alive, as it jostled the ground. It was like an earthquake, and the power from the creature's movement caused them all to lose their footing. With its attackers temporarily immobilised, the monster scurried forward and took a chunk out of the park fence. It spat the metal fence out, and scooped up two of the SWAT team. Even when they were in its mouth, Don could see them firing and shooting. With one gulp though, they were gone, and the firing ceased. Don resumed firing as he lay on the ground, trying to shoot at the thing's legs, body and tail, as it tried to leave the park.

Flashing red and blue lights illuminated the creature as it advanced, and Don heard shouting before suddenly, a fireball erupted on the creature's back. Don was knocked back by the force of the explosion and hurtled into a large, concrete garbage bin anchored to the ground. He heard more shouting and looked up to see the monster crush an ambulance sat right outside the park gates. A helicopter circled overhead and a spotlight shone down upon the monster's head.

Don got up. "Terrick? Terrick, you there?"

A man waved from the other side of the park and then was gone, as the monster's tail whistled through the air and smashed the man into the ground. Don pointed his rifle at the monster as it continued fighting its way out of the park. The bullets sank into the flesh, but had little effect. The grenade on the creature's back hadn't even caused it to bleed, and Don saw it trample over half a dozen police cars as it left the park. Gunshots rang out over the otherwise still night and mingled with the animal's barking, as it carved a path of destruction into the city.

Don's rifle clicked empty and he sank to the ground, defeated. He could smell something rotten and fishy, undoubtedly the leftover pungent aroma of the beast. He watched as it jumped over a building to its right, and then he couldn't see it anymore. He slumped backwards, exhausted, and his head landed on something soft. Reaching around, he picked up an arm that had been torn from its owner. The pale hand still clutched a small card, and Don saw the name on it: Stacy Woodman.

He closed his eyes and swallowed down the bile in his mouth, as he put the arm down gently.

Is this really what You wanted? She was just a kid. What about the others? What about the hundreds dead and injured, the families who had come for entertainment, but ended up being eaten alive? How many homes will be empty tonight? Is this what we deserve?

Don slowly got to his feet. More sirens approached, but all they could hope to do now was find the injured. Wild Seas Park was a morgue. He had to go find Amanda and Meghan. He had so much to do. All around him were dead bodies. There were no more screams. Were there even any injured people? All he could hear was the distant barking of the monster that up until thirty minutes ago, hadn't even existed. Where was Diablo? It wasn't with its parent, and it wasn't likely to be hiding.

Don started walking back towards the security room. He wanted to get more ammo for the rifle and anything else he could still lay his hands on. If Diablo was still around, he wanted to be fully prepared. Soon, the park was going to be awash with cops and crime scene examiners, if not the FBI, and he didn't know how much access he would get once they took over. Don retraced his steps, and as the battle receded behind him, he became aware of an odd sound. Like the mewling of a kitten, it occasionally burst into a series of coughs, before silencing. Don found the door to the janitor's office that he and Amanda had escaped from, and the noise increased. He went into the room and waded down the stairs into the water. Although the roof had caved in, a small portion of the underground corridor was still visible. There, buried beneath the rubble and submerged in the cloudy water, was Diablo. A massive chunk of concrete was embedded in its head, and whenever it moved, blood spilled out, mixing with the salt water.

"You're lucky I don't have any ammo left," said Don. He pulled his walkie out. "This is Don, anyone copy me?"

"Don, this is Sam. Where are you? Are you hurt?"

Don felt the scar above his head. His short hair was grimy with sweat and dirt. "I'm fine. I'm in the storeroom behind the stadium. How're you doing, Sam?"

"Just peachy. I sent as many of the guys out there to help as I could, but...only Selick came back. Everyone else is...gone."

"It's not your fault, Sam. I'm in charge and this is on me."

"Don, it's going crazy here. Apparently, the FBI is on their way. The switchboard is jammed. You don't even want to know what CNN is saying. This is insane. What do I do? What the hell do we do, Don?"

"Sam, listen, we've got a situation here and it needs containing. I need you and Selick to get down here quickly, before the FBI stick their noses in. Bring the lifting crane and flatbed truck. If anyone sees you, tell them you're moving the injured dolphins from their pool to a holding tank."

"Are the dolphins a priority right now, Don? There are so many injured people out there that we..."

"Sam, just do it. It's not for the dolphins, but I don't have time to explain right now. I'm not asking you, I'm telling you to do this. Unless you want more injured people, get off the radio, and get down here with the truck."

"Copy."

Don looked at Diablo as more blood seeped from the animal's wound. "I guess Mommy lost you, huh? Did she get a bit excited, perhaps lost sight of why she was here? Thought she could leave you to finish us off while she went sight-seeing?"

Don knew he was going to have to find Amanda and tell her. He couldn't leave Diablo here and wait for its parent to come back for another go at rescuing its infant. The cops were going to want to speak to him, assuming they weren't too busy chasing a giant monster over the city. He desperately wanted to find Meghan, to know that she was okay, but he also needed to get more ammo while he could. There was so much to do. All because of this hideous brute, hundreds if not thousands of people were dead. Zola was dead. For all he knew, Hamish, Curtis, and Meghan were too.

Don took his rifle butt and jammed it into Diablo's right eye. The creature wriggled around, but was unable to free itself as Don continued blinding it. It was weak from blood-loss and Don took great pleasure as the animal's eye finally burst. "And when I've got you out of there, I'm taking your other eye too, bitch."

CHAPTER 13

OCTOBER SATURDAY 18TH 05:55

"O'Reilly, get over there, now. We're moving on this. You've got a green light."

Don clambered up the side of the bank and the gritty sand stuck to his body. As he nestled low into the dirty shoreline, he tried to ignore the stench that pervaded the air. There was a strong fishy smell mingling with what he could only assume was human excrement. He looked through his goggles and saw Pozden on his left flank, Carter to his right. Don felt the sun warming his back. An invisible force was pushing him along, moving his legs for him toward the crest of the bank as if he were a puppet on a string.

Tufts of coarse Psamma scratched at his legs and arms as he climbed. He knew what was coming over the ridge: the mosque, the faded green door, the stray cat, and a trailer full of dead rotting sharks. He went over the top and first of all, saw the trailer full of carcasses, only this time the sharks had been replaced with people. Women and men of all ages were piled up with their heads missing, their backs broken, and their souls in Hell. Things were moving fast now. He reached for his Heckler and Koch MP5K to find that it had been replaced with a cuddly toy. He looked down at the cute brown bear clutched in his hand. It wore a T-shirt proudly displaying a logo, 'I met Diablo.' Then the bear's head fell off and blood gushed from its neck. Don dropped it in horror and looked back at the mosque as a dog barked in the distance

Do it, do it now.

Three men ran toward him firing their guns. Wilson shot them down as the doors to the mosque burst outwards. Hostages began pouring out, running in all directions as the man in the yellow polo shirt and red bandana raised his weapon. Don fired and the top of the building was lost in a mist of exploding masonry.

He tried to shout, yet every time he opened his mouth, he spewed out only sand. Don watched Robert's left knee shatter as the explosion from the rocket launched Don into the air. His body smashed into the beach and he rolled over. Don lifted himself to his feet, aware his arm was broken. There was a hole in the ground where Wilson had been standing, and suddenly Carter fell at Don's feet. "Blow it, Don, blow them all to Hell."

He pulled the detonator from his pocket and looked at Carter. "The hostages? What about the fucking hostages!"

Carter lay still. "All gone. Do it, do it now, and take those bastards down. They're inside the mosque."

Don gripped Carter's hand. "Where's Robert?"

Carter was dead. Wilson was dead. The CRRC was still there, a few feet away. He could still make it back to the USNS Arctic. He looked at the detonator in his hand again.

Press it. Fuck, Robert, where are you? You're the only one left. FUCK! Do it, do it now.

Carter's words rang around his aching head. A tremor rippled through the sand, and the sun was obscured by a huge form that loomed over him. Diablo was running through the street, eating the dead hostages, and the Ocean King towered above Don as he squeezed his right hand.

Do it.

Bullets ripped into the beach, spraying him with dirt and sending mushroom clouds of gritty sand into his eyes. Carter's body twitched as more rounds tore through him, and Don was sprayed with warm blood. An obtuse shape, no more than a shadow, flitted across his vision and melted into the sand before it could be identified, yet, Don cold feel what it was. The Ocean King was getting closer.

Do it, do it now.

A man's voice spat out urgent commands that Don could not understand. The frantic barking of a rabid dog merged with the barks of the monster standing over him. Its face was coming closer now, closer to Don, its jaws widening. He could feel the beast's warm breath as it opened its mouth to swallow him. He saw shreds of meat and tissue caught between its teeth and incisors dripping with blood. Zola's head toppled out of its mouth and landed with a soft thud into the sand beside him. The man in the yellow polo shirt laughed, and Don's head rang with the sound of death. He knew what he had to do.

A ringing alarm splintered Don's head and he opened his eyes. The monster was gone and the sand around his feet was nothing more than a white duvet. The alarm clock next to him read six a.m., and he fumbled for the off switch. He looked around the room and he remembered why he was here.

In the carnage that had swiftly ensued last night, the monster had run amok in downtown San Diego. FOX was reporting 'Monster Mayhem' amid lurid details of how people had died. The injury list was truly horrifying. CNN had described it as one of the worst days in modern American history, leaving the blame squarely with Wild Seas, and their now deceased GM, Zola Bertoni. Amanda's name had been mentioned only in passing. Many references had been made to Diablo and its current unknown location, but the majority of headlines were concerned with the new monster. A reporter on the BBC had called it the new king of the oceans, and so it had stuck. The New York Times, The Chicago Tribune, The Washington Post, USA Today, and even the Wall Street Journal had all gone with the same theme: 'Where is the Ocean King?' 'Ocean King destroys San Diego.' 'Meet The Ocean King.' A number of blurry and hastily taken photographs had failed to capture the true size of the beast, and it was the news channels that had the most accurate coverage with aerial footage of the monster ploughing through the city, showing graphically, just how big it was.

The army had been called up, but San Diego city centre had been annihilated before they had arrived on the scene. The Ocean King had wiped out billions of dollars' worth of real estate, and the death toll stood in the thousands. Scripps Mercy Hospital had been overrun by midnight with casualties, and the injured had been sent further and further out to get treatment. A triage centre was set up at Paradise Valley Hospital, and a list of the identified dead was established.

Don remembered heading down there with Amanda around ten thirty. Amanda's car escaped the Ocean King's rampage unscathed, and she took them both to her place at first. It was empty, and there was no sign of Hamish. The phone lines were down, of course, and the mobile companies were so overloaded that it took hours before the text messages had come through. They had not talked to each other the whole car journey back. They agreed it would be best to go to the hospital, rather than sit around at home waiting, not knowing. Neither of them wanted to be at home, waiting for a phone call that may never come. Don insisted that on the way to the hospital, they drive by Collwood Lane. Once he had seen that the house was undamaged, they had moved on. Amanda didn't ask why he wanted to look at the house, and he didn't offer any explanation.

Whilst they waited outside Paradise Valley, sitting in the car in silence hoping to get news, Amanda's phone started beeping. As the texts came in, she started weeping.

"Hamish is okay, he's fine," said Amanda. "Oh, thank God."

"What is it?" asked Don. If Hamish had been hurt, he didn't know how he would've comforted Amanda. He knew it was impossible to console someone who had just lost someone they loved. "There's something else, isn't there?"

"It's his father, Curtis. He was badly hurt. He's in a coma now. They've got him at Alvarado. Hamish is there now with his mother. I've got to talk to him."

Don watched Amanda get out of the car and sit on the bonnet. She kept looking at her phone as she tried to get through, and finally, Don knew she had been connected. She broke down as Hamish explained what had happened, and told Don later how Curtis had been crushed under Diablo, as he had run through the stadium.

Don sat patiently in the car. They had been there with hundreds of others, waiting for the injury and death toll to be updated. Finally, with Amanda still on the phone, he saw a doctor in green scrubs leave the foyer and pin two notices up on the front door. There were four armed guards to ensure that the access-way was kept clear, and there was a surge of people as the doctor left. Don got out of the car and sauntered over to the doors. People were jostling to get to the updated lists, and more were crying as they filed past Don away from the hospital.

Do you really want to look at it? Go home. That's where she is. She'll have gone back to the Old Station, or home. If she can, she'll find you. Go back to Amanda. She needs you now. There's no time for this. Meghan made it out. She's at home, probably trying to call me, being consoled by her stupid flatmates. If anything, she's probably in this crowd somewhere, trying to find out how I am.

Don checked his phone, but it was silent: no texts, no missed calls, and not one voicemail. Trying not to think the worst, he approached the two pieces of paper pinned up on the hospital doors. From the crowd, a tall man emerged in a black smock sporting a wild grey beard. He held a sheaf of paper out to Don as he neared the building. Don batted it away.

"The time has come. The time has come for us all. His is the only way. Only through Him can we seek blessed salvation and sanctuary in Heaven. He has sent his messenger. God is waiting for you."

Don pushed the tall man away and stood in front of the door. He looked down the list of injured people. There were several new names on the list, highlighted in red, but he didn't know any of the names and he felt relief. She was okay, she wasn't here. Don began to let himself breathe again. He looked across to the list of dead, and scanned down it. Three from the bottom was the name Meghan McCabe. He read it again, looking up and down the list. Three from the bottom: Meghan McCabe. It couldn't be. He traced his finger over the name and shivered.

Don turned around and pushed his way through the thinning crowd back to the car. She was gone. Just like that, she was nothing more than a name on a list, third from the bottom. He could still smell her sweet perfume, and still remember her lips on his. It was Zola's fault. It was Diablo's fault. But mostly, it was his fault. He didn't even know her family. He couldn't do anything to fix this. He wanted her back.

Meghan, where are you? Don't leave me now.

Don reached Amanda's car. She was behind the wheel and he got in as she started the engine.

"Do you mind if we go? Hamish is going to meet me at my house. You want me to drop you anywhere? You want to go home and see if Meghan is there?"

Don shook his head. Last night was so fresh and clear in his mind that it was as if he hadn't even slept. They had got back to Amanda's house, and Hamish had swept Amanda up into his arms the second she'd got home. They had talked, briefly, and decided on what had to be done. Hamish wanted no part of it. He wanted to stay at his father's bedside, as Curtis wasn't predicted to last more than a few days. Don had convinced Hamish at least to help. Then he had crashed in Amanda's spare room. He hadn't wanted their sympathy over Meghan, nor did he want to hear his own grief. He set the alarm, and had slept fitfully since.

Don got up, still dressed in yesterday's clothes. They stank of salt water, blood, and guilt. There was a knock on the door as he pulled on his shoes.

"Come in." Don saw Amanda enter the room. She had changed into fresh clothes, and wore plain jeans with a dark sweater. The bags under her eyes suggested she had not slept either. He was hardly surprised, given the circumstances.

"Did you sleep?" she asked him.

"A little." Don didn't want the conversation that came next. He was going to have to tell Amanda that Meghan was gone, and then Amanda would tell him she was sorry, and then he would probably break down. That was not how he wanted it to be, and he couldn't handle it right now. There was only one thing he wanted to do, one thing he *needed* to do. "We should get moving, before…"

"Don, we have to go by Alvarado hospital first."

"Damn it, Amanda, we don't have time. We discussed this last night. Hamish has his own car. You and I need to…"

"Don." Amanda stepped into the room and shut the door behind her. "Curtis died last night. He didn't make it through the night. The doctors thought he was…" Amanda looked to the ceiling and her bottom lip trembled. "Hamish is…"

Don hugged Amanda and let her cry. Her body was warm and he just held her, waiting for the pain to subside. He held her until she got her emotions under control and the crying stopped. He kept his mind blank, as she shook against him, unable to let his mind go to that dark place as well.

"Go," he said to her. "Go with Hamish. I've got Sam to help me. We'll manage. I'll get a cab and call you later."

Amanda pressed a set of keys into Don's hands and then walked away. She said nothing, nodding and rubbing her eyes as she left the room.

I need a drink. I could get the cab to stop at Mama Kitty's on the way to the park. No, better to stop by mine, so I can get a real drink.

OCTOBER SATURDAY 18TH 08:34

Wild Seas Park was now permanently closed. As Don looked out of the truck's window, he saw the devastation left behind by Diablo and his uninvited killer parent. It was a horrifying scene, and one he was all too familiar with. Death was a close friend of Don's, no matter how much he tried to leave her behind. Many of the buildings were ruined, either destroyed by the monsters, or burnt down overnight. Several places in the park, including the main office and restaurant, were waterlogged and would be demolished. The park had no future now. They had tried to protect animals, to nurture them back to health and educate people, only for it all to be torn down in one night. Don saw the Freshwater Aquarium, now just a hollow in the earth. The fish inside were all dead, either eaten by Diablo, or suffocated when the aquarium had been destroyed.

Getting into the park had been much easier than Don had anticipated, which was a small mercy. He had been dreading having to argue and force his way in, or not getting in at all. The park was closed, and there were some police cars stationed outside to ensure that there were no trespassers or photographers looking for an unsavoury scoop for the front page. The clean-up operation hadn't started in earnest, even though several hundred dead bodies still littered the grounds. The reality was that the city had been taken by surprise and no civil defence plan could prepare for a marauding Kaiju. Evidently, the city had been under attack for several hours last night, and the Wild Seas Park was only the first in a long line of casualties. Downtown San Diego looked like a warzone. There simply weren't enough police to cover the ground required. They were spread so thinly that looking after a marine park full of the dead was low on the list of priorities. The Symphony Towers, the Hyatt, the Union Bank of California, and the Hilton, were high-profile skyscrapers that were no more than piles of rubble now. A state of emergency was called and the city was effectively a no-go zone. Don passed through two checkpoints from Amanda's to the park. Each time, he plainly explained how he was on the way to the park to secure the animals that were still there, and help with the clean-up operation. There was no reason to doubt him, and so Don arrived at the park early. He picked Sam up on the way, who was one of his few living guards.

At the park entrance, Don used the same reason for needing entry. While most of the aquariums and buildings had been destroyed, a few were still intact, including the Petting Zoo and Sea-Lion stadium. It was a lie, but the police on guard had no idea which parts of the park were still standing, and so had let them through. It sounded feasible that the animals still needed feeding and looking after, and Don still had his Security ID card, so they asked no questions.

Whilst the local authorities desperately tried to deal with the overwhelming number of dead and dying, the army was being called up to help. The marines were first in attendance, and their priority was to find the monster and kill it. In the confusion, somewhere between the bombs and missiles that had rained down over the city overnight, it had escaped. It was agile, and had caused chaos everywhere. There were theories that it had been killed, perhaps crushed by one of the skyscrapers it had brought down. Others thought it had sought refuge in the San Diego River, while some thought it might even have gone as far as Lake Murray or the Sweetwater Reservoir. With so much ground to cover, nobody was looking at Wild Seas.

Don steered the semi-trailer left onto the Kumeyaay Highway. His cargo was quiet and still, and it needed to stay that way for the next hour, or it was going to become a very interesting journey. The first thing Don had done, on arriving at the park, was send Sam to gather up as many weapons as possible. Meanwhile, he had gone searching for more barbiturates or sedatives, anything he could use to keep Diablo silent. Don had used a tranquiliser gun last night to shoot three large rounds of Midazolam into Diablo, to make sure he stayed put in the holding tank that Sam and Selick had helped him move Diablo into. This morning, Diablo had been so still that Don thought he was dead. He had jammed the butt of a rifle into the creature, and soon found it was very much alive. It had lost a lot of blood, and was traumatised, but still breathing. Don pumped it full of more sedatives, and then unloaded a full clip into its other eye. Diablo was blinded, which was exactly how Don wanted it. He didn't want the thing dead, not just yet.

"Don, you sure about this?" asked Sam. "Shouldn't we just leave it to the army? They're scouring the city looking for this thing, and we've got it in the back of a truck. I don't think this is such a good idea."

"You didn't think that way last night, Sam. You said you wanted to hurt this thing, to get revenge for Terrick and James and everyone else it had killed. You can't back out on me now." Don drove slowly down the highway, not wanting to draw attention to his unusual cargo. He turned onto San Diego Freeway to bypass the city centre and any more roadblocks. A lot of the city's roads were blocked anyway, and the highway was the quickest route to where he needed to be. Don was also hoping to avoid any more potentially awkward questions, especially from men with guns, and so kept the truck at a steady sixty. "Look, your part in this is nearly over anyway. I won't make you come with me any further than the Port. Once we're unloaded and get it tied down, you can leave."

Sam looked at Don. "Are you okay, Don? I mean, is this really a wise move? Look, why don't we just put it out of its misery. We can cut its throat and dump it in the harbour. No one will even know it was us."

"Put it out of its misery? Are you kidding me? This thing's parent turns up and together they kill thousands of people. They killed Zola, Terrick, our colleagues and friends, people close to us. People close to me died, and you want to put it out of its misery? No way. I want this fucker to suffer. I want its mommy or daddy to *know* it's suffering."

"Don, this is insane. You can't do this alone. Come on, man, just think about what you're doing."

"That's *all* I've done, Sam. I'm thinking about the people who have died. I'm thinking about Meg...about lots of things. This is something I have to do, so don't try to talk me out of it. I'm not expecting you to do anything more."

They left the highway and entered the Port area where the smaller roads were surrounded by a cluster of low-rise buildings and warehouses. Don could see the harbour ahead. The last few days had been glorious sunshine, yet now, the sun had deserted them and a bank of dark clouds had rolled in, making the morning gloomy and cool. A slight mist trickled through the buildings as they drove past, and Don slowed as they drove close to the water's edge. Eventually, Don pulled up next to a battered looking fishing trawler.

"This it?" Sam frowned. "The Mary-Jane. Looks like a heap of junk."

Don got out of the cab and jumped down onto the ground, grasping the keys in his hand. "This is it. She'll do fine." He jumped onto the trawler and noticed the thick rope and tethers that had originally brought Diablo here. He was going to use the same ones to take it back. Amanda had been almost right; they should take it back out into the ocean and dump it. But Diablo had one more job to do before then.

Don instructed Sam to start uncoupling the semi and check on their freight, as he jogged up to the wheelhouse on the trawler. He looked at the wheel, the array of instruments and equipment, and suddenly doubted he could pull this off. It had been twenty years since he had last taken charge of a boat, and that had not been a commercial fishing trawler. He sat down on a cushioned seat and looked out at the open water. With the clouds brewing, there might even be a storm coming. He really didn't know what he would do if there was.

Sam's right, I should leave it alone. I don't know how to drive this thing. If only Curtis hadn't died last night. Damn, how selfish is that. You only want him alive so you can use his son. Maybe I'm not being selfish. Maybe I just want some freaking help. How can you leave me, Meghan, just when things were starting? Where are you now? I wish I could see your face again. I wish for a lot of things, but they never come true. I wish things had gone differently twenty years ago. I wish I had a beer in my hand and not the keys to a fucking trawler I don't even know how to start. I need help. To hell with it. I'm not wishing for things anymore, I'm going to make things happen myself.

Don took his phone out of his pocket and scrolled through the call log. Finding the number he wanted, he dialled, and hoped he would get an answer. Ryan picked up on the second ring.

"Don? Jesus, what happened?" Ryan sounded scared.

"You were right, Ryan. That beast came to the city. There are a lot of dead. A lot."

"Jesus."

The line went quiet and Don wasn't sure if he should be asking Ryan for help, but he had to. He didn't like to admit his deficiencies, but he wasn't going to be able to do this on his own.

"Ryan, where are you? Did they pick you up last night? You back in town?"

"No, I'm still on San Clemente."

"They didn't get you? Did you ring Ravensbrook?"

"Yeah. He was going to send a troop over to see how bad it was. I was going to catch a ride back to the mainland with them, but they never showed. I guess things got a bit wild over there, and they had bigger things to deal with."

"Are you okay?"

"Yeah, I found a corner of the mess-hall to sleep in. I started making myself useful and cataloguing what wasn't damaged. There are plenty of supplies still here, and half of the guys didn't even get to discharge their weapon before that thing... Anyway, would sure be nice to get home."

"Well, I was going to ask you for a favour, but it seems like you're the one who needs a hand. I'll try to get hold of Ravensbrook, see if we can't get you sorted out. Hang tight, Ryan. Call me if you need anything."

"Thanks."

Ryan hung up and Don felt very old. He ran a coarse hand over his head. He hoped Ryan might be able to help him with the trawler, but it looked like he was going to have to figure it out himself. Ryan was stuck on the island, and Don needed someone right here in the city. He went back down to the deck, and then over the gangway to the harbour where Sam was unlocking the back of the truck.

"Any movement in there?" asked Don.

Sam swung the back doors of the truck open and climbed down beside Don. "Nothing. I think it's still out cold."

"Good, that'll make our job easier. There's a crane on the trawler. We can move it with that. Once we get it on board, do you mind helping me tie it down? Then you're free to go."

"Sure." Sam looked at Don. "I need to get home. Kelly would kill me if she knew what I was doing."

Don patted Sam on the back. "Thanks for doing this. We'd better get…"

A car pulled up behind them and screeched to a stop. Don turned around to see the three occupants get out, expecting to see a squad car with guns pointed at him. Instead, the driver was Amanda, and the two passengers were Hamish and Jay.

"Amanda? What are you doing here?" Don felt something was wrong. She was coming to put a stop to it. She was going to make him take Diablo back and hand it over to the authorities. Hamish and Jay were the muscle in case he argued back. If only he had gotten Diablo onto the boat a few minutes earlier, he would be home free.

"Don, how are you?" asked Hamish shaking his hand.

"I'm sorry to hear about Curtis," said Don, shocked. "Um Hamish, this is Sam, he was just helping me. He's got nothing to do with this."

Jay merely nodded and hung back, and Hamish let Amanda speak.

"Don, we're not here to bust you. We're here to help."

"But you said...what about, you know... Hamish has just lost his father. You shouldn't be here. It's dangerous and..." Don didn't know what to say. He couldn't believe they had all come to help with his crazy plan.

"Don, my father died last night, and I've got the rest of my life to spend grieving for him," said Hamish. "That monster you've got hidden in the back of that truck though, is the reason my father died. I owe it to him to get justice. I owe it to my mother, who is devastated and right now can't stop crying."

"Hamish, I can't ask you to..."

"You don't have a choice, Don. Amanda told me what you're planning. I think it's insane. I also think it's not only the best thing to do, but the *only* thing we can do. Plus, the Mary-Jane is my boat, and I'm the captain. So you want to take it, you've got to answer to me." Hamish took the keys from Don's hand and marched off toward the boat as his voice cracked.

Don looked at Amanda. "He's right. There's nothing we can do for Curtis now, except try and sort this mess out. We created it, and we're ending it." Amanda pulled back the truck's other back door and pinned it into place. "Sam, right? You want to help? Go help Hamish with the crane. I've got this. Jay, get up here."

Don watched in amazement as Amanda and Jay prepared the harness with Diablo cradled inside, and heard the trawler's engine kick into life. He jumped up into the back of the truck to help them attach the cables, so that they could get Diablo back on the boat.

"Amanda, I can't promise how this is going to go down, you know? Anything could happen out there. I'm not sure you should be..."

"Don, shut up and hand me that lock. I'm not doing this for you, or for Hamish, or for Zola, or anyone else. I'm doing it because I have to. If I'd spoken up or made Zola listen to me, I could've stopped this. I believe that by keeping Diablo as we did, its mother came looking for it. Somehow, it tracked her infant here. I have to take some responsibility for this whole mess. If I didn't at least try, I don't think I could live with myself."

Don knew there was no talking her out of it. He felt the same obligation that she did. He had seen that fiery look in her eyes before. With Diablo securely trussed up, the crane started to lift him out of the truck. Don watched as the monster was slowly moved onto the trawler. He wondered if it knew what was happening. It sure couldn't see anything; he had made sure of that.

"You think it was its mother? That giant last night was Diablo's mother?" asked Don.

"Why not? Is there any more protective bond than that of a mother and her young? We see it all the time. Dolphins and whales behave in the same way, so why not this? Whether it's some long-lost relative of a Metoposaurus or not, its basic instincts are the same. It was trying to protect its young."

"Was that what it was doing when it ate Zola? When it killed Meghan?"

"I think that was something else. Who's to say animals can't have cognitive reasoning or a conscience? Maybe it remembered Zola. If we could understand how they communicated, we could understand what was going on in their heads. I guess we'll never know for sure. The Ocean King is pure evil as far as I'm concerned, but it's also intelligent. I think it knew what it was doing."

Amanda began walking to the trawler and Sam jumped up into the cab.

"Good luck. I'm outta here," said Sam.

"Appreciate it, Sam. See you soon, buddy," said Don. He turned to Amanda as Sam pulled the truck away. "Well, it's too late to study Diablo now. If its mother is in the city somewhere, she's going to be pissed. We've got her baby tied up again, and I'm not giving it back."

"We should make a move before someone sees what we're up to," said Amanda. "And I don't like the look of that sky. I just want to get this over with." She walked down onto the deck, carefully avoiding Diablo who was curled up on board. His tail was squashed up against the port side and his head against the starboard. It was difficult to get past without getting worryingly close to its huge jaws. Jay stood guard over it with one of the ASM-DT Amphibious Rifles they had brought from the park.

"I just need to make a quick call," said Don. "I've got an idea."

Amanda watched Don sidestep Diablo and then put his phone to his ear.

"Hey, yeah, it's Don. Ryan, I'm on a boat and heading your way if you fancy a lift. Listen, you said you were making an inventory of what was still on the island. Think you could get your hands on some explosives?"

Shortly after Don had hung up, the Mary-Jane sailed out into the Pacific for her final voyage.

CHAPTER 14

OCTOBER SATURDAY 18TH 12:02

The Mary-Jane idled in the calm water, and they waited. Hamish killed the engine when they were far enough away from shore, and joined the others down in the cabin. It was over three hours since they'd left San Diego, and whilst the storm had never materialised, the weather had not really cleared either. A dark sky loomed over the ocean and mist wrapped itself around the trawler. Amanda, Don, Hamish, Jay, and Ryan, were cooped up in the cabin around the small table listening to the radio. They wanted to keep abreast of what was happening in the city, in case the Ocean King resurfaced. Most of the music stations had kept the airwaves clear for updates and announcements, so there was little else to listen to except what was going on in the city. They were currently hearing from a reporter in a news chopper.

"From my vantage point, nearly a thousand feet above the city, I can see the downtown area and I have to report that it does not make for comfortable viewing. So many structures have fallen down since the Ocean King's attack last night that the whole area is now cordoned off. Palm trees and vehicles were flattened, whole buildings came down, and I can see a small boat on the top of the Electra building. The mayor of course was one of the casualties of last night, and the city is now under martial law.

"The US Army is trying to contain the collateral damage, but they are leaving no stone unturned in their quest to find the monster. There has been a noticeable increase in the number of troops deployed on the ground in the last two hours, and any civilians not requiring medical attention, are advised to stay in their homes. San Diego has officially been declared a major disaster area and perimeters are being set up all around the city to stop anyone from leaving or entering the city unnecessarily. I have heard of sporadic reports of looting, but with such a huge loss of life, it seems the people of California are rallying around in this time of need."

"Turn it off," said Don. "It's not there. We're not going to learn anything we don't already know. The Ocean King is not hiding beneath the Hilton, it's gone."

Amanda turned the radio down, but not off completely. She wasn't convinced the animal wasn't still in the city somewhere. "We can't predict their behaviour. This is not an animal that's been studied; this is a fossil, a dinosaur. Trying to guess what it'll do next, would be like trying to predict next week's lottery numbers. If it stayed close to shore, we would've known about it by now. It must have sought refuge somewhere, perhaps in one of the caves nearby, or a lake. Who knows? It might have been so badly hurt that it crawled into a hole somewhere and died."

"That's wishful thinking," said Don. "No, she's out there. She's just picking her moment."

"Where did it come from? It's weird, don't you think, how it just came out of nowhere? It was like a Hollywood movie. I was there on the cliff top, then all of a sudden, this fucking monster appeared. It was nuts, seriously nuts," said Ryan.

"My guess is they were living out in the deep sea somewhere, possibly near the Bering Sea. Could be that's why it seems to have disappeared, that it's gone home." Amanda looked over at Jay. "If the Ocean King thinks its infant, Diablo, is dead, it might have left. You think it's gone back to where it came from?"

"No, if we let it, I think it will be here to stay. It definitely took some hits last night, okay, not lethal or hard enough to stop it, but we hit it and it kept going. You know as well as I do that when a predator finds a healthy food supply, it doesn't retreat. There are shallow waters, caves, canyons, kelp forests, shipwrecks - plenty of places it could go. Plus, if it associates this place with its young, maybe it just doesn't want to leave. It'll find somewhere to call home, somewhere deep, safe...hidden."

Don noticed that Jay spoke without looking at anyone. He was a quiet man, and without Zola to back him up, probably didn't think anyone would take notice of him. Don was suspicious of Jay's motives for coming along, but he had encountered worse than Jay before and could handle him. Was Jay feeling guilty? Or did he just not want to miss out on all the drama?

"Well, the ocean's a big place. Where do we start looking?" asked Hamish. "I could have a look at some maps, see if I can't figure something out? Amanda, you want to help me? I know the area, but you know these creatures better than anyone."

"I guess Hamish came upon Diablo by chance, and its mother tracked it down," said Jay. "It was just a fluke really. You were in the wrong place at the wrong time."

"A fluke," said Don absently. He glanced over to the wall and noticed a map of the western seaboard stuck up crudely by sticky tape.

"I suppose the park is beyond saving?" asked Ryan. "I never got to go, but I was hoping to one day. Did any of the animals make it? How bad is it?"

"I got a text from Sam," said Jay. "They're gone: the seals, otters, manta rays, the penguins, everything. They're all gone. He said they found a couple of penguins alive, but they were badly injured and were put down. Even Poppy and Pete, that's our resident dolphins, were dead, crushed in their tanks." Jay balled up his hands into fists. "Damn it, why did I listen to her? I was so stupid."

"Good question," Amanda said accusingly. "Why *did* you listen to her, Jay? I told you not to do it, but you ignored me. Don't you think..."

"This is not *all* my fault," said Jay. He angrily looked over at Hamish. "Your boyfriend dragged that fucking thing back here. Why don't you have a go at him?"

"You want to try to pin this on me?" Hamish looked at Jay incredulous. "My father died this morning with a crushed spine and I never even got to say goodbye, you little shit. Maybe you should rethink your career options, now that you've killed all the animals you worked with."

As Amanda, Hamish and Jay started arguing, Don ignored them. He kept staring at the map on the wall. "We should've seen it coming."

Don got up and pulled a large map from the cabin's wall. The corners ripped and stayed behind on the wall with the sticky tape, and he laid out the main body of the map over the cabin table. It was faded and curling up, having hung on the wall for several years, so he asked Amanda, Hamish and Jay, to take a corner each and hold it down. As they debated whose fault it was that things had gone so badly wrong, they didn't hear him and he tried again, without success. Eventually, Don climbed up onto his seat and hollered as loudly as he could. "Shut up! Everyone; just shut it!"

All three of them stopped arguing and yelling immediately, shocked at Don's manner. He composed himself and then coolly got down. Again, he asked them to take a corner of the map each and hold it in place.

"I'm sorry, but come on guys, let's keep it together. If you want to blame anyone, you can drop it on me. I'm in charge of security, so ultimately, the buck stops with me. Normally, I would vote for Zola, but as she's not with us anymore, it would be a bit unfair of me to put it on her." Don looked around the room stony-faced. His friends and colleagues were glum; their anger was forgotten, replaced by misery, shame, and mourning. Don didn't want to see any more evidence that they had all helped in some way to create this mess. Zola was a part of it too, but as she was in the stomach of the beast now, her body being digested, it seemed ungracious to talk about her. He had to take charge. He knew he had to take responsibility and try to figure out a way of sorting things out.

"Amanda, where was that seal colony? You know the one that was wiped out, somewhere up the coast of British Columbia, right?" Don flattened the map with his palms and studied the map closely.

"Err, it was somewhere near Ucluelet I think. Yeah, just over there." She pointed it out and Don grabbed a red marker pen. He put a big cross through the point on the map.

"What about that ocean liner? That was found approximately a thousand miles east of Hawaii, right? So that would place it about...here." Don drew another large X on the map.

Ryan got up to examine the map. "Look, Don, I don't know what you're thinking, but..."

"Ryan, you asked where it came from. I think I know. This is us right, and this is San Clemente." Don drew two more large crosses on the map.

"Yeah, but what's that got to do with anything?" asked Ryan.

"I think I see it," said Hamish. His furrowed brow relaxed, and he let out a quiet expletive.

Don had aroused their curiosity, and the heated argument from earlier had been forgotten. He drew a line with the marker from the cross at the top of the map by Ucluelet, down through where the liner had been roughly found, through San Clemente, and finally stopping at Wild Seas. The line formed a perfect arc.

"The seal colony was wiped out a week ago. The cruise ship was found earlier yesterday, and San Clemente was hit yesterday evening. We all know what happened later," said Don.

"It followed us," said Hamish in a muted voice.

"What?" asked Amanda. "What did you say?"

"It followed us back. This wasn't a fluke or an accident. This monster didn't just appear out of nowhere. The Ocean King followed us all the way here. I brought this." Hamish let go of the map and it slowly began to curl up into the centre of the table. He sat down and stared at Amanda blankly.

"Somehow, it was able to track down its infant," said Jay. "I mean that's what it is, isn't it? We had the young here all this time. Somehow, it was like a honing beacon. Maybe it left pheromones, maybe it was able to communicate to its mother, who knows? I think it's apparent that we inadvertently caught the infant of the species, and now we have an adult, the Ocean King, rampaging across California."

"And mommy's pissed." Don sat down too, letting go of the map. It began to wrinkle and he watched the red line he had drawn out slowly disappear as the paper wrapped itself up.

"You're telling me that monster tracked her child all the way here?" asked Amanda.

"It's possible, you know it is," said Jay.

"It fits." Don looked at Amanda, searching her eyes for clues. "It all fits. We've seen what that thing can do. It stands to reason, if it could wipe out Wild Seas, then a small island of seals would stand no chance. I think the Ocean King made its way down here and it was just unfortunate that the cruise ship got in its path. Let's face it, that monster could take down a ship in seconds if it wanted to."

"I need some air," said Amanda. She left the cabin and went out onto the deck. Cold wind bustled into the cabin as she went through the door.

"Hamish, you mind looking over those maps with Ryan? I need some air too," said Don.

"What can I do?" asked Jay.

"I don't know about you, but I'm thirsty. Perhaps you can ask Hamish where he keeps the beer."

Don left the warmth of the cabin behind and found Amanda up on the deck looking over Diablo. The creature was perfectly still and quiet, and its breathing was laboured.

"He's lost both his eyes, you know. Even if we did release it back into the ocean, I'm not sure it would last long without vision," said Amanda.

"True," said Don. "I guess it was more injured than we realised." Amanda didn't need to know the details of how Diablo had lost his sight. Don knew she had her suspicions, but she said nothing. He wasn't about to lie if she asked him the truth, but he wasn't about to tell her when it was irrelevant anyway. He had no more intention of letting Diablo go than of sprouting wings and flying to the moon.

"He asked me to marry him," said Amanda. She pushed her hair over her ears and looked at Don. "This morning, at the hospital. He told me he was planning on proposing at some restaurant he'd booked for Sunday lunch. He wanted his parents there too, but with Curtis... So he proposed in the hospital room."

"What did you say?" Don felt like smiling. He knew this was for the best, that Hamish would look after her. They were the perfect couple, and yet, Amanda wasn't smiling back. Her eyes, so usually vivacious, were dull.

"I said I'd have to think about it. I mean, his father has only just died, and his mother was in pieces. What could I say? I don't think he was thinking straight. He's grieving, he shouldn't be thinking about me, not now."

"Don't confuse guilt with love, Amanda. You said he was going to propose anyway, so it's not like his father's death clouded his judgement or anything. It might not be the most romantic proposal I've heard, but it's the most honest. He wanted his father there when he asked you to marry him. Do you know how much guts that takes? Hamish is stronger than you think. How did his mother take it?"

"She was happy for a while, when he asked I mean. When I said I had to think about it though..." Amanda lent over the side of the boat. "I feel sick."

Don put a hand on her shoulder and lent beside her. The murky water was quiet as the mist slowly evaporated, shifting silently across the ocean. Tendrils of low cloud snaked across the surface like dancing shadows, flitting in and out of existence, waiting for inevitable death. Don saw his reflection in the water, his face shifting in and out of focus. For a moment, his face flowed with the current, and he felt like he was being swept out to sea, to swim at the bottom of the ocean with the hundreds who had died on the cruise ship.

As he rubbed Amanda's back, it felt as if this was the final time they would be together alone. There was no logic to the way his mind was working, but everything was telling him to talk to her. He needed to tell her. "When you find someone, Amanda, don't let them go. Don't try to second guess them, or over-think it. If someone you love asks you to marry them, you say yes. You don't want a lifetime of regrets and wondering what if you had done something else. I'll never have that. I'm not saying I wasted my life, but I definitely missed out on a few things. I don't know what would've happened with Meghan, but I know I'll never get the chance to find out. She didn't make it. I found out last night, but I wasn't sure of when to tell you. Grief can be overwhelming. It can take a grip on your heart and not let go. Trust me, I know. When you feel it squeeze, you have to fight it."

Amanda looked at Don with red eyes. "Meghan? Oh no, Don, I'm so sorry."

Don continued to rub her back. He knew it would help to alleviate the nausea, and he also understood it wasn't from seasickness. He had to get it out, while he could, while they had this moment of peace. The storm could be on them at any moment. He didn't need Amanda grieving Meghan for him.

"It gets harder every year. I can't let it go, as much as I try to. Fuck, I can't lie to you, Amanda. I don't try to let it go at all. I just hide from it. I've spent my whole life hiding. My father died when I was young and my mother didn't cope so well after I found him. I was the eldest, so I guess I bore the brunt of her frustrations. I talked to her a couple of days ago, at the graveside. It wasn't good."

"I thought your mother was…"

"No, I just let you think that. I let everyone think that she was dead. It's easier that way. It means I don't have to explain why she hates me."

"Your mother might have issues with you, Don, but I'm sure she doesn't hate you."

Do it, do it now.

Don removed his hand from Amanda's back and absently traced a finger over the scar on his head. "We don't see each other, apart from awkward conversations once a year in the cemetery. I put money in her account every month so she has enough to get by. She doesn't know. I tried offering her money, but she said she wouldn't take blood money from me, so I have to keep it secret. I don't like it, but I don't want her living in poverty either. I check on her from time to time, and she seems all right for the most part. She has her church group and she can still drive, so…"

"What else are you hiding from, Don? It's not just your mother is it?" Amanda asked him.

Just then, Hamish appeared with two cold beers. "I thought you might want these."

Amanda took them both. "Thanks, honey, can you just give us a minute. I'll be inside shortly."

They kissed and Hamish went back into the cabin. Amanda passed Don a beer and he drank it down without pausing.

"I didn't tell you about my brother, did I?"

"No," said Amanda. "I know you were close, but you never said what happened to him. All I know is you visit his grave once a year on the sixteenth. You don't have to tell me, Don, it's up to you."

Don took in a large lungful of sea air. It was so fresh and clean, he couldn't remember the last time the air had felt so good. "We joined up together. He was a year behind me, but he kept up, and we were admitted at the same time. We went through training together and even got into the same unit. Being in the SEALS was our dream. I don't think you could say either one of us wanted it more. We were equals. Some people found it odd that two brothers could be so close, but my father's death made us closer. It drove a wedge between my mother and me, but I loved my brother more than anything. We were inseparable until...

"Anyway, that was the final straw for my mother. I came home after and he didn't. There was never even a body to bury. His grave is full of his medals, schoolbooks, photographs, and stuff like that, just personal things. They put the video online when he was killed. They didn't need to do that. Do they really think it's going to inspire an uprising or recruit more people to their cause? He was just a man, a regular guy. They had no right to do that. I had to watch it. I had to know how it ended. After they cut off his head, I just...

"It took years for me to accept he was gone, and even now, I can't really believe it. Without having him come back, it's like he might still be out there. I know he's dead, but to me, he's still missing. I just want to be able to talk to my brother again and tell him I'm sorry. I still talk to him, but it's not the same. I like to think he's around sometimes. My mother has never accepted the way it happened. She blames me. Nothing I ever said changed her mind, and in the end, I gave up. I couldn't deal with her anymore. Her anger was ruining his memory for me. Now Meghan's gone too, and...the snakes in my head keep going round and round, Amanda. It's like a whole bag full of them up there, hissing and fighting and biting, poisoning my mind. I need them out. I can't live like this anymore. I can't go on without him, knowing that what I did... I know it now. It will be different this time though. I have another chance, Amanda."

Don turned to look at Amanda. She was crying. Her blonde hair was damp and straggly, and her eyes shone despite the tears. Don knew he was keeping Amanda from Hamish. He had to let her go too. Don looked at the sleeping monster on the deck. "I'm going to finish this. The responsibility is mine now. I'm going to kill Diablo, and then I'm going to kill the Ocean King. He's waiting for me, I can feel it. We're close now. I'm close. He's waiting. This is the end, Amanda. He's out there waiting for me."

Amanda put her arms around Don. "Please, Don, you're scaring me. I'm so sorry, I didn't know. I wish you had told me. We've been friends for so many years, and I never knew."

Don held Amanda, and looked at Diablo. It needed finishing.

"Amanda, get inside with Hamish. I'll be there in a moment. I need to talk to all of you about how we're going to kill the Ocean King."

"You'll be okay?"

Don nodded and watched Amanda retreat to the cabin. Once she was inside and the door was closed, he unlocked the chest they had brought onto the trawler from San Clemente. Inside was a small armoury. He saw two Colt M4 Carbines, one HK MP5 with three clips, two ASM-DT amphibious rifles, one AK47, six grenades, one detonator, and a kilo of C4.

Good boy, Ryan, I have to say I'm impressed. Uncle Taggart was right about you. I just hope I get you out of this alive. You'll be heading home with a Medal of Honor if this goes right.

Don picked up the Colt M4 and checked the mag. Then he walked over to Diablo and stood by the creature's centre. Its body was rising in a regular pattern, as if it was having a gentle nap. Its eyes were gelatinous cavities, and thick rope was wound over it so that it couldn't escape. Don unloaded a full mag into the creature's side, grinning as he did so. Diablo thrashed and bucked beneath the ties, but was powerless to free itself. Its jaws snapped up and down and Don heard the pathetic barking it made as he continued to rip it apart. Blood dripped out onto the deck, forming a slick trail of death. When the mag was empty, he threw the gun down and walked calmly back to the cabin.

"What the hell's going on?" shouted Hamish.

"Jesus, that barking is horrible, can't you shut it up?" asked Jay. "Why'd you have to go and do that?"

"Relax," said Don entering the cabin. He saw the startled faces staring back at him. "We've waited too long already. If mommy wants her baby back, she's going to have to come get him. It seems to me she was having trouble finding him, so I thought she might need a bit of help."

"And you thought shooting Diablo was a good idea?" asked Jay. "Have you gone insane?"

Don held his arms out. "Do you see the Ocean King anywhere? Do you notice any monsters out there? It's about time we stopped sitting around waiting, and gave it an incentive to get out here. Let's get this done."

As Diablo continued banging on the deck and barking madly, Don sat down at the table. "Now, we probably don't have long before mommy arrives. I suggest we go over the plan of how we're going to kill this bitch."

CHAPTER 15

OCTOBER SATURDAY 18TH 12:33

"Maybe Lady Luck will pay us a visit and the Ocean King's gone home, just gone back to where it came from," said Jay.

"Doubtful," said Amanda. "If it has lost its only child, it might want to stick around. Plus, it knows there's a plentiful food supply. We'll need more than luck to beat it."

Don shook his head in disagreement. "I don't need to put my faith in luck or anything else. We can beat this thing, but we use our heads. We can outsmart it, outthink it."

"Don's right," said Hamish. "Look, if there's one thing my father taught me, it's that the ocean is a dangerous place, just as dangerous as being on land. With this Ocean King swimming around, it just got a whole lot worse. You make your own luck out here, so we're going to do things my way. I'm the captain of this boat now, and if we all go shooting off doing our own thing, somebody's liable to get hurt.

"I remember, I was about twelve, Dad came home one day and said he'd caught a tuna, the biggest one he'd ever caught. This big, he said." Hamish held his arms out as far as he could and Don smiled. "I remember Mom saying he must have had a good day, been real lucky to land it. At first, he said nothing and then he lost it. He kept saying how it wasn't luck that had put food on the family table for the last fifteen years, that it wasn't luck he and Mom had met, or had a healthy boy. He said life was what you made it, you worked hard, you took your opportunities, and if rabbit's feet and horseshoes had anything to with it, then why were the Irish so fucking miserable all the time."

Don looked at Amanda. She was watching her boyfriend with a look of fascination and awe. There was a huge serving of love in those eyes too, and Don knew they were meant for each other.

Hamish continued. "Anyway, then Mom told him off for swearing in front of me, and I don't know what happened after that. That was about as close to fighting as my folks ever got." Hamish paused and then sighed. "I sure miss him."

Amanda leant across the table and squeezed Hamish's hand. They looked at each other warmly, and then let go, aware they had company and unsure of how much affection they could display.

"You could argue it was sheer luck that we didn't get nailed out there at the park. You could say God had an eye on us. I sure know that's what my mother would've said." Don yawned. Sleep had been hard to find last night and he felt exhausted. "Do you think it's lucky that we're still here when so many are dead? We do this as planned and we can come out of this. Let's go over it, I don't want to be caught short." Don squeezed his right hand. It was like a tic, something he did from time to time without even knowing why. "That bitch could surface anytime and I want to be ready. I believe in what I can see. We have a monster coming for us, and we are going to be more than ready for it when it does."

Ryan spoke up. "I don't know about this, Don. I wasn't sure if I should tell you, but while you were outside, I got a call from Ravensbrook. He said the army is assembling all along the coastline and erecting barricades from Tijuana to La Jolla. They're preparing for an attack again. They think the monster is biding its time, and that it'll strike San Diego. Once it shows its ugly face, they are going to blast it into a million pieces."

"Well, I'm pleased they're taking precautions, but they're wrong. The Ocean King isn't going to go back to San Diego. The only way to get to it is to lure it out, and the best place for that is well away from the major population centres. That monster is going to come after us, after her child."

"What if it does go back to the city? What if the military do capture it?" asked Jay.

"Well, I think the first thing they'll do is try and figure out a way of controlling it. A monster like that? Imagine if it was fighting for us, not against us," said Ryan. "It has an incredible natural power."

"It doesn't matter," said Don, "they won't find it, they won't capture it, and they won't kill it. The army is looking in the wrong place. Diablo is screaming his head off out there. The Ocean King is coming this way."

"How can you be so sure? They've got armour-plated bullets, fighter jets flying overhead loaded with ballistic missiles, and the best soldiers in the God damn world," said Ryan.

Don shook his head. "They won't get it. This monster is bigger and badder than we are, true, but it's clever. It's not a dumb animal. It knew what it was doing when it came here. It's not going to stay in hiding near Wild Seas or the city. It'll go back to where it can survive, where it won't be noticed. I wouldn't be surprised if it had survived by hiding in one of the underwater canyons. No, when it's ready, there's only one thing that it wants, and we have it."

"And what if you're just blinded by revenge?" asked Jay. "Have you thought this through clearly? What if you're wrong?"

Don looked at Jay with contempt. "If I'm wrong, then what are you doing here? I thought you wanted to make this right? If you're so convinced everything we're doing is wrong, why didn't you stay in the city? You seem to believe the Ocean King is going to be a no-show. You'd be nice and safe back in San Diego, surrounded by soldiers who would die for you. Then you wouldn't have to get your hands dirty. That's what this is about for you isn't it, Jay? Amanda told me what you did to Diablo last night, how you pumped it full of drugs. You knew what you were doing was wrong, but you did precisely what Zola told you to do, and look what happened. You're a coward."

Jay stood up wagging his finger at Don. "You've no right. You don't know what you're talking about. I don't know what's going on in your head, Don. This is some sort of crusade you're on and you're going to get us all killed. Fuck this." Jay stormed out of the cabin leaving the room in relative silence. Only the faint chattering from the radio and Diablo's barking could be heard.

"That went well," said Don. "Right, well if anyone else thinks we're barking up the wrong tree here, let's get it out now and clear the air."

Nobody spoke a word. Don wondered what Jay thought he was going to achieve. There was nothing he could do out there, no way back to the mainland without all of them going. He was better off staying outside where he could sulk. Better to let him cool off than confront him now.

"Right, assuming The Ocean King is on its way, we need to be ready."

"So how exactly do we kill it?" Hamish put his arm around Amanda. "Like you said, it could've taken down that cruise ship in seconds, and my boat is not even a quarter the size. It could smash us into oblivion before we even knew it was here."

"True, but they weren't expecting it, we are. We all know why it came to Wild Seas last night. We still have what it wants. We have a hostage."

"I see now," said Amanda. "The Ocean King won't attack us as it knows we have Diablo. It wants its young back. If it destroys the boat, it destroys its child. You're putting a lot of faith in this theory of yours, Don."

"As long as we have Diablo tied up out there, we have the upper hand. It's going to be mighty pissed off, but it'll keep its hands off until it gets Diablo back." Don unfurled the map they had looked over earlier and pointed to La Jolla Canyon. "If it was hiding around here, then it should be here soon. Very soon."

"And what do we have to kill it?" asked Hamish.

Don turned to Ryan. "Glad you asked. That's where my cousin comes in."

"Thanks for picking me up by the way. I was beginning to feel a bit like Tom Hanks in that movie," said Ryan. "Anyway, that chest I brought aboard with Don? It's full of weapons we can use to kill it. I gathered up everything I could find, which wasn't as much as I'd hoped, but it should be enough."

"It'll be enough," said Don. "We've got two Colt M4's, an AK47, two ASM-DT's, grenades, and some C4."

"I've also got an S37 combat knife tucked away, just in case," said Ryan lifting his shirt to reveal a ripped torso and the hilt of a blade.

"Hamish and Amanda, I want you two to take the amphibious rifles. If this bitch gets out of the water, or stays in it, either way, we can take her out. When we see it, we arm up and take it down. We have to wait 'til it's close enough, and aim for the head. Go for the eyes. If it can't see us, it can't get to us. It can't touch the trawler with Diablo on board, so it'll make a lot of noise, try to scare us, but we can't buckle. When the time comes, unload everything you've got at it. When it's weakened, I'm going to untie Diablo and let him go."

"Let him go? But..."

"Don't worry, I've not gone all soft on you," said Don. "He's going to have the C4 strapped to him, and when he snuggles up to mom, kaboom. The Ocean King will be shark food."

Hamish cracked open a beer and offered the others one, yet, only Don took one. Hamish took a swig. "Sounds like a plan to me. You might want to show me, Amanda, and Jay, how to use these weapons, Don, we're not used to them like you and Ryan."

"And when they're both dead, then what?" said Amanda.

"Then we go home," said Ryan.

The trawler rocked gently from side to side as they drank their beer and contemplated what lay ahead. It almost sounded easy. Shoot the big guy, blow up the little guy, and be home for supper. Amanda turned up the radio, but there was no more news on the whereabouts of the Ocean King. The station had opened up to callers and they listened as a young man called to say he had seen it in the Sleep Train Amphitheatre, which had quickly been discredited as a crank call. Somebody else phoned in to say the monster was moving across the US to Washington, that it was a message from God and it was going to eat the President. "God is waiting," they'd said before being cut off.

Another caller believed it was the start of an alien invasion and the creature had flown down from the dark side of the moon. Don wished it was an alien, but he knew it was all too real. In times of crisis, there were always a few crackpots who came out with their theories and odd beliefs. Ultimately, it was flesh and blood, and it could be killed. He intended to make sure it died today, one way or another. He finished the beer and then asked everyone out onto the deck. He had to make sure they could all shoot when the time came. Ryan was schooled in the basics of how to use the weapons, but the others had no idea where to start.

Don opened the cabin door, and led them all up onto the deck. Diablo's barking was louder outside, and it was a wonder the Ocean King hadn't attacked them already. He glanced up at the cloudy sky. The brittle wind cut and sliced through the air, snapping at Don's flesh as if it were armed with pincers and razor blades. He drew his jacket up to his neck and stared at Jay as he approached the chest.

"Jay, what the hell are you doing?" Don saw him standing over Diablo's tail, sawing through one of the ropes. The tie came away and Jay stood up, triumphantly holding it above his head before throwing it into the sea.

Most of the creature's tail was now free, and it was whipping back and forth like an untended pressure hose. It also meant the ties around Diablo's body had become looser, and its body was hammering onto the deck, bouncing up and down as it tried to break completely free. There was no easy way to get to Jay now, who was at the stern. Diablo's body filled the deck, and his head was at the front, near the cabin.

"Jay, stop!" shouted Amanda, as he leant over and began to cut through another of the tethers that held Diablo in place.

"You're wrong," said Jay. "We can't defeat the Ocean King. The only thing we can do now is let Diablo go. Let the army deal with this. If we let Diablo go, she'll leave us alone. We just need to give her back her child, and we can go back to land."

"Jay, you idiot, stop. This is my boat, and I'm telling you to stop right now!" Hamish tried to manoeuvre past Diablo's head, but there was no room. With the ties becoming looser, it gave Diablo just enough leeway to angle his head and block any path down to the stern of the boat. Its jaws snapped from left to right. "What do we do, Don, we can't let Diablo go, not now."

"Ryan, open the chest," said Don coolly. He watched as Ryan lifted the lid. "Pass me the AK47, please."

Don took the weapon from Ryan and aimed it squarely at Jay. "Jay, look at me."

Jay glanced up from his work. His hands were sore from gripping the rough rope and knife. He saw the gun trained on him and stood up. Confusion rippled through his eyes. "Don, you know this is the only thing we can do. I have to do it." Jay bent down slowly over Diablo.

"Jay, listen to me, there is more at stake here than our own lives, and you know it. If we let Diablo go now, then it's over. It wins. The Ocean King is already coming for us. And if we don't have Diablo safely tied up on this boat, then we are all dead. You understand? So drop the knife, stand up, and nobody has to get hurt."

Ryan pulled out the two amphibious rifles and loaded them. He passed one each to Hamish and Amanda. "Just in case," he whispered.

Jay began to saw at another piece of rope. "Don, I can't let you do this. You're not going to shoot me."

Don felt the pressure in his head building. Jay wasn't insane or angry, he was just scared. But they couldn't let Diablo escape before they were ready, or the plan was lost, and with it any chance of killing the Ocean King. "Jay, I'm not giving you another chance. Drop the knife now."

As Jay continued to cut through the rope, Don fired the weapon mere inches above Jay's head.

"Fuck!" Jay screamed and jumped up. "What the fuck? You nearly killed me, Don."

"I'm not telling you again, Jay. Next time, I won't miss." Don kept the gun pointed at Jay.

"You're a madman. You would actually rather shoot me, than this fucking monster?" Jay kicked Diablo's body over and over. He repeatedly kicked it and punched it, and Diablo grew more agitated.

"Jay, quit it," said Don. Now the man didn't look scared anymore. He was losing it.

Jay looked at Don. He was out of breath from the exertion of beating the monster. He took a step up onto Diablo's back and straddled it, holding the knife above his head. "This is for the best, Don."

"Jay, don't do it. Don't you do it." Don was trying to offer the man a way out. He really didn't want to shoot him, but there was no other way. If Jay killed Diablo, then it was game over for all of them.

Don tightened his finger on the trigger and watched as Jay prepared to hammer the knife down into Diablo's back. As if sensing what was happening, Diablo pressed himself flat against the deck, and then bucked wildly, sending Jay tumbling backwards as he fell off Diablo. Jay caught hold of Diablo's tail to stop himself from falling into the ocean, and then Diablo spun his tail quickly around, flicking Jay across the deck and slamming him into the side of the boat. Diablo sent his thick tail smashing into Jay over and over, pinning him against the side and pulverising his body.

"Jay!" screamed Amanda. She turned away, unable to watch as Jay was crushed. His pleas for help soon stopped as he received a blow to the head and fell unconscious.

"Hamish, Ryan, get that tarpaulin and throw it over Diablo. Then make as much noise as you can and distract it." As soon as the tarp was over the monster's head, Don jumped over the thing's jaws and dived towards Jay. The shouting seemed to divert Diablo's attention just enough for Don to reach Jay. He grabbed Jay's hand and pulled him clear of the tail. Then Don threw him over his shoulder and carried him back to the others, all the time avoiding getting too close to Diablo. Once he was clear, he laid Jay down on the deck, propping him up against an oil drum.

"Jesus, is he…" Amanda knelt down and felt for Jay's pulse. "It's weak, but he's still alive." She looked over the man's broken body and doubted if he would ever walk again. Any recovery would take years. His legs and arms were broken and he was bleeding from so many wounds it was hard to know where to start. His face was a mess and only a loose flap of skin indicated where his nose had been. Jay's breathing was ragged, and as his head lolled forward, blood and teeth slipped from between his lips. "We need to get him inside. We need to stop this bleeding."

They carried him down into the cabin and laid him out on the table. Hamish brought out two first aid kits, and Amanda began patching him up, dressing the wounds and bandaging the cuts. Don took his jacket off and balled it up to make a pillow for Jay. Ryan found a blanket and when they were done, he placed it gently over Jay.

"Will he be okay?" Ryan asked.

Amanda was covered in Jay's blood. "I don't know. He needs to get to a hospital. He's got a lot of broken bones, probably internal bleeding...we need to get back to the mainland and get him to a hospital."

"No," said Don, "we're not going anywhere."

Amanda held up her hands. They were bright red, dripping with Jay's blood. Her face was angry and Don was pleased to see there was no fear in her eyes anymore. "You see this, Don? He's going to die if we don't get him to a doctor. We have to go now."

"No. We stick to the plan. He made his choice."

Amanda turned to Hamish. "You can't go along with this, surely? I don't condone what Jay did, but we can't leave him like this."

"I'm not sure, honey. Don does kind of have a point. Jay brought it on himself, acting like he did," said Hamish.

"And you, Ryan?" Amanda turned to Ryan who was stood in the doorway of the cabin.

"I think I need to show you how to use those guns. The Ocean King will be here soon."

"Incredible." Amanda wiped her hands on her jeans and left the cabin infuriated.

Don looked at Jay. The man probably wasn't going to last long, which was true. But he was damned if he was going to let one man's stupidity jeopardise this mission. The objective was to take down the Ocean King, and everything else was secondary.

"Got any more beers?" Don asked Hamish, breaking the silence.

Hamish shook his head. "I'm all out. Only had a few. I hadn't planned on coming out for long. The pantry's nearly bare. Just a few tins of beans, nothing much really."

Don sat down and watched Jay's chest rise and fall. "Ryan, do me a favour and show Hamish and Amanda how those guns work. It won't be long now. I'm just going to keep an eye on Jay. I'll be up soon."

Ryan left the cabin and Hamish went to follow him.

"Hamish, before you go, I just wanted to tell you something," said Don. "Look after her. You've got a special one there. Don't fuck it up. She loves you."

Hamish nodded and left the cabin. Don waited. He had to be right about this. He knew Jay was unlikely to make it back to shore alive, and he didn't want anyone else to suffer the same fate. Should he feel bad about Jay? He didn't want the man to die, but he hadn't made him do anything. So much depended on him being right that Don's head felt like a water balloon about to burst. What if he was wrong? What if the Ocean King was still on land, hiding in a creek or a river somewhere, nursing its wounds until it was ready for round two. What if it didn't track Diablo to the trawler? Perhaps the monster would head back to California. It had found plenty to eat on its last visit, so why would it bother with a small fishing trawler.

Jesus, Don, this is no time to doubt yourself. Think how much has changed in the last few hours. Not everything is in my hands. Poor Meghan, she was so sweet and carefree. That's what it must be like to live free of guilt and grief. At least you got to know her briefly. She's free now. She's waiting for me.

Don hung his head and let the tears come for Meghan. There were so many other things he should be thinking about, so many other people relying on him, but he couldn't hold it in anymore. Why was she dead and he still alive when he was old and useless? What was the point? Don wiped his face and looked at Jay. He had been stupid, but now Jay was going to die too. How many more people had to suffer?

Don looked out of the window. The storm had not developed, and the sky was clearing. A wisp of cloud scattered on the horizon separating the crisp blue ocean from the sky. And yet, the boat was being buffeted about strongly enough to make him uncomfortable. They'd been at sea for hours, yet, it felt like days. He just wanted it over with. Why was the boat rocking so much, when the clouds were fading and there was no wind? Don suddenly raced outside.

Swirling mist gave way to an increasingly turbulent ocean. Foaming waves bit at the hull of the Mary-Jane, casting serious concerns into Don's mind. The choppy waves were only close to the boat. A few hundred feet away and the ocean remained calm. He looked down into the water, ignoring the others who were examining the weapons. Diablo was still barking, but the sounds were weak. Don hoped it was dying. It just had to hang on to life a little longer.

Over the rail, Don watched the water churn and swirl, leaving a trail of foamy wake behind it. "Hamish?"

Hamish came over to Don carrying the AK47 over his shoulder.

"Hamish, this is no storm. There's no wind, and look at the shore. The water's calm, almost flat. So why are we rocking like this?"

Hamish looked puzzled too. "I could take us further out. Maybe there's a rip current, although we're too far from shore for..."

The trawler suddenly tipped as the water below swelled. They grabbed the rails until the trawler settled down again.

"I don't get it," said Amanda joining them. "What's going on?"

"Underneath us," said Don realising what Hamish was saying.

"Something's knocking around down there, churning the water up."

"You think it's found us?" asked Amanda.

"Could be...but I don't understand what it's doing down there if..."

Don saw the water churning and turning red, and then the first piece of meat bobbed to the surface. A huge chunk of flesh with strands of loose tissue like red seaweed hit the side of the boat. One side was dark grey, the other pink and ragged, as if something had taken a bite out of a hunk of beef and then spat it out. Another piece floated to the surface, smaller in size to the last, and the water calmed down. The body of a shark drifted to the surface. It was easily twenty feet long, and its mouth was open. Several teeth had been torn from its gums, and it was obvious where the chunk of meat had come from, as one side of the shark had been gored.

"Jesus," whispered Ryan as he looked over the side of the trawler. "It's here."

CHAPTER 16

OCTOBER SATURDAY 18TH 13:50

The Great White rose up through the foaming water. As Don looked closer, he could see its belly slit open and its innards were spewing out. Seagulls cartwheeled and cawed overhead, spying the food. Hamish saw deep lacerations on its skin, and half of its massive jaw had been ripped off. The shark flipped over in the water and drifted away from the trawler.

"How much longer?" asked Amanda. She fidgeted nervously with her hair, winding it around her fingers, letting it go, and then winding it up again.

"Not long now," said Hamish, "it's toying with us. It's as if it knows it can't just come up here and kill us or take the boat down. It knows we've got something nasty waiting for it. Maybe it took a peek when we weren't looking and saw what we did to Diablo. Maybe it saw we've got enough C4 to blow its ass back to hell."

"Maybe." Amanda felt her nausea rising once more. The boat had stopped rocking and settled down into the natural waves, tipping faintly to the left and right. The ocean looked calm again. "You think it's gone?"

Don shook his head. "I doubt it. It's beneath us, working out what to do. That shark just got in the way. She'll show her face soon."

"Well then, good," said Amanda resolutely. Despite her sickness, the swell was subsiding, and she was feeling more confident about things. She looked at Hamish. "If – *when* – it comes back, we'll do better next time. I'm not out here to catch a cold. I'm out here to kill it."

Hamish opened his mouth to answer, to tell Amanda he was impressed with her resolve and that he loved her, when a large bubble floated to the surface of the ocean, at least seven feet across, and popped, causing him to hesitate. He expected the creature to surface, but not just yet. He had assumed it would wait a while, draw the game out. When a cat played with its food, it didn't eat it straight away. No, it would mess with it, tease it, and even cajole it into thinking it could get away right before those sharp teeth dug in. A bubble breaking the surface like that wasn't natural. And if it came from the creature, then it wasn't far away at all.

"Look at that," said Ryan who was seeing the same thing. "The water's all milky and...gross."

Don looked down into the creamy white water that was circling around where the bubble had burst. There was nothing else to see, but it was certainly unusual. A dull shadow flitted briefly below the surface, and then the water started churning again, faster and faster until the milky substance began frothing up.

Hamish took Amada's arm. "I don't like this. Something's going on."

"Get your guns," said Don. He raced to the chest and pulled the C4 and detonator out. "Ryan, get up to the wheelhouse. Concentrate your fire on its eyes. Hamish, Amanda, stay close to me. Remember, we have limited ammo, so aim for its head and don't fire until it's close enough."

The three of them stood on the deck, waiting. A minute passed and Don could feel the sweat trickling down his back. He could sense the tension amongst them all. He wasn't alone in worrying what was going to happen. Another minute passed, and nothing happened. The Ocean King had not appeared, and made no attempt to engage them.

Come on, where are you? Show yourself. Come and get your child. What are you waiting for? Where are you?

A third minute passed, and Don could see the fear on Ryan's face. The boy had faced the monster before and lived. Clearly, he was having doubts he was going to live through their second encounter. Hamish and Amanda were side by side, facing the ocean. Don was proud of them. He still didn't know Hamish well, but the man had just lost his father and here he was, putting his grief to one side to support Amanda.

Just then, Don heard the unmistakeable bark of the Ocean King. It was close enough to make the hairs on his arms bristle and a shiver run down his spine. "The wolf is at the door," he said quietly, as he ran his eyes over the water, trying to find the source of the noise. The vivid memory of all the death and destruction at the park yesterday came flooding back into his mind. Wild Seas was gone now and half the city destroyed. There were so many dead, so many people who were in the hospital now with missing limbs and deceased family members. So many children in the crowd who never made it home. So many husbands, wives, and lovers...

Another bark indicated the thing was closer now, yet, Don couldn't see the advancing creature, only the distant Californian coastline. He wondered if his mother was okay, if she was watching events unfold on television, or if she knew he was about to face the deadly monster. He wondered if she would pray for him. He knew it wasn't that his mother was a cruel person, but she had decided what she wanted to believe, and nothing he could ever say or do would change that. God knows he had tried. Every year, he vowed he would have no more to do with her; it was pointless trying to reason with her, and the unsavoury scene at the grave last week had reminded him of that. Margaret O'Reilly had forgiven her neighbour for stealing her cable for twenty years, she had forgiven her priest for sodomising those poor boys, and she had forgiven Bush for every war crime committed under his watch. But she could not forgive her eldest son for not bringing her youngest home. So every month he paid his dues, depositing hundreds of dollars into her account and driving past her house most evenings to make sure she was safe. Don began to wonder if there were any beers down in the galley, and he smacked his lips together just with the thought of it. His mother seemed more like a memory than a real person. He couldn't envisage seeing her or her house again.

As Don's mind wandered, he barely even noticed the next bark. Its hollow ring bounced off the trawler's hull, echoing back across the water. If he had heard it, he would've realised the thing was much closer now. It was as if it wanted them to know it was coming for them. The Ocean King was announcing its arrival, showing no fear, only a driving hunger, and a burning desire to reach its prey. It didn't care if they knew it was coming now. There would be only one winner in this battle, and a rusted fishing trawler was no match for the Ocean King.

Don was stirred into reality when another bark came. There was no doubting now that the sea monster was not headed for the mainland, but straight for the boat. Don straightened up and looked dead ahead. A smooth dark shape manifested itself. Like Daniel headed into the Lion's Den, Don couldn't help but feel the odds were against them.

"Amanda, Hamish! Get ready!" he shouted. Don gripped the handrail of the trawler and watched, as a bulbous dark-green shape emerged, rising from the water. It was almost close enough to touch. He could smell it now too. The aroma of rotting fish came foremost, followed by the sting of salty seawater. Droplets cascaded down onto Don as the Ocean King drew itself up and loomed over him. He felt himself get colder as it reared up out of the water, a hundred feet in the air.

The monstrous creature seemed to hover in front of him, its wet body standing tall and proud before him, and Don looked up. The thing's head was bending over, examining the ship, and he could see its yellow eyes scanning the length of the trawler, probably weighing up how many bites it would take to sink it. Its jaws opened wide, so wide you could fit a tank inside, and silvery rivulets of seawater dripped onto the deck below. The monster let rip, bellowing loudly, and sending waves of fear crashing through Don. When he had seen it at the park, it had almost been unreal, as if he was watching some old Godzilla movie from the fifties. But now, he was right in its sights. The roar filled his ears and he winced as the noise whistled through his head. The smell as it roared was terrible, unnatural, reminding him of rotting meat left out in the midday sun. Don's knuckles whitened and his stomach clenched, as the behemoth rose from the depths further and threatened to engulf the trawler entirely. It had propelled itself up by its long tail, and its two front feet were clear of the water. Don knew there was no backing out.

"Hail Mary, Mother of God," he whispered. Without thinking, he unloaded a full clip from the Colt he held into the creature's belly. With his feet locked and back braced against the trawler's side, he kept squeezing the trigger until there was nothing left. He tried to lift the gun as he fired, but the head was too high to reach. He couldn't see the thing's face anymore, so decided he would try to wound it, perhaps open up its stomach. The bullets hardly scratched its skin, and Don watched as the things flabby white underbelly just absorbed the bullets, as if they were nothing more than marshmallows sinking into jelly. He watched as the others fired as well. All three of them fired round after round into the beast. It bellowed and Don saw blood. Finally, the Ocean King's blood began to flow, oozing from the gunshot wounds. The plan to shoot it in the head had disappeared as soon as it had loomed up over them. It was too big, too tall, and too quick: they had to hit it wherever they could and not be picky about their target.

The monster barked as it fell, crashing back into the water right beside the boat. Don grabbed the railing as the boat was tossed furiously on the wave, and almost pulled under as the creature disappeared beneath the surface. Don watched as the monster's tail followed it, sending a massive wave of icy cold seawater over him.

"That all you got?" he shouted. "That it?" Don began reloading his gun quickly, vaguely hearing shouting from Amanda and Hamish. With the gun ready again, he pointed it out to where the monster had been. The water sloshed around, but there was no sign of it. He stepped up to the edge of the boat, looking all around for it. Then he saw it. About a hundred yards out to sea, it was coming at them head on. Its snout was pushed to the surface of the ocean, and Don could see its telltale yellow eyes above that massive jaw bearing down on him. It snaked through the water elegantly and quickly, flicking its tail from side to side. It would be on them in seconds.

Don sneered and raised the Colt to sea level. "Come and get it, you fucking bitch."

When the Ocean King was no more than fifty feet from the trawler, Don fired, but the monster did not slow. If anything, it sped up and Don knew it wasn't going to stop, no matter how many bullets they put in its head. Its mouth was agape as it descended on them, its jaws spread wide in a sinister smile.

"Brace!" He saw Amanda and Hamish grab the railing, and managed to get one hand on a length of rope as the monster hit. The tremendous impact sent the trawler hurtling across the water and everyone was knocked off their feet. Don saw Hamish cling to Amanda as they fell to the deck. Ryan had been standing on top of the steps leading to the wheelhouse, and when the monster smashed into the boat, he was sent flying through the air. Don watched as the boy somersaulted through the air and landed at least a hundred feet away in the water.

The Ocean King had rammed them head on, and then dived underneath the boat, leaving a hole in the side. Water gushed onto the deck and Don struggled to bring himself upright, as the trawler slowed. He had dropped the Colt, and felt for the C4. Thank God, he still had it. Luckily, he had the foresight to put it with the detonator in a pouch and tie it to his belt.

"Hamish, Amanda, you okay?"

They nodded as they got to their feet.

Don grabbed a life preserver and threw the rubber ring toward Ryan. "Quick, get to it and we'll bring you in," he shouted.

Ryan was treading water and had lost his gun in the ocean too. He began swimming towards the ring, his dazed expression turning to panic as he realised where he was.

Hamish tried to manage the water flooding onto the deck, but the gaping hole was too big to patch up, and with Diablo still tethered to the deck, there was little he could do. He knew they were going down.

"Don look." Amanda pointed beyond Ryan. The water was rising, and then the two golden orbs appeared as the Ocean King turned around and headed back to the boat.

"Ryan, swim. Don't look back," shouted Don.

"Hurry, Ryan!" screamed Amanda.

"Do you still have your rifles? Either of you?" Don looked at them frantically, but they had both dropped them when the boat had been hit.

Don looked around for another weapon, but there was nothing left apart from the C4. He ran to the chest that lay on its side. He fished around inside, but the grenades had gone, lost in the battle. There was the HK MP5 and Don stuffed it into his waistband. He didn't even know if it was loaded and then he saw the tip of a gun near Diablo, and grabbed it. It was the AK47 and there was half a mag left. Don raced back to the railings. Amanda and Hamish were up to their ankles in water now, and the boat was beginning to keel over. It would take some time, but the Mary-Jane had been dealt a lethal blow.

The Ocean King was a full ten feet out of the water now, following Ryan back to the trawler. Don fired a couple of shots at it, trying to warn it off, but they had no effect. He could see it was too late. Ryan was still trying to get to the life preserver and Don fired the AK47 again, but they had no effect on the Ocean King. Just when it looked like it was about to swallow Ryan, it dove under the water out of sight.

"Where did it go? asked Amanda.

"I don't know" said Don. "Ryan, hurry, it's gone. You can still…"

And then Ryan was gone, just like that. The Ocean King zoomed up out of the water like a rocket. A towering inferno of rage, it flew from the ocean and Ryan disappeared in a huge plume of water. He hadn't even had time to scream. Seawater cascaded down from the beast and Don knew the boy was gone.

"No." Don stepped back from the railing. "No, not Ryan."

The Ocean King dominated the sky as it hung over them, watching the three tiny figures on the boat below it. Hamish dragged Amanda back from the railing and gave her a life jacket.

Don strode over to Diablo and pulled the tarpaulin off its head. The animal was still barking and yapping like a terrified dog. Don pointed the AK47 at Diablo's skull. "Is this what you want?" he screamed. He looked up at the Ocean King. "Is this what you came for?"

Don unloaded everything he had into Diablo at point blank range, obliterating its face. Pieces of green skin and brain covered him as he blew Diablo apart. The Ocean King roared and then belly-flopped into the water, sending a tidal wave to the trawler. Don slipped on the deck as the wave hit, and he grabbed hold of Diablo's jaws to stop himself from slipping into the ocean. With its last ounce of life, Diablo seized Don's left arm and crunched down. Don cried out in pain and tried to free himself, but his arm was encased in the monster's jaws, and its teeth were firmly embedded into his bone. The AK47 was empty, and Don pulled the HK MP5 from his belt. He fired into Diablo and only stopped when the chamber was finally empty. The pressure on his arm lifted, and Don could feel Diablo going. The monstrous body jerked, and then lay still. Diablo was dead.

Don tried to prise apart the dead creature's jaws with his free right arm, but he was too weak. Hamish joined Don and pulled on Diablo's upper jaw, allowing Don to wriggle free. When he finally retrieved his left arm, it was a mess, a tangle of flesh and muscle, splintered bone and nerve endings.

Amanda walked up to them holding a serrated cobalt knife. "This is all I could find." She drove it into Diablo's mangled skull, right between its eyes. She screamed as she unleashed her pent up emotions, screaming and cursing, as she smashed the knife repeatedly into Diablo's disintegrated skull and bloody mashed brains.

Hamish grabbed her arm and she dropped the knife, collapsing into him. "It's over," he said.

Amanda kissed Hamish and looked at Don. She grabbed a torn piece of tarpaulin and wrapped it around Don's shoulder. Blood rapidly soaked through the makeshift tourniquet and then Hamish removed his shirt, tying it around Don's shoulder and pressing down to stem the bleeding. Thankfully, at some point between being released from the monster's vice-like grip, and Diablo dying, Don had passed out.

"Hamish, we have to get Don to a hospital."

Hamish rested beside Amanda on the bloody deck. The water lapping at the hull was still, but the trawler was slowly going down. "You think it's safe? You think it's gone?"

Amanda looked out at the mainland. The sky was hazy and lights twinkled in the distance like stars on the horizon. She nodded. "Its baby is dead now. I don't know where it'll go, but it's not our problem anymore. I think it'll either head home, or back to the city. It knows it defeated us. We failed. Let the military find it. We need to get Don to a Doctor."

Hamish looked across the quiet ocean. "I'll check on Jay and then radio for help. The Mary-Jane is going nowhere." He got up and leant on the railings, looking down at Amanda holding Don. "I think you're right. It's gone. There's no sign of it out there. Maybe it's headed inland now."

Amanda wiped Don's brow, and swept his hair from his face. He was coming round and she was going to need to get him to the first aid kit inside. She looked up at Hamish to ask for help, and screamed. Behind him, the Ocean King had silently risen from the water and its evil face blocked out the sun like a dark planet. Its teeth lowered themselves over Hamish as it towered over the boat.

Hamish looked up in awe and then the Ocean King snapped its jaws once. As the monster grinned and hissed, Hamish's decapitated body took two steps forward. A fountain of blood gushed from the headless body as it crumpled. Hamish's dead body twitched and then slipped into the water, out into the ocean.

Amanda screamed again as the monster's jaws latched onto the trawler and it started to pull at it, trying to drag it under the water. The trawler started moving backwards, and the deck began to fill rapidly with more water.

"Amanda!" shouted Don. He had awakened to see Hamish killed, and knew Amanda was hyperventilating. She was going into shock, desperately clinging to Don, as the beast continued munching on the trawler's hull, as though it were made of nothing stronger than cardboard.

Amanda looked at Don, blinking away salt tears from her eyes. "What... Hamish..."

"Amanda, listen to me, you have to get off the boat. The life raft is right behind you. Just reach over and grab it. Get the hell out of here, as far as you can."

"I can't, I can't leave Hamish, I can't..."

Don grabbed Amanda with his remaining right hand, and ignored the pain coursing through his body. He looked her in the eyes. "Amanda. Hamish is gone. Go. You need to go, now."

"If I get in the water with that thing, it'll get me, it'll get me. Like Ryan and Hamish and…"

"Trust me," said Don as the trawler began to splinter. A wooden plank flew over their heads as the boat began to break up. Diablo's lifeless body began to slip back into the ocean and Don watched as the Ocean King paused. As Diablo was swept into the Pacific, his mother watched silently. Don wanted to kill it more than anything. The Ocean King was gunning for revenge now. It had ruined so many lives that just killing its infant wasn't enough anymore.

Together, they wrestled the life raft out from its holding straps and threw it over the side, away from the Ocean King that was quietly watching its young disappear beneath the surface. It had gouged out a huge part of the starboard hull and the trawler was listing.

"I'm not leaving you, Don. I can't. I can't lose you too."

Don felt Amanda shaking and he put his arm around her. He pressed his face into her neck, his mouth next to her ear. "We don't have long. Look at me, Amanda. I'm done. My left arm is gone. I've lost so much blood I wouldn't even make it back to shore if I did get off this boat. The beast doesn't want you. It wants this boat. It won't even notice you. You're too small for it to bother with. You saw it. Its focus is here. It wants to tear this boat apart. I'm going to make sure it's the last thing it does."

Amanda used the rails as support to lift Don up. She saw the life raft a few yards away in the water and prepared to jump. She looked back at Don questioningly. "Don, I can't, this is too much. I don't want to drown. I can't do this." She broke down and began sobbing. "I want Hamish. I don't want to go without him."

"Amanda, it's time to go. I've got to go. She'll come back in a minute, and you need to be off this boat when she does." Don stepped back. "There are more guns in the galley. I stashed them down there earlier. I'm going to get them and unload them into her brain. Get out of here."

Amanda put a foot on the rail and looked at the whirling ocean below. "Don…"

"Go!"

Amanda looked over her shoulder to see Don hobbling across the deck to the cabin door. He didn't look back.

Amanda jumped and plunged into the ocean. As she slipped beneath the waves, the coldness caught her breath and she fought to control her nerves. The water felt like shards of ice plucking at her skin, and she frantically kicked out, trying to resurface. Her foot made contact with something solid and she looked down. The beast was directly beneath her, ploughing a direct line underneath her to the boat. Screaming, she kicked again and spiralled to the surface, choking out seawater as she did so. The slipstream of the beast almost pulled her under again, but she kept kicking and made it to the raft. She pulled herself up the boarding ladder and there was an awful groaning sound, as she saw the monster take another bite out of the Mary-Jane. The stern was caught in its jaws and the trawler was more below the water than above it now. The boat listed wildly as the beast thrashed around, shaking it like a toy. The waves created by the monster's movements rocked the life raft, and its savage throes threw her back onto the soft rubber under the canopy. Amanda lay there as the raft was tossed around on the ocean, crying and spitting out seawater. She remembered Hamish's smile before he was devoured. She remembered Don's fierce determined face. There was nothing more she could do now, except hope and pray.

OCTOBER SATURDAY 18${}^{\text{TH}}$ 14:16

The ship tilted alarmingly, but then righted. It was like riding a rollercoaster in a storm, yet, Don knew he couldn't give up. Now was the time. He had to do what he had come here to do. Amanda should be safe by now, trussed up in the life raft, and he couldn't wait any longer. The pain shooting through his body was telling unconsciousness to take over, to let oblivion drown out the pain, and slip quietly into the dark.

The guns weren't in the galley. There was nothing. It had been a lie to get Amanda off the boat. Better that, than to have her die with him. Don grabbed an oil drum and shoved it toward the cabin door. It rolled down the short steps and into the pantry. He pulled on another drum and summoned up his last ounce of energy to send it tumbling down into the pantry to join the other. Don could see Jay on the galley floor. He had fallen off the table and probably never regained consciousness. Only his feet were visible now beneath the foot of water on the floor. It didn't matter whether he had died of his injuries or drowned, he was just another poor soul killed by the Ocean King. Don felt the boat tilt and he lost his balance. Unable to hold onto the doorway for support with his only good hand, he fell down into the bowels of the boat. He ended up in the pantry and banged his head against one of the oil drums. His left arm didn't hurt too much now. It was going numb and Don could feel his temperature dropping. It wasn't just the fear, or the seawater. He was losing too much blood.

Synapses sparked in Don's head, connecting the dots in his subconscious; random thoughts and memories collided as his hand reached for the pantry door. He couldn't reach it, and kicked it shut with his feet. With a resounding snap, the door shut, enclosing Don in darkness. He nestled back against an oil drum and sat up. There were awful moaning sounds from outside. Some were from the Mary-Jane as she fought against the titan, dragging her down into the ocean, the others from the angry grieving Ocean King. Ignoring the cold and the pain, Don reached around for the pouch at his waist. He needed the C4 and detonator. His chest ached and he suspected he had broken a couple of ribs. His left arm was shredded, and the bone was exposed at the elbow. He was actually grateful for the darkness, so he didn't have to see how bad he looked.

The ship tilted and he slid along with the oil drums until he crashed into the wall. This time the boat did not roll back.

Finally, Don thought, *finally she's going for it. She's going to pull us under. Go for it bitch, I'm ready now.*

A wave of happiness and terror filled him as the boat creaked and groaned. It tilted further and he felt it being pulled downward. Whether it was the current of the ocean, or the monster tearing it apart, it didn't matter anymore. He had to do this, now. The monster was so close there was no time to think anymore. He could hear it barking, emitting urgent deep sounds that had no place or right to exist on Earth.

The C4 was in his right hand and he reached into the pouch for the detonator. He banged his head back against the oil drum and a metallic clanging sound reverberated around the small galley.

"Fuck," he said. "Fuck!" He placed the C4 between his knees and began fishing around in the water that lapped at his legs. The detonator was gone. How could he not have it? Had it fallen out when he'd killed Diablo, or when he'd tripped down into the pantry? His fingers came across a variety of useless instruments: cutlery, salt and pepper pots, canned beans and broken glass. His right hand began to bleed as he cut his fingers in the darkness, but he paid no attention to the pain, as he continued searching for the detonator.

Please God, let it be here. Let it be right here.

But there was nothing. He let his hand rummage around in the darkness a moment more and then gave up. There was nothing. The Ocean King was going to win. It would destroy the trawler, take Don, and then go back to the mainland for more. Don was surrounded by explosives and he had no way of setting them off. The C4 without a detonator was as useful as a lump of sodden earth. One of the oil drums was leaking, and the smell was irritating. It had a small hole in the base from when it had landed in the pantry. All he needed was a gun or a match, anything to create a flame and ignite it. If he did, then it might be enough to ignite the C4 too. If the monster was close enough, he could kill it. At the very least, the Ocean King was going to go away with a serious headache.

A tearing sound reached his ears and more water started to come in from under the pantry door. It trickled at first, soaking his legs and back. Then the icy water started to pour in through the whole of the doorframe. The boat was at such an angle now that Don knew it was almost completely submerged. The monster could've destroyed it in a second, yet, it was taking its time, as if it wanted them to know it held all the power. It was relishing in Don's inevitable death, making him pay for its dead infant.

Do it, do it now.

Don heard another crack, another, and another, and the sea water began to fill up the pantry. He put the C4 on the oil drum over his shoulder and let his hand fall to his side. It was over. He had failed again. He was going to join the long list of dead created by this prehistoric monster. He only hoped Amanda had gotten far enough away to escape being pulled down with the trawler.

As his hand fell to his side, he brushed his pant leg and felt something small and hard tucked into the inside pocket. He pulled it out and clasped it in his hands. It was pitch black now and he had to work out what it was by touch. His thumb caressed the three-inch long plastic and he laughed. He could picture it now, the naked woman sunbathing on that tropical island. He laughed again, and felt a rush of cold water swarm over his legs, completely taking his breath away.

Thank you, Stacy.

He flicked the wheel down and a tiny flame erupted from the tip of the lighter. Don's shaking hand carried it toward the oil drum. Any moment now and...when he was all but half an inch away, the flame went out, caught by a droplet of flying water. As the water rose higher, up to his chest, there was another creaking sound and he thought the galley door was going to give way. It held, just, but the pressure on it had undoubtedly increased, and he knew he only had seconds left. The dark room was abruptly pitched into silence. The monster's barking stopped and the only sound Don could hear was the beating of his own heart.

As he held the lighter up above the seawater, he felt the warmth on his back. The strong African sun took away the chill of the water. All around him was gunfire and shouting. It was chaos and he didn't know if the bullets whistling past his head were friendly or not. Someone yelled in his ear to detonate, but he knew he couldn't. His brother was still inside the mosque, and the terrorists were too close. If he blew them up, he would take his brother out too.

Robert, where are you?

The detonator was right there, all he had to do it was push it. But, Robert was there. He couldn't do it. He couldn't blow it up, not now. He had to go and save his brother. There was a chance he could make it. There was always another chance.

Guilt and tears welled up inside him as the churning seawater numbed his lower body. His left arm was broken, useless, and his head pounded. He held the lighter and his thumb rested on the ignition wheel. If the monster didn't find him in the next five seconds, then the churning rushing water would. The pantry would flood and Don's lungs would fill with seawater. The world would turn icy black and the trawler would sink to the depths with the Ocean King free to roam the seas of the world. All Don had to do was flick the ignition and unleash the payload. The oil would erupt as long as it still had enough oxygen to ignite.

Do it, do it now.

Don's salty tears shimmied down his face and fell into the ocean's saltwater. His brother whispered in his ear.

I'm sorry, Robert. Forgive me. I'll see you soon, brother. I'm waiting for you. It's not your fault. I can't do this again.

It was a no-win situation; that was what the debriefing had revealed. The insurgents had rigged the mosque with enough explosives to level it twice over.

"Perhaps, if O'Reilly had blown up the outer doors when he had the chance though," said the prosecutor, "well then, perhaps more would've lived. Navy Seal, Robert O'Reilly, would certainly have been spared the agonising death we all saw he suffered and his brother would not have his own brother's blood on his hands."

Cold water mingled with African sunshine and Don shivered. Fear had paralysed him before, and couldn't let it happen this time. His fear and shame and guilt dissipated, flowing out of him like the blood flowed from his arm. Don felt clean and knew what he had to do. The man in the yellow shirt smiled and waved. Don's eyes glazed over as the galley door gave way and a thunderous tumult of water crashed into the black room.

I'm sorry, Mom. I couldn't do it. I'm sorry, Robert, I couldn't save you. I'm letting you go now, but I'll see you soon, brother.

The Ocean King appeared, its jaws drooling with excitement, and the wooden walls splintered apart as the galley collapsed. Don briefly saw the gigantic teeth of the Ocean King approaching, as he calmly flicked the lighter's wheel and the tiny flame erupted for one last time. It caught onto the oil and there was a spark as the oil drums ignited. The last of the oxygen in the room was sucked up into the explosion and Don closed his eyes. The world went a hellish, fiery black.

The End

Acknowledgements

The impetus to write 'The Ocean King' came from my fantastic publisher at Severed Press. I urge you to check them out along with the innumerable quality novels they have produced at www.severedpress.com

This story and all the characters are fictional, but there are undoubtedly outside influences that affect my thought process, and can lead the plot in directions I would never have thought of. I have to thank my wife for standing behind me and putting up with the nightmares.

Finally, if you have enjoyed this, then please consider leaving a review. Thank you. Feel free to visit my website www.russwatts.co or view my other titles by Severed Press:

The Afflicted
The Grave
Devouring the Dead
Devouring the Dead 2: Nemesis

6828970R00116

Printed in Great Britain
by Amazon.co.uk, Ltd.,
Marston Gate.